Works by Alain Robbe-Grillet
Published by Grove Weidenfeld

The Erasers
For a New Novel: Essays on Fiction
In the Labyrinth and *Jealousy: Two Novels*
La Maison de Rendez-vous and *Djinn*
Last Year at Marienbad
Project for a Revolution in New York
Recollections of the Golden Triangle
Topology of a Phantom City
The Voyeur

THE ERASERS

by

Alain Robbe-Grillet

Translated from the French
by Richard Howard

*"Time that sees all has found
you out against your will."*

—*Sophocles*

GROVE WEIDENFELD
NEW YORK

Published by Grove Weidenfeld
A division of Wheatland Corporation
841 Broadway
New York, NY 10003-4793

Originally published by Les Editions de Minuit, Paris, France, as *Les Gommes*, copyright © 1953 by Les Editions de Minuit

ISBN 0-8021-5086-1

Library of Congress Catalog Card Number 61-11766

Manufactured in the United States of America

Printed on acid-free paper

First Evergreen Edition 1977

20   19   18   17   16   15   14   13   12   11

PROLOGUE

1

In the dimness of the café, the manager is arranging the tables and chairs, the ashtrays, the siphons of soda water; it is six in the morning.

He has no need to see distinctly, he does not even know what he is doing. He is still asleep. Very ancient laws rule every detail of his gestures, saved for once from the uncertainty of human intentions; each second marks a pure movement: a side-step, the chair eleven inches out from the table, three wipes of the rag, half-turn to the right, two steps forward, each second marks, perfect, even, unblurred. Thirty-one. Thirty-two. Thirty-three. Thirty-four. Thirty-five. Thirty-six. Thirty-seven. Each second in its exact place.

Soon unfortunately time will no longer be master. Wrapped in their aura of doubt and error, this day's events, however insignificant they may be, will in a few seconds begin their task, gradually encroaching upon the ideal order, cunningly introducing an occasional inversion, a discrepancy, a confusion, a warp, in order to accomplish their work: a day in early winter without plan, without direction, incomprehensible and monstrous.

But it is still too early, the street door has just been unbolted, the only person on the scene has not yet recovered his own existence. It is the moment when the dozen chairs gently come down from the imitation marble tables where they have spent

the night. Nothing else. An automaton's arm puts the setting back in place.
When everything is ready, the light goes on. . . .

A fat man is standing here, the manager, trying to get his bearings among the tables and chairs. Over the bar, the long mirror where a sick image floats, the manager, greenish, his features blurred, liverish and fleshy in his aquarium.

On the other side, behind the mirror, the manager again who dissolves slowly in the dawning light from the street. It is no doubt this silhouette that has just put the café in order; now it need only disappear. In the mirror flickers the reflection of this ghost, already almost completely decomposed; and beyond, increasingly undecided, the wavering rigmarole of shadows: the manager, the manager, the manager. . . . The manager, a mournful nebula, drowned in his halo.

Painfully the manager emerges. He fishes up again some random snatches that are still floating around him. No need to hurry, there's not much current at this hour.

He leans on both arms against the table, body tilted forward, not wide awake, his eyes staring at something: that fool Antoine with his Swedish calisthenics every morning. And his pink tie the other day, yesterday. Today is Tuesday: Jeannette's coming later.

Funny little spot; this marble's no good, everything stains it. It looks like blood. Daniel Dupont last night; a stone's throw from here. Funny business: a burglar would never have gone into a lighted room on purpose, the man must have wanted to kill him. Revenge, or what? Clumsy in any case. That was yesterday. Look for it in the morning paper. Oh yes, Jeannette's coming later. And have her buy . . . no, tomorrow.

An absent-minded wipe of the rag, as an excuse, over the funny spot. One way or another vague masses pass, out of reach; or else they're just holes.

Jeannette will have to light the stove right away; it's getting cold early this year. The pharmacist says it always does if it rained on July fourteenth; maybe he's right. Of course that other fool, Antoine, who's always right, just had to prove the opposite. And the pharmacist was beginning to get mad, four or five glasses of white wine are enough for him; but Antoine doesn't see anything. Fortunately, the manager was there. It was yesterday. Or Sunday? It was Sunday; Antoine had his hat; it makes him look sharp, that hat. His hat and his pink tie! No, wait, he had his tie on yesterday too. No. Besides, what difference can it make?

A peevish wipe of the rag once again wipes yesterday's dust off the table top. The manager straightens up.

Against the glass he notices the reverse of the sign "Furnished Rooms" from which two letters have been missing for seventeen years; for seventeen years he has been going to put them back. It was already like that in Pauline's time; they had said when they first came . . .

Besides, there is only one room to rent, so in any case it's ridiculous. A glance at the clock. Six-thirty. Wake the man up.

"Get to work, slacker!"

This time he has spoken almost aloud, with a grimace of disgust on his lips. The manager is not in a good mood; he has not had enough sleep.

To tell the truth, he's not often in a good mood.

On the second floor, at the end of a hallway, the manager knocks, waits a few seconds and, since he hears no answer, knocks again, several times, a little louder. On the other side of the door an alarm clock goes off. His right hand frozen in its gesture, the manager keeps listening, spitefully waiting to discover the sleeper's reactions.

But no one turns off the alarm. After a minute or so it stops of its own accord with astonishment on a few last abortive sounds.

The manager knocks again: still nothing. He cracks open the door and puts his head inside; in the dim morning light he sees the unmade bed, the room in disorder. He walks in and inspects the premises: nothing suspicious, only the empty bed, a double bed, without a pillow, with a single depression marked in the middle of the bolster, the blankets thrown back toward the foot of the bed; on the dresser, the enamel basin full of dirty water. All right, the man has already left, it's his business after all. He went out without going through the café, he knew there wouldn't be any hot coffee yet and after all he didn't have to say anything. The manager leaves with a shrug; he does not like people who get up ahead of time.

Downstairs, he finds someone waiting, an ordinary-looking man, a little shabby, not a regular customer. The manager goes behind his bar, turns on an extra lamp and stares at the customer rudely, ready to spit in his face that it's too early for coffee. But the other man merely asks:

"Monsieur Wallas, please?"

"He's gone," the manager says, scoring a point all the same.

"When did he leave?" the man asks, rather surprised.

"This morning."

"What time this morning?"

An anxious glance at his watch, then at the clock.

"I haven't any idea," the manager says.

"You didn't see him leave?"

"If I had seen him leave, I'd know when it was."

A pitying pout emphasizes this easy success. The other man thinks for a few seconds and then says:

"Then you don't know when he'll be coming back either?"

The manager does not even answer. He attacks on new grounds:

"What can I serve you?"

"Coffee—black," the man says.

"No coffee this early," the manager says.

Definitely a good victim, a sad little spider's face, perpetually reconstituting the tatters of his frayed intelligence. Besides, how could he know that this Wallas came last night to this obscure bar in the Rue des Arpenteurs? It's unnatural.

Having played all his cards for the moment, the manager is no longer interested in his visitor. He dries his bottles with an absent-minded expression and, since the other man is not drinking anything, he turns off the two lamps, one after the other. There's plenty of daylight now.

The man has gone, mumbling something incomprehensible. The manager finds himself back among his wreckage, the spots on the marble, the varnish of the chairs which the dirt makes sticky in places, the mutilated sign on the glass. But he is the victim of more insistent specters, spots darker than those of the wine disturb his vision. He tries to brush them away, but it is no use; at every step he bumps into another. . . . The movement of an arm, the music of idle words, Pauline, sweet Pauline.

Sweet Pauline, who died so strangely, so long ago. Strangely? The manager leans toward the mirror. What's so strange about it? A spiteful contraction gradually distorts his face. Isn't death always strange? The grimace grows worse, freezes in a gargoyle mask that stares at itself for a moment more. Then an eye closes, the mouth twists, one side of the face contracts, a still more hideous monster appears and dissolves immediately too, giving way to a calm and almost smiling image. Pauline's eyes.

Strange? Isn't it the most natural thing of all? Take this Dupont, how much stranger it is that he is not dead. The manager begins laughing softly, a kind of voiceless laughter without gaiety, like a sleepwalker's laugh. Around him the familiar specters imitate him; each has its own grin. They even strain a point somewhat, guffaw, nudging one another with their elbows and slapping one another on the back. How can he make them shut up now? There are a lot of them. And they are quite at home.

Motionless in front of the mirror, the manager watches himself laughing; he tries as hard as he can not to see the others that are swarming across the room, the jubilant troupe, the wild legion of minor heartaches, the refuse of fifty years of badly digested existence. Their racket has become intolerable, the horrible concert of brays and yelps and all at once, in the silence that has suddenly fallen again, a young woman's clear laugh.

"Go to hell!"

The manager has turned around, wrenched from the nightmare by his own cry. No one is there, of course, neither Pauline nor the others. He glances with weary eyes around the room that calmly awaits the people who will come, the chairs where the murderers and their victims will sit, the tables where the communion will be served to them.

Here is Antoine; it's starting well.

"Have you heard the news yet?"

Not even a nod in answer. He is not an easy customer this morning, the manager. Let's give him a try, anyway.

"A man named Albert Dupont, murdered last night, here, right at the end of the street!"

"Daniel."

"Daniel what?"

"Daniel Dupont."

"No, I said it was Albert. Right here . . ."

"First of all, no one was murdered."

"That's what you say. How do you know anyway, without ever leaving your bar?"

"She telephoned from here. The old housekeeper who works for them. Their line was out of order. Flesh wound in the arm."

(Poor fool who always knows everything.)

"Well, he's dead anyway! Look at the paper: he's dead, I tell you."

"You have a paper?"

Antoine looks through his overcoat pockets, then he remembers:

"No, I left it for my wife."

"All right, never mind, it doesn't matter anyway: his name's Daniel and he isn't dead at all."

Antoine does not look happy. He stands there wondering what he might do that would be more convincing than an ironic sneer, but the bartender does not give him time.

"Are you drinking something, or getting the hell out?"

The dispute is likely to grow nastier, when the door opens again and lets in a cheerful, plump, and gesticulating person, almost in rags.

"Good morning, boys. Say, I have a riddle for you."

"All right, we know that one," Antoine says.

"No, boy," the cheerful man says, undiscouraged, "you don't know this one. No one does. No one, you hear? Bartender, a glass of white wine!"

Judging from the man's face, his riddle must be a really good one. So no one will miss a word of it, he enunciates it as if he were giving dictation:

"What is the animal that in the morning . . ."

13

But no one is listening to him. He has already had one too many. He's funny, of course, but the other two don't have the heart for jokes: what concerns them is a man's life!

2

The Rue des Arpenteurs is a long straight street, bordered on each side by houses that are already old, whose inadequately tended two- or three-storied façades suggest the modest circumstances of the tenants they shelter: laborers, office workers, or merely fishermen. The shops are not very prosperous looking and even the cafés are few and far between—not that these people are particularly sober, but they choose to do their drinking elsewhere.

The Café des Alliés (Wines & Liquors. Furnished Rooms) is located at the end of the street, number 10, only a few houses from the Boulevard Circulaire and the city proper, so that the proletarian character of the buildings in its vicinity is somewhat tempered by bourgeois features. At the corner of the parkway stands a big stone apartment building, well kept up, and opposite, at number 2, a small two-story private house with a narrow strip of garden around it. The structure does not have much style but gives an impression of comfort, even of a certain luxury; a fence and behind it a spindle-tree hedge clipped to a man's height complete its isolation.

The Rue des Arpenteurs extends eastward, interminable and less and less prepossessing, to quite out-of-the-way neighborhoods that are obviously those of the poor: a checkerboard of muddy paths between the shacks, rusty corrugated iron, old planks, and tarpaper.

To the west, on the other side of the parkway and its canal, stretches the city proper, the streets somewhat cramped between the high brick houses, the public buildings without unnecessary ornament, the churches stiff, the shopwindows somber. The whole effect is solid, occasionally substantial, but austere; the cafés close early, the windows are narrow, the people are serious.

Yet this mournful town is not monotonous: a complicated network of canals and ponds brings in from the sea, which is only six kilometers north, the smell of kelp, the gulls, and even a few boats of low tonnage, coasters, barges, small tugs, for which a whole series of drawbridges and locks opens. This water, this movement keep people's minds open. The freighter whistles reach them from the harbor, over the tow docks and depots, and at high tide bring the space, the temptation, the consolation of possibility.

Since their heads are on their shoulders, temptation is enough: possibility remains simply possible, the whistles have long blown without hope.

The crews are recruited elsewhere; men around here prefer to go into business, on land, the most daring among them scarcely venturing farther than thirty miles from the coast to the herring fisheries. The rest are content to listen to the ships and estimate their tonnage. They do not even go to see them, it's too far. The Sunday walk stops at the Boulevard Circulaire: one comes out into the parkway along the Avenue Christian-Charles, then follows it along the canal to the New Dairy or to the Gutenberg Bridge, rarely below.

Farther south, on Sundays, one meets, so to speak, only neighborhood people. On weekdays, the calm here is disturbed only by the army of bicycles on their way to work.

At seven in the morning, the workers have already gone past; the parkway is virtually deserted.

15

At the edge of the canal, near the drawbridge at the end of the Rue des Arpenteurs, there are two men. The bridge has just opened to let a trawler through; standing near the winch, a sailor is about to close it again.

The other man is probably waiting for him to finish, but he cannot be in much of a hurry: the footbridge joining the two banks a hundred yards to the right would already have allowed him to continue on his way. He is a short man dressed in a long, rather old greenish coat and a shapeless felt hat. His back is to the sailor, he is not watching the boat; he is leaning against the iron railing at the end of the bridge. He is staring straight down at the canal's oily water.

This man's name is Garinati. He is the one who has just been seen going into the Café des Alliés to ask for that Wallas who was no longer there. He is also the clumsy murderer of the day before, who only slightly wounded Daniel Dupont. His victim's residence is that little house with the fence around it at the corner of the street, just behind his back.

The iron fence, the spindle-tree hedge, the gravel path around the house . . . He has no need to turn around to see them. The middle window of the second floor is the study window. He knows all that by heart: he studied it enough last week. For nothing, moreover.

Bona was well-informed, as usual, and all Garinati had to do was follow his orders carefully. Would have had, rather, for everything has just been ruined because of Garinati's blunder: probably no more than scratched, Dupont will soon be able to return behind his spindle trees and dive back into his files and index cards among the green calf bindings.

The light switch near the door, a porcelain button with a metal plate. Bona had said to turn off the light; he did not do this, and everything was ruined. The tiniest flaw . . . Is it so

16

certain? The hallway had remained lighted, of course; but if the bedroom had been in darkness, Dupont might not have waited to open the door wide to turn on the light. Maybe? Find out! Or would he have really done it? And the tiniest flaw was enough. Maybe.

Garinati had never gone into this house before, but Bona's information was so exact that he could just as well have moved around inside it with his eyes closed. At five to seven he has reached the house, calmly walking down the Rue des Arpenteurs. No one around. He has pushed open the garden gate.

Bona had said: "The buzzer won't work." Which was true. The bell has remained noiseless. Yet that very morning, when he had passed in front of the house ("There's no use your prowling around there all the time"), he had surreptitiously pushed open the gate, just to see, and he had distinctly heard the bell. No doubt the wire had been cut during the afternoon.

It was already a mistake to have tried the gate in the morning; coming in this evening, he was afraid for a second. But the silence has reassured him. Had he ever really had any doubts?

He has carefully closed the gate, but without letting the latch catch, and walked around the house on the right side, keeping on the lawn to avoid making the gravel crunch. In the darkness, he could just make out the path, paler between the two flowerbeds and the well-clipped top of the spindle trees.

The study window, the one in the middle of the second story on the canal side, is brightly lighted. Dupont is still at his desk. It's all just the way Bona said it would be.

Leaning against the wall of the shed, at the back of the garden, Garinati waits, his eyes fixed on the window. After a few minutes the bright light is replaced by a fainter glow: Dupont has just turned out the big desk lamp, leaving only one of the bulbs on in the ceiling fixture. It is seven o'clock: he is coming downstairs to eat.

The landing, the staircase, the hall.

17

The dining room is to the left, on the ground floor. Its shutters are closed. At the back of the house, the kitchen shutters are closed too, but a faint light filters through their slats.

Garinati approaches the little glass door, being careful not to expose himself to the light coming from the hallway. At the same moment the dining room door is closed again. Dupont already? He has come down quickly. Or else the old housekeeper? No, she's coming out of the kitchen now. So it was Dupont.

The old woman moves off toward the other end of the hall; but her hands are empty; he will have to wait longer. She comes back almost at once, leaving the dining room door open. She goes back into her kitchen and soon reappears carrying an enormous tureen in both hands, comes back into the dining room and this time closes the door behind her. Now is the moment.

Bona said: "You have almost five minutes to get upstairs. The old woman waits until he has finished his soup." Probably she is taking orders for the next day; since she is rather deaf it probably takes some time.

Noiselessly, Garinati slips inside. "The hinges will creak if you push the door too far." Violent desire, suddenly, to try all the same; to push it open a little farther, only a little; just to see how far he can go. A few degrees. Just one degree, one single degree; a little margin for error . . . But the arm stops, sensible. On the way out, instead.

They are not very careful in this house: anyone could come in.

Garinati has closed the door without a sound. He walks carefully on the tiles where his crepe soles make an almost imperceptible hissing noise. On the steps and upstairs there are thick carpets everywhere, that will be even easier. The hall is lighted; the landing too, upstairs. No more difficulty. Walk up, wait until Dupont comes back, and kill him.

On the kitchen table there are three thin slices of ham spread out on a white plate. A light dinner: fine. Provided he doesn't empty the whole tureen. You shouldn't overeat if you want to sleep without dreaming.

Things take their immutable course. With calculated movements.

The perfectly adjusted machinery cannot hold the slightest surprise in store. It is merely a matter of following the text, reciting phrase after phrase, and the words will be fulfilled and Lazarus will rise from his tomb, wrapped in his shroud. . . .

He who advances like this, in secrecy, to carry out the order, knows neither fear nor doubt. He no longer feels the weight of his own body. His footsteps are as silent as a priest's; they glide over the rugs and tiles, as regular, as impersonal, as definitive.

A straight line is the shortest distance between two points.

. . . footsteps so light they leave no trace on the surface of the sea. The stairs in this house have twenty-one steps, the shortest distance between two points . . . the surface of the sea . . .

Suddenly the limpid water grows cloudy. In this setting determined by law, without an inch of land to the right or left, without a second's hesitation, without resting, without looking back, the actor suddenly stops, in the middle of a phrase. . . . He knows it by heart, this role he plays every evening; but today he refuses to go any farther. Around him the other characters freeze, arm raised or leg half bent. The measure begun by the musicians goes on and on. . . . He would have to do something now, speak any words at all, words that would not belong to the libretto. . . . But, as every evening, the phrase begun concludes in the prescribed form, the arm falls back, the leg completes its stride. In the pit, the orchestra is still playing with the same vigor.

The stairs consist of twenty-one wooden steps, then, at the

very bottom, a white stone step, noticeably wider than the rest and whose rounded outer edge bears a brass column with complicated decorations and, as a finial, a jester's head wearing a cap with three bells. Higher up, the heavy, varnished banister is supported by turned wooden rails flaring slightly toward the base. A strip of gray carpet, with two garnet stripes at the edges, covers the stairs and extends, across the hall, to the front door.

The color of this carpet has been omitted in Bona's description, as well as the detail of the brass finial.

Another man, in this same place, weighing each step, would come . . .

Above the sixteenth step, a small painting is hanging on the wall, at eye level. It is a romantic landscape representing a stormy night: a flash of lightning illuminates the ruins of a tower; at its foot two men are lying, asleep despite the thunder or else struck by lightning? Perhaps fallen from the top of the tower. The frame is made of carved and gilded wood; both painting and frame seem to be of rather ancient date. Bona has not mentioned this painting.

The landing. Door to the right. The study. It is just as Bona has described it, even more cramped maybe and more crowded: books, books everywhere, those lining the walls almost all bound in green leather, others, paper-backed, piled carefully on the mantel, on a stand, and even on the floor; still others lying casually on the end of the desk and on two leather armchairs. The desk, of dark oak, long and monumental, virtually fills the rest of the room. It is completely covered with files and papers; the big desk lamp, set in the middle, is out. A single bulb is turned on in the ceiling fixture.

Instead of walking straight across the small free area of green carpet, between the door and the desk (the floor creaks there), Garinati passes behind the armchair, squeezes between the stand and a pile of books and reaches the desk from the other side.

"Standing behind the desk and holding the back of the desk chair in front of you with both hands, you will take note of the position of all the objects and of the door. You have time: Dupont doesn't come back up before seven-thirty. When you are perfectly sure of everything, you'll go and turn out the ceiling light. The switch is against the door jamb; you have to push it toward the wall, if you push it in the other direction two more bulbs go on. Then you'll come back, still by the same way, and stand behind your chair in exactly the same position as before; you'll wait, the loaded revolver in your right hand, your eyes fixed on the doorway. When Dupont opens it, he will be silhouetted clearly in the opening against the lighted hallway; invisible in the darkness, you'll take aim easily, resting your left hand on the back of the chair. You'll fire three times at his heart, and you'll leave, without excessive haste; the old woman will have heard nothing. If you meet her in the hall, don't let her get a good look at your face; push her aside, but not roughly. There will be no one else in the house."

The only distance between two points.

A kind of cube, but slightly misshapen, a shiny block of gray lava, with its faces polished as though by wear, the edges softened, compact, apparently hard, heavy as gold, looking about as big around as a fist; a paperweight? It is the only trinket in the room.

The titles of the books: *Labor and Organization, The Phenomenology of the Crisis* (*1929*), *Contribution to the Study of Economic Cycles,* and the rest in keeping. Not interesting.

Light switch against the door jamb, porcelain and chromium-plated metal, three positions.

He had been writing, four words at the top of a sheet of blank paper: "which can not prevent. . . ." It was just then that he

21

went downstairs to eat; he must not have found the word that came next.

Footsteps on the landing. The light! Too late to reach it now. The door opening and Dupont's stupid stare . . .

Garinati has fired, only one shot, trusting to instinct, at a fragment of an escaping body.

The tiniest flaw . . . Maybe. The sailor has just finished cranking the winch; the drawbridge is back in place.

Leaning over the handrail, Garinati has not moved. He watches the oily water ripple at his feet in a recess of the quay; a few pieces of flotsam have accumulated here: a piece of tar-stained wood, two old corks, a piece of orange peel, and smaller fragments, half decomposed, difficult to identify.

3

You don't die so fast from a flesh wound in the arm. Come off it! The manager shrugs his massive shoulders in a gesture of denial tempered with indifference: they can write whatever they want, but they won't make him believe that, with their stories made up on purpose to fool people.

"Tuesday, October 27.—A daring burglar made his way at nightfall yesterday into the residence of M. Daniel Dupont, number 2 Rue des Arpenteurs. Caught red-handed by the owner, the criminal, as he escaped, fired his revolver several times at M. Dupont. . . ."

The old woman arrived all out of breath. It was just before eight o'clock; the café was empty. No, the drunk was still here, half asleep in his corner; there was no one left for him to pester with his riddles: the others had finally all gone home to eat. The old woman asked if she could use the telephone. Of course she could; the manager pointed to where it was, on the wall. She was holding a sheet of paper which she looked at to dial her number while she went on talking: there was no way of calling from her house, something wrong with the phone since Saturday. "Home" was the little house at the corner, with a hedge around it. It was hard to say just whom she was speaking to. Probably to him, since the drunk obviously took no interest in the matter, but she seemed to be trying to reach a wider audience beyond, like a crowd in a public square; or else trying to affect something deeper in him than the sense of hearing. Since Saturday, and no one had come to fix it yet.

"Hello! Doctor Juard, please?"

She was shouting even louder than when she was telling her misfortunes.

"The doctor has to come right away. Someone's hurt. Right away, you hear? Someone's hurt! Hello! You hear? . . ."

In any case, she herself did not seem to be hearing very well. Finally she handed him the extra earphone and he had to report what the clinic was saying to her. Probably deaf. She followed the words on his lips when he spoke.

"Monsieur Daniel Dupont, two Rue des Arpenteurs. The doctor knows."

Her eyes questioned him.

"All right. He's coming."

She went on talking as fast as ever while she paid for the call. She did not seem hysterical, only a little overexcited. When he left the table Monsieur Dupont had found a criminal in his study—some people have their nerve—in his study which he had just left; where the light had even been left on. What did he want, anyway? To steal books? Her employer had had just time enough to dash into the next room where his revolver was;

his arm had only been grazed by a bullet. But when he had come back into the hallway, the criminal had already escaped. And she had heard nothing, seen nothing, that was the worst! How had he even got in? Some people have their nerve. "A daring burglar made his way . . . ." The phone had not been working since Saturday. And she had taken the trouble to go to the office, so someone would come to take care of it; of course no one had come. Sunday, all right, that was a holiday—and still, there should have been some kind of emergency repair service for such cases. Besides, if the repair service was any good, someone would have come right away. As a matter of fact Monsieur Dupont had waited all Saturday afternoon for an important call; and he did not even know if he could receive outside calls, since the phone had not rung since Friday. . . .

A plan of general reform of the telephone and telegraph system. Article one: a permanent repair service for emergency cases. No. Sole Article: Monsieur Dupont's telephone will be kept perpetually in perfect working order. Or more simply: everything will always work normally. And Saturday morning will stay quietly in its place, separated from the following Monday evening by sixty hours of sixty minutes each.

The old woman would have gone back at least as far as September if the drunk had not interrupted, awakened by her exclamations. He had been staring hard at her for a few minutes and took advantage of a moment's silence to say:

"Say, grandma, do you know what's the worst thing for a telephone lineman?"

She turned toward him.

"Listen, boy, there's nothing for you to brag about."

"No, grandma, that's not it, I'm not bragging, not me! I'm asking if you know what's the worst thing for a telephone lineman?"

He expressed himself formally, but with some difficulty.

"What's he saying?"

The manager tapped his forehead in explanation.

"Oh! That's it. These are strange times we're living in, all the same. I'm not surprised things go so badly nowadays, at the telephone offices."

Meanwhile Jeannette has lighted the stove and the café has filled up with smoke. The manager opens the street door. It's cold outside. The sky is overcast. It looks as though it were going to snow.

He steps out onto the sidewalk and looks toward the parkway. The fence and the hedge of the corner house are in sight. At the canal's edge, at the end of the bridge, a man is leaning on the railing, with his back to the street. What is he waiting for? A whale to pass? All that can be seen of him is a long shabby coat; like the one the man was wearing this morning. Maybe he's waiting there for the other man to come back!

What does this story about the burglary mean? Was there a more serious wound the old woman did not know about? Or didn't she want to say so? A burglar! It doesn't make sense. Besides, what difference can it make to him anyway?

The manager picks up his paper again:

". . . The victim, critically wounded and taken at once to a nearby clinic, died there without regaining consciousness. The police are investigating the identity of the murderer whose traces, up to now, have not been found.

"Daniel Dupont, *croix de guerre, chevalier du Mérite,* was fifty-two years old. Formerly a professor at the School of Law, he was also the author of many works on political economy known for their original views, notably concerning the problem of the organization of production."

Died without regaining consciousness. He hadn't even lost consciousness. Another shrug. Flesh wound in the arm. Come off it! You don't die so fast.

4

After a pause, Dupont turns toward Doctor Juard and asks: "And what do you think about it, Doctor?"

But the latter shrugs evasively; it is obvious he does not think anything.

Dupont continues:

"Speaking as a doctor, you don't see any disadvantage in this trip? This (he indicates his left arm, wrapped in a bandage), this doesn't bother me when I move around, and I won't be driving the car. Besides, you won't have any trouble with the police: they'll receive this morning—or they may have received it already—the order not to bother about me ny more, simply to file the death certificate you sent them and to let my "body" be taken to the capital and disposed of there. You'll just hand over to them the bullet you've removed. It's supposed to have hit me in the chest: you'll make up some position that makes it all more or less plausible. They don't need anything else for now, since there's not supposed to be a real inquest. Do you have any objections?"

The little doctor makes a vague gesture of denial, and it is the third person in the room who speaks in his place. Sitting at the head of the wounded man's bed, on an iron chair, he has kept his overcoat on; he does not seem very comfortable.

"Isn't it . . . a little . . . you know . . . romantic? Wouldn't it be better to make . . . to say . . . I mean, to make less of a mystery about it?"

"On the contrary, you see, it's out of discretion that we're obliged to behave this way."

"For outsiders, for the public, I understand. The release to the press and the secret kept even here in the clinic—fine. But I wonder if the secret *is* being kept . . . actually. . . . This room may be isolated. . . ."

"Yes it is," Dupont interrupts. "I tell you I haven't seen anyone except the doctor and his wife; and no one else ever comes to this part of the building."

The doctor makes a small sign of acquiescence.

"Of course . . . Of course," the black overcoat continues, not quite convinced. "But still, with the police, is it really worth . . . worth keeping . . . observing the same . . ."

The wounded man raises himself a little in his bed:

"Yes, I've already told you! Roy-Dauzet has insisted on it. Outside the group he can't count on anything right now, not even on his police. Moreover it's only a temporary thing: the leaders—at least certain ones—will be told, here and elsewhere; but at present you can't really know who's to be trusted in this city. Until we hear differently, it's better that I should be dead, for everyone."

"Yes, all right . . . And old Anna?"

"They told her this morning that I had died during the night, that it was one of those strange wounds which seem harmless at first but end up being fatal. I hesitated giving her such a shock, but it was better. She would have got her lies all mixed up if someone had questioned her."

"But you told the papers: 'Died without regaining consciousness.' "

This time the doctor intervenes:

"No, I didn't tell them anything of the kind. It's an embellishment that must have been added by some police official. Some papers didn't even print it."

"In any case it's . . . yes it seems troublesome to me. There are one, even two, two people who know you didn't lose consciousness: old Anna and the man who fired at you."

"Anna doesn't read the papers; and besides she's leaving the city today to go to her daughter's, she'll be out of the way of indiscreet questions. As for my murderer, he only saw me lock myself into my room; he couldn't know where he hit me. He'll be all too happy to learn of my death."

"Of course, of course . . . But you say yourself that they're so perfectly organized, that their information service . . ."

"Their main advantage is that they believe in their strength, in their success. We'll help them believe it this time. And since the police have been quite powerless up to now, we'll do without them, at least temporarily."

"All right, all right, if you think . . ."

"Listen, Marchat, I talked to Roy-Dauzet tonight on the phone, for almost an hour. We've weighed our decision and all its consequences. It's our best chance."

"Yes . . . Maybe . . . And suppose your conversation had been tapped?"

"We've taken the necessary precautions."

"Yes . . . precautions . . . of course."

"Let's get back to those papers: I absolutely have to take them with me tonight and I obviously can't go back there myself. I've sent for you to ask you to do this favor for me."

"Yes, yes . . . of course . . . But here again, you see, it's really a policeman's job. . . ."

"Not really, not at all! Besides, it's impossible now. What have you to be afraid of, anyway? I'm giving you the keys and you'll go there quietly this afternoon, after Anna leaves. All you have to do is fill a couple of briefcases. You'll bring them straight back here. I'll leave from here around seven, in the car Roy-Dauzet is sending; I'll be at his place before midnight."

The little doctor stands up and straightens his white smock.

"You don't need me now, do you? I'm going to see one of my expectant mothers. I'll stop by again later."

The timorous overcoat stands up too and shakes his hand:

"Good-bye, Doctor."

"My pleasure, Monsieur."

"Do you trust that man?"

The wounded man glances at his arm:

"He seems to have done his work well."

"No, I'm not talking about the operation."

Dupont makes a broad gesture with his good arm:

"What do you want me to tell you? He's an old friend; besides, you've noticed he's not very talkative!"

"No, not . . . certainly not very talkative."

"What do you think? That he's going to turn me in? Why? For money? I don't think he's stupid enough to get mixed up in this business more than he has to. All he asks is to see me leave as soon as possible."

"He looks . . . He doesn't seem . . . how can I put it? . . . He looks wrong."

"Don't exaggerate. He looks like a slightly overworked doctor, that's all."

"They say . . ."

"Of course, they say! Besides, they say it about every gynecologist in the country, or just about. And besides, what does that have to do with it?"

"Yes . . . of course."

A pause.

"Marchat, tell me the truth, you really don't want to go get those papers, do you?"

"Yes I do . . . oh yes. . . . I just think it isn't . . . exactly safe."

"It is for you! That's just why I'm not asking someone in the group to do it. They don't have anything against you! You know they don't kill just anyone whenever they feel like it. In the last nine days there's been a murder committed regularly, between seven and eight at night, every day, as if they had made this little detail into a rule. I'm yesterday's victim and my case seems to have been closed. Today they've chosen their new victim, and it's obviously not you—it probably won't even be in this city. Besides, you'll be going to my house in broad daylight, when no one has anything to fear."

"Yes, yes . . . Of course."

"Will you go?"

"Yes, I'll go . . . as a favor to you . . . if you think it's essential. . . . I don't want to look like I'm working for your group either. . . . This is no time to seem to be on too good terms with you . . . is it? Don't forget, I've never agreed with you on fundamental issues. . . . I'm not saying this in defense of . . . of these . . . of this . . . ."

The doctor listens to the regular breathing. The young woman is sleeping. He will come back in an hour. It is just eight. Dupont will not leave the clinic until seven tonight, he said. Why did Dupont have to call him in? Any doctor . . . Bad luck.

Seven tonight. A long day. Why do people always call him in for things like this? Refuse? No, he has already accepted. He will do what is asked of him one more time. And then? With the other one, he had not had any choice! All he needed was this new problem. . . .

The other one. It's not so easy to get away from him. Wait. Until seven tonight.

Why does Dupont have to get his friends mixed up in a mess like this! Marchat decides it's just nerve; and he is supposed to seem pleased into the bargain! What about his wife? Why couldn't she go? He has plenty of time to meet her; she or anyone else, until seven tonight.

About to leave the little white room, he turns back toward the wounded man:

"And your wife—she knows about this?"

"The doctor has informed her of my death by letter. It was more correct. You know we haven't met for a long time. She won't even ask to see 'my remains.' On that score, everything's going to be fine."

Evelyn. What is she doing now? Maybe she will come anyway, why not? A dead man's not exactly her type, though. Who else might try? But no one will know which clinic. They just have to say it's not this one. Until seven tonight.

5

Since they all agree, it's perfect. Commissioner Laurent closes the dossier and lays it with satisfaction on the pile to the left. The case is closed. Personally, he has no desire to get involved with it.

The investigations he has had made already have not produced the slightest result. Many distinct fingerprints left all over the place, as though intentionally, have been picked up; they must belong to the murderer, but they do not match any-thing registered in the enormous police file. The other details collected have offered no suggestion as to what lead to follow. Nothing has been brought in by the usual informers either. Under such conditions, where do you start? It's highly unlikely that the murderer belongs to the criminal circles of the port or the city: the file is too complete and the informers too numerous for a criminal to be able to escape their networks altogether.

Laurent knows this from long experience. At this hour he would normally have heard something already.

What then? A chance beginner? An amateur? A lunatic? Such cases are so rare; and besides, amateurs always leave traces and can be picked up right away. One solution, obviously, would be that they were dealing with someone coming from far away just to commit this murder, and then leaving immediately after. Yet his work seems a little too well done not to have required a good deal of preparation. . . .

After all, if the central services want to take the whole thing over themselves, even to the point of taking away the victim's body before an inquest, it's all right with him. He is certainly not going to complain. For him, it's as if the crime had never happened. After all, if Dupont had committed suicide it would have come down to exactly the same thing. The fingerprints could be anyone's, and since no one alive saw his attacker . . .

Better still: nothing at all has happened! A suicide still leaves behind a corpse; and now the corpse is vanishing without a word, and his superiors are asking him to keep out of it. Perfect!

No one has seen anything, heard anything. There is no victim. As for the murderer, he has fallen from the sky and must be far away by now, well on his way back to wherever he came from.

6

The scattered fragments, the two corks, the little piece of blackened wood: now they look like a human face, with the bit of orange peel for the mouth. The oil slick finishes off a grotesque clown's face, a Punch-and-Judy doll.

Or else it is some legendary animal: the head, the neck, the breast, the front paws, a lion's body with its long tail, and an eagle's wings. The creature moves greedily toward a shapeless prey lying a little farther on. The corks and the piece of wood are still in the same place, but the face they formed a moment ago has completely disappeared. The greedy monster too. Nothing remains, on the canal's surface, but a vague map of America; and even that only if charitably interpreted.

"And suppose he turns the light on again before opening the door wide?" Bona, as usual, was not willing to admit the objection. There was nothing to argue about. Still, it turned out, as a matter of fact, as if Dupont had turned the light on again: even if Garinati had been able to turn out the light in plenty of time, suppose Dupont, coming in, had turned on the light again before pushing the door all the way open—it came down to the same thing. He would have been seen in the room with the light on, anyway.

Besides! Bona has made a mistake in any case: Since he—to whom the job had been entrusted—had not turned out the light.

Forgotten? Or done on purpose? Neither one nor the other. He was going to turn out the light; he was going to do it just at that moment. Dupont came back upstairs too soon. What time was it exactly? He did not act fast enough, that's all; and all things considered, if he did not have time enough, it was still a mistake in calculation, a mistake of Bona's. How is he going to fix that now?

Dupont was wounded, apparently. But not seriously enough to keep him from running away, getting out of danger; Garinati distinctly heard him turning the key in the lock. There was nothing else for him to do but leave. The gray carpet, the twenty-two steps, the shiny banister with its brass finial at the end. Things lost a little of their consistency again. The revolver shot made such a funny noise; unreal; phony. It was the first time he had used a silencer. Ping! Like an air pistol; not loud enough to scare a fly. And right afterward everything was filled with cotton.

Maybe Bona knows already. From the papers? It was too late for the morning papers; and who would bother to report this nonexistent crime? "Attempted murder: a marauder fired a silent pistol at a harmless professor. . . ." Bona always knows.

Coming home the night before, Garinati found a note in his chief's handwriting. "Why didn't you come afterward, the way we'd planned? I have a job for you: they're sending a special agent. A Monsieur Wallas who'll take a room in the theater of operations. You should have come this morning! Everything's going fine. I'll expect you Tuesday morning at ten. J.B." It was as if he had already heard about the success of the job. The fact is, that he does not imagine that it could have failed. When he has made up his mind about something, it can only happen the way he has planned. "You should have come this morning." No! It's time for him to come now.

He has not had much trouble catching up with him, this Wallas, but he missed him, him too. He'll find him again easily. But for what? To tell him what? Early this morning, methodically looking for him in the neighborhood, Garinati kept feeling he had something urgent to tell him; he no longer knows what it was. As if he had been told to help him in his task.

All right, first of all he would have to decide how he was going to make up for yesterday's bad luck. Rendezvous at ten. Bona attached a lot of importance to the day and the time when Dupont was supposed to have been killed. Too bad; for once he will have to put up with it. And the others Garinati does not know, the whole organization around Bona, even above him, that huge machine—is it going to be stopped just because of

34

him? He will explain that it was not his fault, that he did not have time, that it did not work out the way it had been planned. But nothing is lost: tomorrow, tonight maybe, Dupont will be dead.

Yes.

He will go back and wait for him behind the spindle-tree hedge, in the study full of books and papers. He will go back there freely, clearheaded and revived, careful, "weighing each of his footsteps." On the desk is lying the cube of stone with its rounded corners, its faces polished by wear. . . .

The ruined tower lit up by the storm.

Twenty-one wooden steps, one white step.

The tiles of the hallway.

Three slices of ham on a plate, through the half-open door.

The dining room shutters are closed; the kitchen shutters too, a faint gleam filtering through their slats.

He walks on the lawn to avoid making the gravel crunch on the path, which he could see because it was paler than the two flower beds on either side. The study window, in the middle of the second story, is brightly lighted. Dupont is still up there.

The buzzer that makes no noise, at the gate.

Five to seven.

The endless Rue des Arpenteurs, invaded by the smell of herring and cabbage soup, from the dark suburbs and the muddy checkerboard of paths between the miserable shacks.

At nightfall, Garinati has wandered around, waiting until it's time, among this filthy vegetation of latrines and barbed wire. He has left Bona's written instructions, long since learned by heart, in his room.

These papers—exact sketches of the garden and the house, minute descriptions of the premises, details of the operations to be performed—these papers are not in Bona's handwriting; he has written out only certain items concerning the murder proper. As for the rest, Garinati does not know who the author is; who the authors are, rather, for several people must have gone into the house to make the necessary observations there, discover the arrangement of furniture, study the domestic habits, and even the behavior of each board underfoot. And someone has silenced the buzzer at the gate during the afternoon.

The little glass door has made a deep creak. In his rush to escape, Garinati has opened it a little wider than he should have.

It still remains to be seen if . . .

Go back without waiting. The old deaf woman is alone now. Walk back up there and find out for himself. The room being in darkness, find out at exactly what moment the unexpected hand turns on the light.

Anyone else, in his place . . . Unexpected. His own hand.

The murderer always returns. . . .

And if Bona finds out? He shouldn't be hanging around here either! Bona. Bona . . . Garinati has straightened up. He starts across the bridge.

It looks as though it were going to snow.

Anyone else in his place, weighing each of his footsteps, would come, clearheaded and free, to carry out his task of ineluctable justice.

The cube of gray lava.

The buzzer silenced.

The street that smells of cabbage soup.

The muddy paths that disappear, far away, among the rusty corrugated iron.

Wallas.
"Special agent . . ."

CHAPTER ONE

1

Wallas is leaning against the rail, at the end of the bridge. He is still a young man, tall, calm, with regular features. The clothes he is wearing and his idle air provide, in passing, a vague subject of remark for the last workmen hurrying toward the harbor: at this time, in this place, it does not seem quite natural not to be wearing work clothes, not to be riding a bicycle, not to look hurried; no one goes for a walk on Tuesdays early in the morning, besides, no one goes for a walk in this neighborhood. Such independence of the place and the time has something a little shocking about it.

Wallas himself thinks how chilly it is and that it would be pleasant to warm himself up by pedaling across the smooth asphalt, swept on by his own momentum; but he stands where he is, clinging to the iron railing. The heads, one after the other, turn toward him. He adjusts his scarf and buttons his overcoat collar. One by one the heads turn away and disappear. He has not been able to get breakfast this morning: no coffee before eight in that café where he has found a room. He glances mechanically at his watch and notices that it has not started again; it stopped last night at seven-thirty, which has not made things easier for his trip or for anything else. It stops every once in a while, he does not really know why—sometimes after a shock, not always—and then starts again afterward, all by itself, with no more reason. Apparently there is nothing broken inside, it can also run for several weeks at a stretch. It is unpredictable, which is rather annoying at first, but you can get used to it. It must be six-thirty now. Is the manager thinking about going up to knock at the door as he promised? Just in case, Wallas has wound the traveling alarm clock he had taken the precaution to bring along, but he has awakened a little earlier anyway: since he was not sleeping, he might as well begin right away. Now he is alone, as though left behind by the wave of bicyclists. Before him, vague in the yellow light, extends the street along which he has just walked before turning the corner onto the parkway; to the left an imposing five-story apartment building with a stone façade stands at the corner, and facing it a brick house surrounded by a narrow garden. It was there that this Daniel Dupont was killed yesterday by a bullet in the chest. For the time being, Wallas does not know any more than that.

He arrived late, last night, in this city he scarcely knows. He had been here once already, but only for a few hours, when he was a child, and he does not have any very precise memory of the place. One image has remained vivid to him, the dead end of a canal; against one of the quays is moored an old wreck of a boat—the hull of a sailboat? A low stone bridge closes off the canal. Probably that wasn't exactly right: the boat could not have passed under the bridge. Wallas continues on his way toward the center of the city.

Having crossed the canal, he stops to let pass a streetcar returning from the harbor, its new paint gleaming—yellow and red with a gold coat-of-arms; it is completely empty: people are going in the other direction. Having reached Wallas, who is waiting to cross the street, the car stops too, and Wallas finds himself facing the iron step; then he notices beside him the disk attached to a lamppost: "Streetcar Stop" and the figure 6 indicating the line. After ringing a bell, the car starts up again slowly, its machinery groaning. It seems to have finished its trip. Last night, as he came out of the station, the streetcars were so jammed that he was unable to pay his fare before getting off; the conductor could not walk through the car because of the suitcases. The other riders informed him, with some difficulty, of the stop nearest this Rue des Arpenteurs, of whose existence most of them seemed quite unaware; someone even said that it was not in this direction at all. He had to walk a long time along the badly lighted parkway, and once he found it, he noticed this café that was still open, where they gave him a room, not very luxurious of course, but good enough. He was quite lucky actually, because it would not have been easy to find a hotel in this deserted neighborhood. "Furnished Rooms" was written in enamel letters on the window, but the manager hesitated before answering; he seemed annoyed, or in a bad mood. On the other side of the embankment Wallas turns into a street paved with wood, which must lead toward the center of town; "Rue de Brabant" is written on the blüe plaque. Wallas has not had time, before leaving, to get hold of a map of the city; he plans to do so this morning as soon as the stores open, but he is going to take advantage of this respite he has before going to the police station, where normal service does not begin until eight, to try and find his way alone through the labyrinth of streets. This one seems important despite its narrowness: apparently long, it dissolves into the gray sky in the distance. A real winter sky; it looks as though it were going to snow.

On either side stretch rows of what seem to be brick houses, all similarly constructed, without balconies or cornices or ornament of any kind. Here there is only what is strictly necessary: regular walls pierced with rectangular openings; it does not suggest poverty, only work and economy. For the most part, moreover, these are office buildings.

Severe façades, rows of small, dark red bricks, solid, monotonous, patient: a penny profit made by the "Resinous Wood Corporation," a penny earned by "Louis Schwob, Wood Exporter," by "Mark and Lengler" or by the "Borex Corporation." Wood export, resinous wood, industrial woods, wood for export, export of resinous wood, the neighborhood is completely devoted to this commerce; thousands of acres of pine trees, piled brick by brick, to shelter the big ledgers. All the houses are built the same way: five steps lead to a varnished door, recessed and with black plaques on each side showing the firm's name in gold letters; two windows to the left, one to the right, and four stories of similar windows above. Perhaps there are apartments among all these offices? They cannot be discerned, in any case, by any outer sign. The employees, still not wide awake, who will be filling the street in an hour will have a good deal of difficulty, despite being used to it, recognizing their doors; or else maybe they enter the first one they come to, to export at random the wood of Louis Schwob or of Mark and Lengler? The main thing is that they do their work carefully, so that the little bricks go on piling up like figures in the big ledgers, preparing still another story of pennies for the building; a few hundred tons more of totals and exact business letters: "Gentlemen, in answer to yours of the . . ." ready cash, one pine tree for five bricks.

The row is broken only at the perpendicular, identical crossroads, leaving just room enough to slip between the piles of ledgers and adding machines.

But here is the deeper trench which the water carves through these brick days; along the quay rises the gables' line of defense, where the openings instinctively grow more myopic and the ramparts thicker. Down the middle of this cross street flows a canal, apparently motionless, a straight corridor men have left to the original basin, for barges loaded with wood that slowly move down toward the harbor; last refuge, too, in the suffocation of this drained land, for the night, the bottomless water of sleep, the glaucous water rising from the sea and contaminated with invisible monsters.

Beyond the channels and dikes, the ocean releases its hissing whirlpool of monsters whose coils are here confined between two reassuring walls. Still you have to be careful not to lean too far over, if you want to avoid inhaling them. . . .

Soon the series of brick houses begins again. "Rue Joseph-Janeck." Actually this is the same street that continues on the other side of the canal: the same austerity, the same arrangement of windows, the same doors, the same plaques of black glass with the same gold inscriptions. Silbermann and Son, exporters of pulp wood, capital one million two hundred thousand; main warehouses: four and six Quay Saint-Victor. Along a loading basin, carefully piled logs behind the row of cranes, the metal sheds, the smell of machine-oil and resin. Quai Saint-Victor, that must be somewhere over there, to the northwest.

After a crossroad, the landscape changes slightly: the night-bell of a doctor, a few shops, the architecture a little less uniform, giving the neighborhood a more livable look. A street branches off to the right, forming an angle more acute than the preceding ones; maybe he should follow it? It's better to follow this one to the end, there will always be time to turn off afterward.

A wisp of smoke lingers on the ground. A shoemaker's sign; the word "Provisions" in yellow letters on a brown background. Although the scene remains deserted, the impression of humanity gradually increases. At one ground-floor window, the curtains are decorated with a mass-produced allegorical subject: shepherds finding an abandoned child, or something of

45

the kind. A dairy, a grocery store, a delicatessen, another grocery; for the time being all that can be seen is their lowered iron shutters, and in the middle, outlined against the gray sheet iron, a lace star the size of a dinner plate, like the kind children make out of folded paper. These shops are small but clean, often repainted; almost all are food stores: an ocher butcher shop, a blue dairy, a white fish store. Only their colors and the sign on their pediment distinguishes one from another.

Again, open blinds and that cheap net curtain: under a tree two shepherds in classical costume give ewe's milk to a tiny naked baby.

Wallas continues on his solitary way between the drawn shutters, walking along the brick walls with the same elastic, confident gait. He walks on. Around him life has not yet begun. Just now, on the parkway, he has passed the first wave of workmen riding toward the harbor, but since then he has not met anyone else: the employees, the businessmen. the mothers, the children on their way to school, are still silent inside the closed houses. The bicycles have vanished and the day which they had inaugurated has retreated behind a few gestures, like a sleeper who has just stretched out his arm to turn off the alarm clock and grants himself a few minutes reprieve before opening his eyes for good. In a second the eyelids will rise, the city emerging from its false sleep will catch up at once with the rhythm of the harbor and, this dissonance resolved, it will again be the same time for everyone.

The only pedestrian, Wallas advances through this fragile interval. (Just as a man who has stayed up too late often no longer knows to which date to ascribe this dubious time, when his existence loses its shape; his brain, tired out by work and waking, tries in vain to reconstitute the series of days: he is supposed to have finished for the next day this job begun last night, between yesterday and tomorrow there is no place left for the present. Completely exhausted, he finally throws himself down on his bed and falls asleep. Later, when he wakes up, he'll find himself in his normal today.) Wallas walks on.

2

Without going out of his way or slowing down, Wallas walks on. In front of him a woman crosses the street. An old man drags toward a back door an empty garbage can that had been standing on the edge of the sidewalk. Behind a window are stacked three rows of rectangular platters containing all kinds of marinated anchovies, smoked sprats, rolled and loose herring, salted, seasoned, raw or cooked, smoked, fried, pickled, sliced, and chopped. A little farther, a gentleman in a black overcoat and hat comes out of a house and passes him; middle-aged, comfortable, frequent stomach trouble; he takes only a few steps and immediately turns into an extremely clean-looking café, certainly more appealing than the one where Wallas spent the night. Wallas remembers how hungry he is, but he has made up his mind to eat his breakfast in some large modern restaurant, on one of those squares or boulevards that must, as everywhere else, constitute the heart of the city.

The next cross streets intersect the one he is on at a decidedly obtuse angle, and consequently would lead him too far back— almost in the direction he is coming from.

Wallas likes walking. In the cold, early winter air he likes walking straight ahead through this unknown city. He looks around, he listens, he smells the air; this perpetually renewed contact affords him a subtle impression of continuity; he walks on and gradually unrolls the uninterrupted ribbon of his own passage, not a series of irrational, unrelated images, but a smooth band where each element immediately takes its place in the web, even the most fortuitous, even those that might at first seem absurd or threatening or anachronistic or deceptive; they all fall into place in good order, one beside the other, and the ribbon extends without flaw or excess, in time with the regular speed of his footsteps. For it is Wallas who is advancing; it is to his own body that this movement belongs, not to the backcloth some stagehand might be unrolling; he can follow in his own limbs the play of the joints, the successive contractions of the muscles, and it is he himself who controls the rhythm and length of his strides: a half second for each step, a step and a half for each yard, eighty yards a minute. It is of his own free will that he is walking toward an inevitable and perfect future. In the past, he has too frequently let himself be caught in the circles of doubt and impotence, now he is walking; he has recovered his continuity here.

On the wall of a school courtyard there are three yellow posters side by side, three copies of a political speech printed in tiny letters with an enormous headline at the top: "Citizens Awake! Citizens Awake! Citizens Awake!" Wallas recognizes this poster, distributed throughout the city and already old, some kind of trade-union propaganda against the trusts, or liberal propaganda against the tariff rates, the sort of literature no one ever reads, except, occasionally, an old gentleman who stops, puts on his glasses and carefully reads the whole text through, shifts his eyes back and forth along the lines from the beginning all the way to the end, steps back a little to consider the whole poster with a shrug, puts his glasses back in their case and the case in his pocket, then goes on his way in some perplexity, wondering if he has not missed the point. Among the usual words some suspect term occasionally stands out like a signal, and the sentence it illuminates so equivocally seems for a moment to conceal many things, or nothing at all. Thirty yards farther on can be seen the back of the plaque warning drivers of the school crossing.

The street next crosses another canal, wider than the last, along which a tug is slowly approaching, pulling two coal barges. A man in a dark blue pea jacket and a visored cap has just closed off the bridge at the opposite end and turns toward the free end where Wallas has just started across.

"Hurry up, Monsieur, it'll be opening!" the man shouts.

As he passes him, Wallas nods.

"Not so warm this morning!"

"Winter's coming," the man answers.

With a low moan the tug salutes; under the cluster of metal beams, Wallas glimpses the trail of dissolving steam. He pushes the gate. An electric bell indicates that the workman at the other end is about to set the machinery in motion. At the moment Wallas closes the gate, the roadway behind him comes apart, the platform begins to tip up with a noise of motors and gears.

Wallas finally turns into a wide avenue that looks much like the Boulevard Circulaire he left at dawn, except for the canal, which is replaced here by a central sidewalk planted with very young trees; adjoining houses of five or six stories alternate with more modest structures of almost rural appearance and buildings evidently used for industrial purposes. Wallas is surprised to find more examples of this suburban mixture. Since he has crossed the street to turn right in this new direction, he reads with even more surprise the words "Boulevard Circulaire" on the building at the corner. He turns back, disconcerted.

He cannot have been walking in a circle, since he had gone straight ahead ever since the Rue des Arpenteurs; he has probably walked too far south and bypassed a segment of the city. He will have to ask his way.

People in the street are hurrying past on their errands, Wallas prefers not to delay them. He decides on a woman in an apron who is washing the sidewalk in front of her shop on the other side of the street. Wallas approaches but he is not sure how to ask his question: for the moment he has no precise destination; as for the police station where he is supposed to go a little later, he is reluctant to mention it, less from professional discretion than because of his desire to remain in a convenient neutrality rather than carelessly inspiring fear or merely curiosity. The same is true for the courthouse which, he has been told, is opposite the police station, but whose faint artistic renown is not enough to motivate the interest he would appear to be taking in it. The woman straightens up when she sees him beside her; she stops the movement of her broom.

"Excuse me, Madame, can you tell me how to get to the central post office?"

After a moment's reflection, she answers:

"The central post office; what do you mean, the central post office?"

"I mean the main post office."

This does not seem to be the right question. Maybe there are several main post offices and none located in the center of town. The woman looks at her broom and says:

"You'll find a post office right near here, on the parkway." She points with her chin. "People usually go there. But it's probably closed at this hour."

So his question meant something: there is only one post office with a telegraph office open all night.

"Yes, that's just it, there must be a post office open for sending telegrams."

This remark unfortunately seems to awaken the woman's interest:

"Oh, it's for sending a telegram!"

She glances at her broom, while Wallas tries to get off with a vague "yes."

"Nothing serious, I hope?" the woman says.

The question has not been asked in a specifically interrogative way, rather as a polite, slightly dubitative wish; but then she says nothing more and Wallas feels he must answer.

"No, no," he says, "thanks."

This is a lie too, since a man has died during the night. Should he explain that it is no one in his family?

"Well," the woman says, "if you're not in a hurry, there's a post office here that'll be open at eight."

This is what making up stories gets you into. Now to whom would he send a telegram, and what about? How can he manage to get back where he started? Observing his dissatisfied expression, the woman finally adds:

"There's a post office on the Avenue Christian-Charles, but I don't know if it opens before the others; besides, to get there from here . . ."

She examines him more attentively now, as if she were calculating his chances of reaching his goal before eight; then she glances down at the end of her broom again. One of the bristles, half undone, lets a few sprays of quitch grass stick out on one side. Finally she expresses the result of her scrutiny:

"You're not from around here, Monsieur?"

"No," Wallas admits reluctantly; "I've been here only a little while. If you'll show me how to get to the center of town, I'll find my way."

The center? The woman tries to locate it in her own mind; she stares at her broom, then at the pail full of water. She turns toward the Rue Janeck and points in the direction Wallas came from.

"Just take that street. After the canal you turn left on the Rue de Berlin and you'll come to the Place de la Préfecture. Then you just follow the avenues; it's straight ahead."

The prefecture: that's what he should have asked for.

"Thank you, Madame."

"It's a long walk, you know. You'd be better off taking the streetcar over there, you see. . . ."

"No, no, I'll walk fast; it'll warm me up! Thank you, Madame."

"At your service, Monsieur."

She puts her broom in the pail and begins scrubbing the sidewalk. Wallas starts walking in the opposite direction.

His reassuring course has been re-established. Now the office workers are coming out of their houses, holding the imitation leather briefcases that contain the three traditional sandwiches for the noon meal. They glance up toward the sky as they come out of their doorways and walk off, winding brown knitted mufflers around their necks.

Wallas feels the cold on his face; though the season of cutting frost that freezes the face into a painful mask has not yet begun, something like a shrinking can already be felt in the tissues: the forehead contracts, the hairline draws closer to the eyebrows, the temples try to meet, the brain tends to shrink to a tiny benign mass on the surface of the skin, between the eyes, a little above the nose. Yet the senses are far from being benumbed: Wallas remains the attentive witness of a spectacle which has lost none of its qualities of order and permanence; perhaps, on the contrary, the course is growing stricter, gradually abandoning its ornaments and its slackness. But perhaps, too, this draftsman's precision is only illusory, merely the result of an empty stomach.

The sound of a Diesel engine approaches behind Wallas . . . the vibration finally fills his head completely, and soon passes him, trailing its cloud of asphyxiating smoke—a heavy long-distance transport vehicle.

A bicyclist who has just got off his vehicle is waiting in front of the white barrier, at the end of the drawbridge that is just being lowered again. Wallas stops beside him and both men stare at the under side of the platform which is just disappearing. When they again see the top of the roadway, the man with the bicycle opens the gate and sets his front wheel on it. He turns toward Wallas:

"Not so warm this morning," he says.

"Yes," Wallas says, "winter's coming."

"It looks as though it were going to snow."

"It's still early for that."

"I wouldn't be surprised anyway," the bicyclist says.

Both of them watch the iron edge of the platform, which gradually reaches the level of the street. At the moment it does, the noise suddenly stops; in the silence they hear the electric bell that authorizes them to cross. As he passes through the gate, the bicyclist repeats:

"I wouldn't be surprised."

"Maybe you're right," Wallas says. "Good luck!"

"Good-bye, Monsieur," the bicyclist says.

He jumps onto the seat and rides off. Is it really going to snow? It's still not cold enough, probably; it's only the sudden change in the weather that is surprising. Wallas, halfway across the bridge, passes the workman in the pea jacket who is about to reopen the barrier.

"Back already, Monsieur?"

"Yes," Wallas answers. "I had just time enough while the bridge was opening and closing. The prefecture is over there, isn't it?"

The other man turns back. "Time to do what?" he thinks. He says:

"Yes, that's right. Take the Rue de Berlin: it's the shortest way."

"Thank you, Monsieur."

"Have a good walk, Monsieur."

Why isn't that barrier controlled automatically, from the other end? Wallas realizes, now, that the Rue Janeck is not really straight: actually it curves south by a series of imperceptible angles. On the school sign showing two children carrying schoolbooks over their shoulders and holding hands, he can see the remains of a butterfly pasted on upside down and torn off. After the double door—Girls Boys—the courtyard wall disappears under the Indian chestnut trees, the reddish leaves and the split husks of the nuts; the little boys have carefully gathered the shiny kernels, the source of many games and much commerce. Wallas crosses to look at the names of the streets branching off to the left.

At one intersection Wallas notices opposite him the dyspeptic gentleman he has seen before, crossing the street. He doesn't look any better after having eaten breakfast; perhaps it is worry and not stomach trouble that gives him that expression. (He looks like Fabius!) He is wearing black: he is going to the post office to send a telegram announcing someone's death.

"Oh, it's for sending a telegram. Nothing serious, I hope?"

"A death, Madame."

The mournful gentleman passes Wallas and turns into the cross street: Rue de Berlin; Wallas walks in step with him.

So earlier this morning he should have kept straight ahead, judging by the direction of this street. The black back advances at the same speed as Wallas and shows him the way.

3

The man in the black overcoat passes on the left sidewalk and turns into a narrow street; consequently Wallas loses sight of him. A pity, for he was a good companion. So he was not going to send a telegram from the post office after all, unless he knows a short cut leading directly to the Avenue Christian-Charles. It doesn't matter, Wallas prefers to follow the main avenues, particularly since he has no reason to go to that post office.

It would certainly have been easier to tell that woman right away that he wanted to cover the principal streets of the city, which he was visiting for the first time; but then would not some scruple have obliged him to talk about the other trip?—the sunny little streets where he had walked with his mother, the dead end of a canal between the low houses, the hull of the abandoned boat, that relative (his mother's sister, or half-sister?) they were supposed to meet—it would have looked as though he were hunting down his childhood memories. As for passing himself off as a tourist, aside from the unlikelihood of the excuse at this time of year in a city completely barren of appeal for an art lover, this offered still greater dangers: where would the woman's questions have led him then, since the post office had been enough to create the telegram, quite naturally, in order to avoid new explanations and out of a desire, too, not to contradict her. By trying to be pleasant and discreet, into what imaginary adventures would he finally be dragged!

"You're not from around here, Monsieur?"

"No, I'm a detective and I arrived here last night to investigate a political murder."

That was even less likely than all the rest. "The special agent," Fabius is always repeating, "should leave as few traces as possible in people's minds; it is therefore important for him to maintain a behavior as close as possible to the normal in all circumstances." The caricature, famous in the Bureau of Investigation and in the whole Ministry, represents Fabius disguised as an "idler": hat pulled down over his eyes, huge dark glasses, and an outrageously false beard hanging to the ground; bent double, this creature prowls "discreetly" through the countryside, among the startled cows and horses.

This disrespectful image actually conceals a sincere admiration on the part of his collaborators toward their old chief. "He's failed a lot," his enemies whisper to you sanctimoniously; but those who work with him every day know that despite certain inexplicable obstinacies, the illustrious Fabius remains worthy of his legend. Yet, despite his attachment to somewhat old-fashioned methods, even his adherents reproach him occasionally for a kind of irresolution, a marked discretion that makes him hesitate about accepting even the most established facts. The perspicacity with which he detected the slightest weak point in a suspicious situation, the intensity of impulse that carried him to the very threshold of the enigma, his subsequent indefatigable patience in recomposing the threads that had been revealed, all this seemed to turn at times into the sterile skepticism of a fanatic. Already people were saying that he mistrusted easy solutions, now it is whispered that he has ceased to believe in the existence of any solution whatever.

In the present case, for instance, where the purpose is clear enough (to uncover the leaders of an anarchist organization), he has shown excessive hesitation from the start, seeming to be concerned with it only reluctantly. He has not even bothered to avoid making quite preposterous remarks in front of his subordinates, pretending to consider the conspiracy either as a series of coincidences or as a Machiavellian invention of the government. One day he remarked quite coolly that such people were philanthropists and were merely trying to further public welfare!

Wallas does not like such jokes, which serve only to get the Bureau accused of negligence, even of collusion. Obviously he cannot feel toward Fabius the blind veneration some of his colleagues show: he did not know him during the glorious years of struggle against the enemy agents during the war. Wallas has worked for the Bureau of Investigation only a short time, before that he was in another branch of the Ministry of the Interior, and it is an accident that he happens to have this job. Hitherto, his work consisted mostly in the surveillance of various theosophical societies against which Roy-Dauzet, the minister, had suddenly conceived a resentment; Wallas has spent several months attending meetings of the members, studying their extravagant brochures, and gaining the confidence of semilunatics; he has just finished his assignment with a voluminous report on the activities of these societies, all quite harmless, as it turns out.

As a matter of fact, the role of this marginal police force is generally quite pacific. Established originally with counterespionage as its real purpose, since the armistice it has become a kind of economic police whose chief function is to check the actions of the cartels. Subsequently, each time a financial, political, religious or other group has seemed to threaten the security of the state, the Bureau of Investigation has taken action and proved itself, on two or three occasions, to be of invaluable assistance to the government.

This time, something quite different is involved: in nine days, nine violent deaths have occurred one after another, of which at least six are definitely murders. Certain resemblances among these various crimes, the nature of the victims, as well as the threatening letters received by other members of the organization to which the nine dead men may have belonged, clearly show that it is a single case that must be dealt with: a monstrous campaign of intimidation—or even of total destruction—conducted (by whom?) against these men whose political role, though not official, is no doubt extremely important and who, for this reason, benefit . . . from a . . .

The Place de la Préfecture is a wide square bordered on three sides by buildings with arcades; the fourth side is occupied by the prefecture, a huge stone building ornamented with scrolls and scallops, fortunately few in number—in short, of rather somber ugliness.

In the middle of the square, on a low pedestal protected by an iron fence, stands a bronze group representing a Greek chariot drawn by two horses, in which are standing several individuals, probably symbolic, whose unnatural positions are out of harmony with the presumed rapidity of their equipage.

On the other side begins the Avenue de la Reine, where the skinny elms have already lost their leaves. There are very few people out of doors in this neighborhood; the few bundled-up pedestrians and the black branches of the trees give it a precociously wintry look.

The courthouse cannot be far away, for, aside from its suburbs, the city is certainly not very large. The prefecture clock showed a little after seven-ten, so that Wallas has a good three-quarters of an hour in which to explore the area.

At the end of the avenue, the gray water of an old shunting canal contributes to the frozen calmness of the landscape.

Then comes the Avenue Christian-Charles, a little wider, lined by a few elegant shops and movie theaters. A streetcar passes, occasionally indicating its silent approach by two or three quick rings of its bell.

Wallas notices a signboard showing a yellowed map of the city, a movable pointer in its center. Ignoring this point of reference, as well as the little box containing the street names on a roll of paper, he has no difficulty reconstructing his route: the station, the slightly flattened ring of the Boulevard Circulaire, the Rue des Arpenteurs, the Rue de Brabant, the Rue Joseph-Janeck which joins the parkway, the Rue de Berlin, the prefecture. Now he is going to take the Avenue Christian-Charles as far as the parkway and then, since he has time for it, make a detour to the left, in order to return along the Canal Louis V and then the narrow canal that follows his street . . . the Rue de Copenhague. It is this latter he has just crossed. When this circuit will have been completed, Wallas will have twice crossed the city proper from one side to the other, within the confines of the Boulevard Circulaire. Beyond, the suburbs extend for considerable distances, dense and unattractive to the east and south, but aerated, toward the northwest, by the numerous ponds of the inland waterway and toward the southwest by the playing fields, a woods, and even a municipal park adorned with a zoo.

There was a shorter way of getting here from the end of the Rue Janeck, but it was also more complicated, and the lady with the quitch-grass broom was right to send him back by way of the prefecture. The black overcoat with the disturbed face turned here and vanished into this swarm of narrow twisting alleyways. On the point of walking away, Wallas remembers that he still has to find the courthouse; he discovers it almost at once, behind the prefecture and connected with it by a tiny street that starts on the square, the Rue de la Charte. As a matter of fact, the main police station is located just opposite. Wallas feels less of a stranger in this space thus marked out, he can move about in it with less deliberation.

Farther down the avenue he passes in front of the post office. It is closed. On the enormous door, a white cardboard poster: "The offices are open continuously from eight A.M. to seven

59

P.M." After having turned toward the parkway, he soon comes to the canal which he follows, attracted and sustained by it, absorbed in the contemplation of the reflections and the shadows.

When Wallas enters the Place de la Préfecture for the second time, the clock indicates five to eight. He has just time enough to go into the café at the corner of the Rue de la Charte to eat something quickly. The place is not at all like what he was expecting: this part of the country does not look as though it cared much about mirrors, chromium, and neon lighting. Behind its inadequate windows, supplemented by the timid glow of a few wall brackets, this big café is actually rather mournful, with its dark woodwork and thin banquettes covered in dark imitation leather. Wallas can just barely read the newspaper he has asked for. He quickly glances down the columns:

"Serious traffic accident on the Delft road."

"The city council will meet tomorrow to elect a new mayor."

"The medium deceived her clients."

"Potato production has surpassed that of the best years in the past."

"Death of one of our fellow citizens. A daring burglar made his way at nightfall yesterday into the residence of M. Daniel Dupont. . . ."

It is likely that Laurent, the chief commissioner, will receive him in person once he arrives, thanks to Fabius' letter of introduction. Provided he is not offended by such an intervention: Wallas will have to present matters skillfully; otherwise he risks turning the man into an enemy or in any case losing his cooperation, which is indispensable. As a matter of fact, though the local police have shown themselves absolutely ineffectual in dealing with the eight preceding crimes—not having been able to find a single lead and even classifying two cases as "death by accident"—it seems difficult to avoid their collaboration completely: they constitute, in spite of everything, the only possible source of information concerning the supposed "killers." From another point of view, it would be inopportune to let them suppose that the latter were suspect.

Noticing an open stationery shop, Wallas walks in for no particular reason. A young girl who had been sitting behind the counter stands up to wait on him.

"Monsieur?"

She has a pretty, slightly sullen face and blond hair.

"I'd like a very soft gum eraser, for drawing."

"Certainly, Monsieur."

She turns back toward the drawers that line the wall. Her hair, combed straight up from the back of her neck, makes her look older, seen from behind. She searches through one of the drawers and sets down in front of Wallas a yellow eraser with beveled edges, longer than it is wide, an ordinary article for schoolchildren. He asks:

"Haven't you any supplies just for drawing?"

"This is a drawing eraser, Monsieur."

She encourages him with a half-smile. Wallas picks up the eraser to examine it more carefully; then he looks at the young girl, her eyes, her fleshy, half-parted lips. He smiles in his turn.

"What I wanted . . ."

She tilts her head slightly, as though to pay special attention to what he is going to say.

". . . was something more crumbly."

"Really, Monsieur, I can assure you this is a very good pencil eraser. All our customers are satisfied with it."

"All right," Wallas says, "I'll try it. How much is it?"

He pays and leaves the store. She accompanies him to the door. No, she's no longer a child: her hips, her slow gait are almost a woman's.

Once out in the street, Wallas mechanically fingers the little eraser; it is obvious from the way it feels that it is no good at all. It would have been surprising, really, for it to be otherwise in so modest a shop. . . . That girl was nice. . . . He rubs his thumb across the end of the eraser. It is not at all what he is looking for.

4

By shifting the dossiers on top of his desk, Laurent covers up the little piece of eraser. Wallas finishes his remarks:

"In short, you haven't found much."

"You might say nothing," the chief commissioner answers.

"And what do you intend to do now?"

"Nothing, since it isn't my case any more!"

Commissioner Laurent accompanies these words with an ironically brokenhearted smile. When his interlocutor says nothing, he continues:

"I was wrong, no doubt, to believe myself in charge of public safety in this city. This paper," he waves a letter between two fingers, "orders me in specific terms to let the capital take over last night's crime. I couldn't ask for anything better. And now the minister, you say—or in any case a service that is directly attached to him—sends you here to continue the investigation, not 'in my place' but 'with my cooperation.' What am I supposed to make of that? Except that this cooperation is to be limited to handing over to you whatever information I possess —which I have just done—and therefore to having you protected by my men, if necessary."

With another smile, Laurent adds:

"So now it's up to you to tell me what *you're* going to do, unless of course that's a secret."

Entrenched behind the papers covering his desk, his elbows propped on the arms of his chair, the commissioner rubs his hands together as he speaks, slowly, almost cautiously, then he sets them down in front of him on the scattered sheets of paper, spreading his short, fat fingers as far apart as possible, and waits for the answer, without taking his eyes from his visitor's face. He is a short, plump man with a pink face and a bald skull. His kindly tone is a little forced.

"You say the witnesses," Wallas begins. . . .

Laurent immediately raises his hands to stop him.

"There are no witnesses, properly speaking," he says, rubbing his right palm over his left forefinger; "you can scarcely call the doctor who has not restored the wounded man to life a witness, or the old deaf housekeeper who has seen nothing whatsoever."

"It was the doctor who informed you?"

"Yes, Doctor Juard telephoned the police last night around nine o'clock; the inspector who received the information wrote down what he said—you've just looked at the record—and then he called me at home. I had an immediate examination of the premises made. Upstairs, the inspectors picked up four sets of fresh fingerprints: those of the housekeeper, then three others apparently made by men's hands. If it's true that no outsider has come upstairs for several days, these last could be (he counts on his fingers) first of all, those of the doctor, faint and few, on the stair banister and in Dupont's bedroom; second, those of Dupont himself, which can be found all over the house; third, those of the murderer, quite numerous and very clear, on the banister, on the doorknob of the study, and on certain articles of furniture in this study—mainly the back of the desk chair. The house has two entrances; the doctor's right thumbprint has been found on the front doorbell, and the hypothetical murderer's on the knob of the back door. You see that I'm giving you all the details. Lastly, the housekeeper declares that the doctor came in through the front door and that she found the back door open when she went upstairs to answer the wounded man's call—even though she had closed it a few moments before. If you want me to, I can have Doctor Juard's fingerprints taken, just to be sure. . . ."

"You can also get the dead man's prints, I suppose?"

"I could, if I had the body at my disposal," Laurent answers sweetly.

Seeing Wallas' questioning look, he asks:

"Haven't you heard? The body was taken away from me at the same time as the control of the investigation. I thought it was sent to the same organization that sent you here."

Wallas is obviously amazed. Could other services be concerned with this case? This is a supposition Laurent receives with obvious satisfaction. He waits, his hands lying flat on his desk; his kindly expression is tinged with compassion. Without insisting on this point, Wallas continues:

"You were saying that Dupont, after being wounded, had called to the old housekeeper from upstairs; for the latter to have heard him, deaf as she is, Dupont would have had to shout quite loudly. Yet the doctor describes him as greatly weakened by his wound, almost unconscious."

"Yes, I know; there seems to be a contradiction here; but he might have had strength enough to go get his revolver and call for help, and then have lost a lot of blood while waiting for the ambulance: there was a relatively large bloodstain on the bedspread. In any case, he wasn't unconscious when the doctor got there, since Dupont told him he hadn't seen his attacker's face. There's a mistake in the account published by the papers: it was only *after* the operation that the wounded man didn't recover consciousness. Moreover, you'll obviously have to go see this doctor. You should also ask for details from the housekeeper, Madame . . . (he consults a sheet from the dossier) Madame Smite; her explanations are somewhat confused: she told us, in particular, some elaborate story about a broken telephone that seems to have nothing to do with the case—at least at first glance. The inspectors haven't made a point of it, preferring to wait until she calms down; they haven't even told her her employer was dead."

The two men do not speak for a moment. It is the commissioner who resumes, delicately rubbing his joints with his thumb.

"He may perfectly well have committed suicide, you know. He has shot himself with the revolver once—or several times—without managing to finish himself off; then he has changed his mind, as so often happens, and called for help, trying to disguise his unsuccessful attempt as an attack. Or else—and this would be more in accord with what we know about his character—he has prepared this setting in advance, and managed to give himself a mortal wound that allowed him a few minutes' survival in order to have time to bequeath the myth of his murder to the public. It's very difficult, you'll say, to calculate the consequences of a pistol shot so exactly; he may have fired a second shot while the housekeeper was going for the doctor. He was a strange man, from many points of view."

"It must be possible to verify these hypotheses from the position of the bullets," Wallas remarks.

"Yes, sometimes it's possible. And we would have examined the bullets and the revolver of the supposed victim. All I have here is the death certificate the doctor sent this morning; it's the only thing we can be sure of, for the time being. The suspect fingerprints can belong to anyone who came during the day without the housekeeper's knowing it; as for the back door she mentioned to the inspector, the wind might have opened it."

"You really think Dupont committed suicide?"

"I don't think anything. I find it's not impossible, according to the facts I have. This death certificate, which is drawn up quite correctly, by the way, gives no indication as to the kind of wound that caused death; and the information furnished last night by the doctor and the housekeeper is all too vague in this regard, as you've seen. Before anything else, you'll have to clear up these few details. If necessary, you could even get the additional details that might interest you from the coroner in the capital."

Wallas says:

"Your help would certainly have made my job easier."

"But you can count on me, Monsieur. As soon as you have someone to arrest I'll send you two or three good men. I'll be eager to get your telephone call; just ask for one-twenty-four —twenty-four, it's a direct line."

The smile on the chubby face widens. The little hands spread out on the desk, palms smooth, fingers wide. Wallas writes: "C. Laurent, 124-24." A direct line to what?

Wallas again considers the isolation of his situation. The last bicyclists ride off in a group toward their work; standing alone, leaning on a railing, he abandons this support as well and begins walking through the empty streets in the direction he has decided on. Apparently no one is interested in what he is doing: the doors remain closed, no face appears in the windows to watch him pass. Yet his presence on these premises is necessary: no one else is concerned with this murder. It's his own case; they have sent him to solve it.

The commissioner, like the workmen earlier this morning, stares at him with astonishment—hostility perhaps—and turns his head away: his role is already over; he has no access, on the other side of the brick walls, to the realm in which this story is happening; the sole purpose of his speeches is to make Wallas feel the virtual impossibility of entering it. But Wallas is confident. Though at first glance the difficulty is even greater for himself—a stranger in this city, and knowing neither its secrets

nor its short cuts—he is sure he has not been asked to come
here for nothing: once the weak spot is found, he will unhesitatingly advance toward his goal.

He asks, just to make sure:

"What would you have done, if you had gone on with the investigation yourself?"

"It's not in my line," the commissioner answers, "which is
why they took it away from me."

"Then what is the responsibility of the police, in your
opinion?"

Laurent rubs his hands a little faster.

"We keep criminals within certain limits more or less fixed
by the law."

"And?"

"This one is beyond us, he doesn't belong to the category of
ordinary malefactors. I know every criminal in this city:
they're all listed in my files; I arrest them when they forget
the conventions society imposes on them. If one of them had
killed Dupont to rob him or even to be paid by a political
party, do you think we would still be wondering, more than
twelve hours after the murder, whether it wasn't a suicide after
all? This district isn't very big, and informers are legion here.
We don't always manage to prevent crime, sometimes the criminal even manages to escape, but there's never been a case
where we haven't found his tracks, whereas this time we're left
with a lot of unidentified fingerprints and some drafts that open
doors. Our informers are no help here. If we're dealing, as you
think, with a terrorist organization, they've been very careful
to keep from being contaminated; in this sense, their hands are
clean, cleaner than those of a police that maintains such close
relations with the men they're watching. Here, between the
policeman and the criminal, you find every grade of intermedi-

ary. Our whole system is based on them. Unfortunately the shot that killed Daniel Dupont came from another world!"

"But you know there's no such thing as a perfect crime; we must look for the flaw that has to exist somewhere."

"Where are you going to look? Make no mistake about it, Monsieur: this is the work of specialists, they've obviously left few things to chance; but what makes the few clues we have useless is our inability to test them against anything else."

"This case is already the ninth," Wallas says.

"Yes, but you'll agree that only the political opinions of the victims and the hour of their deaths have allowed us to connect them. Besides, I'm not so convinced as you that such coincidences correspond to anything real. And even supposing they do, we're not much further: what use would it be to me, for instance, if a second murder just as anonymous were committed in this city tonight? As for the central services, they don't have any more opportunities than I do to get results: they have the same files and the same methods. They've taken the body away from me, and it's all the easier for me to abandon it to them since you tell me they have eight more they don't know what to do with. Before your visit, I already had the impression that the case didn't have anything to do with the police, and your presence here makes me sure of it."

Despite his interlocutor's evident prejudice, Wallas insists: the victim's relatives and friends could be questioned. But Laurent has no hopes of finding out anything useful from this quarter either:

"It appears that Dupont led an extremely solitary life, shut up with his books and his old housekeeper. He seldom went out and received only rare visits. Did he have any friends? As for relatives, there seem to be none, except for his wife. . . ."

Wallas shows his surprise:

"He had a wife? Where was she at the time of the crime?"

"I don't know. Dupont was married only a few years; his wife was much younger than he and probably couldn't endure his hermit's life. They separated right away. But they still saw each other now and then, apparently; by all means ask her what she was doing last night at seven-thirty."

"You're not saying that seriously?"

"Certainly I am. Why not? She knew the house and her ex-husband's habits well; so she had more opportunities than anyone else to commit this murder discreetly. And since she was entitled to expect a considerable inheritance from him, she's one of the few people I know of who could have any interest in seeing him dead."

"Then why didn't you mention her to me?"

"You told me that he was the victim of a political assassination!"

"She could have played her part in it anyway."

"Of course. Why not?"

Commissioner Laurent has resumed his jocular tone. He says with a half-smile:

"Maybe it's the housekeeper who killed him and made up all the rest with the help of Doctor Juard, whose reputation—let me tell you in passing—is not so good."

"That seems rather unlikely," Wallas observes.

"Even altogether unlikely, but you know that never kept anyone from being a suspect."

Wallas feels that this irony is in bad taste. Furthermore, he realizes he will not learn much from this official, jealous of his authority but determined to do nothing. Isn't Laurent really trying to wash his hands of the whole affair? Or else would he like to discourage his rivals in order to make his own investigation? Wallas stands up to say good-bye; he will visit this doctor first. Laurent shows him where he is to be found:

"The Juard Clinic, eleven Rue de Corinthe. It's on the other side of the prefecture, not far from here."

"I thought," Wallas says, "that the newspaper said 'a nearby clinic'?"

Laurent makes a cynical gesture:

"Oh, you know the papers! Besides, it's not so far from the Rue des Arpenteurs."

Wallas writes down the address in his notebook.

"There is even one paper," the commissioner adds, "that mixed up the first names and announced the death of Albert Dupont, one of the biggest wood exporters in the city. He must have been quite surprised to read his obituary this morning!"

Laurent has stood up too. He winks as he says:

"After all, I haven't seen the body; maybe it *is* Albert Dupont's."

This idea amuses him enormously, his overfed body shakes from fits of laughter. Wallas smiles politely. The chief commissioner catches his breath and holds out his hand amiably.

"If I hear anything new," he says, "I'll let you know. What hotel are you staying at?"

"I've taken a room in a café, Rue des Arpenteurs, a few steps away from the house itself."

"You have! Who told you about that?"

"No one; I found it by chance. It's number ten."

"Is there a telephone?"

"Yes, I think so."

"Well, I'll find it in the book if I have anything to tell you."

Without waiting. Laurent begins leafing quickly through the phone book, licking his index finger.

"Arpenteurs, here we are. Number ten: Café des Alliés?"

"Yes, that's the one."

"Telephone: two-zero-two-zero-three. But it's not a hotel."

"No," Wallas says, "they only rent out a few rooms."

Laurent goes to a shelf and picks out a ledger. After a moment of fruitless search, he asks:

"That's strange, they're not registered; are there many rooms?"

"No, I don't think so," Wallas answers. "You see, your facts aren't so exact after all!"

A broad smile lights up the chief commissioner's face.

"On the contrary, you have to admire our resources," he says. "The first person to sleep in this café comes to tell me about it himself, without even giving the landlord a chance!"

"Why the first person? Suppose the murderer had slept there last night, what would you know about it?"

"The landlord would have registered him and reported to me, as he'll do for you—he has until noon."

"And if he doesn't?" Wallas asks.

"Well, in that case, we would have to admire your perspicacity in having found the only clandestine rooming house in town so quickly. It would even be bad for you in the long run; you'd be the first serious suspect I've found: recently arrived in town, living twenty yards from the scene of the crime, and completely unknown to the police!"

"But I only arrived last night, at eleven!" Wallas protests.

"If you weren't registered, what proof would there be?"

"At the time the crime was committed, I was a hundred kilometers from here; that can be verified."

"Of course! Don't good murderers always have an alibi?"

Laurent sits down again behind his desk and considers Wallas with a smiling expression. Then he suddenly asks:

"Do you have a revolver?"

"Yes," Wallas answers. "This time I took one, on the advice of my chief."

"What for?"

"You never know."

"Right, you never know. Would you show it to me please?"

Wallas hands him the gun, a 7.65 millimeter automatic revolver, a common model. Laurent examines it carefully, after having removed the clip. Finally, without looking at Wallas, he says in the tone of an obvious comment:

"One bullet's missing."

He hands the weapon back to its owner. Then, very quickly, he clasps his hands, separates the palms though keeping the fingers interlaced, brings his wrists together again and rubs his thumbs against each other. The hands separate and stretch; each doubles over with a faint clapping sound, opens once more and finally comes to rest on the desk, lying flat, the fingers spread apart at regular intervals.

"Yes, I know," Wallas answers.

In making room for his ledgers, the commissioner has shifted the dossiers that cover his desk, thereby causing the piece of grayish eraser to reappear, an ink eraser probably, whose poor quality is betrayed by several worn, slightly shiny places.

5

Once the door is closed, the commissioner walks slowly back to his chair. He rubs his hands with satisfaction. So it is Roy-Dauzet who has had the body taken away! This kind of conspiracy story is worthy of the old lunatic's grotesque imagination. And now he is sending his clan of secret agents and detectives all over the country—even the great Fabius and his consorts.

Political crime? That, of course, would explain the complete failure of his own investigation—in any case it is a good excuse —but Laurent greatly distrusts the minister's tendency to hysterical storytelling, so that he is delighted to see others besides himself set foot on this dangerous path. He has no difficulty imagining the mess they will be getting into: it is apparent, to begin with, that the confidential agent sent to the scene of the crime hadn't heard of the hasty transfer of the body to the capital—his surprise was not made up. He seems full of good will, this Wallas; but what could he do with it? Besides, just what is his job anyway? He has not been very talkative; what does he really know about these "terrorists"? Nothing probably; and with good reason! Or has he been given orders to keep quiet? Maybe Fabius, who is the best sleuth in Europe, proved to him that Laurent himself was in the gang's pay? You have to expect anything from these geniuses.

First of all, they operate as if their chief concern is to see the police stop their investigations (that was what they were most anxious about, they even ordered him to abandon the house without so much as sealing it or stationing a man there, even though the old servant who is still there alone does not seem to have all her wits about her) and then they pretend to come and ask his advice. Well, they will have to continue to get along without him.

Before sitting down, the commissioner straightens up his desk a little; he puts back the phone book, replaces the loose sheets in the dossiers. The one marked "Dupont" joins the left-hand pile, that of closed cases. Laurent rubs his hands again and repeats to himself: "Perfect!"

But a little later, when Laurent is finishing his mail, the man on duty announces Doctor Juard. What does this one want now! Can't they leave him in peace about this case he's not even supposed to be concerned with?

When he has the doctor shown in, Laurent is struck by his exhausted look.

"Monsieur," the latter begins, almost in a whisper, "I'm

here about the death of this unfortunate Dupont. I'm Doctor Juard."

"Of course, Doctor, but we've already worked together once, if my memory doesn't deceive me?"

"Oh, 'worked'!" the little doctor says modestly. "My cooperation was so insignificant. I didn't think you would even remember it."

"We've all done what we could, Doctor," the commissioner says.

After a slight pause, the doctor continues, as though reluctantly:

"I sent you a death certificate, but I thought you might want to see me anyway. . . ."

He stops. Laurent watches him calmly, his hands lying on the desk which he absent-mindedly taps with one finger.

"Of course, Doctor, I'm glad you did," he says at last.

This is a purely formal encouragement. Doctor Juard is beginning to regret having rushed here so soon, instead of waiting until the police sent for him. He wipes his glasses to gain time, and continues with a sigh:

"All the same, I don't know what I could tell you about this strange crime."

If he has nothing to say, why has he come? He has preferred to come of his own accord rather than seem to be afraid of questioning. He thought we were going to ask him specific details—for which he has prepared himself—and now we're letting him get out of it by himself, as if he were the one in the wrong.

"Why 'strange'?" the commissioner asks.

He doesn't think it's strange. It's the doctor he thinks strange, sitting there stringing out his empty phrases instead of simply saying what he knows. What he knows about what? He hasn't been called to give evidence. He has been particularly afraid that the police would come and rummage through his clinic: that's why he's here.

"I mean: out of the ordinary; there aren't murders in our city very often. And it's extremely rare that a burglar making his way into an inhabited house should be so upset at the sight of the owner that he feels it necessary to shoot him."

Another thing that has kept him from staying home is his need to find out exactly what the others know and don't know.

"You say 'a burglar'?" Laurent asks in surprise; "did he take anything?"

"Not that I know of."

"If he didn't steal anything, he's not a burglar."

"You're playing with words, Monsieur," the little doctor insists: "he probably had every intention of stealing."

"Oh, 'intention'! You're moving a little too fast."

Fortunately the commissioner decides to say something and asks:

"It was the housekeeper who called you, wasn't it?"

"Yes, old Madame Smite."

"Didn't you think it was odd that she should call in a gynecologist to take care of a wounded man?"

"Good lord, Monsieur, I'm a surgeon; I performed many such operations during the war. Dupont knew it: we had been friends since college."

"Oh, Daniel Dupont was your friend? I'm sorry, Doctor."

Juard makes an almost protesting gesture:

"Let's not exaggerate; we knew each other for a long time, that's all."

Laurent continues:

"You went to get the victim by yourself?"

"Yes, I didn't want to take an orderly: I have a very small staff. Poor Dupont didn't seem in any danger; Madame Smite and I were able to hold him up, going down the stairs . . ."

"Then he could still walk? Didn't you say, last night, that he was unconscious?"

"No, Monsieur, I certainly did not. When I arrived, the wounded man was waiting for me on his bed; he spoke to me and because he was so insistent, I agreed to take him without a stretcher, so as to lose as little time as possible. It was during the trip in the car that he suddenly grew weaker. Up till then he assured me that it was nothing serious, but at that moment I realized that his heart had been touched. I operated immediately: the bullet had lodged in the wall of the ventricle, he could have recovered from that. The heart stopped when I performed the extraction; all my efforts to revive him remained useless."

The doctor sighs, with a look of great exhaustion.

"Perhaps," the commissioner says, "there was some cardiac difficulty to complicate matters?"

But the practitioner shakes his head.

"You can't be sure: a normal man can succumb to a wound of that type too. Actually, it's a matter of luck."

"Tell me, Doctor," Laurent asks after a moment's thought, "can you suggest at about what distance from the body the shot was fired?"

"Five yards . . . ten?" Juard says evasively. "It's difficult to give an exact figure."

"In any case," the commissioner concludes, "for a bullet fired by a man running away, it was carefully aimed."

"Chance . . ." the doctor says.

"There wasn't any other wound, was there?"

"No, only the one."

Doctor Juard answers a few more questions. If he hasn't telephoned the police at once, it is because the phone in Dupont's house was out of order; and once he reached the clinic, the wounded man's condition gave him no opportunity. It was from a nearby café that Madame Smite had called him. No, he doesn't know the name of this café. He also confirms the removal of the body by the police van, and hands the commissioner, in conclusion, the only piece of evidence he has left: a tiny ball of tissue paper. . . .

"I've brought you the bullet," he says.

Laurent thanks him. The police magistrate will probably need the doctor's testimony.

They separate after a few more friendly words.

Laurent stares at the tiny cone of black metal, a 7.65 projectile that could just as well have come from Wallas' pistol as from any weapon of the same type. If only the cartridge shell had been found too.

This Doctor Juard certainly has something suspicious about him. The first time Laurent had any dealing with him, he could not quite dismiss this impression: the doctor's embarrassed phrases, his peculiar explanations, his reticence had finally made Laurent suspect some sort of intrigue. He sees now that this is the man's normal behavior. Is it his glasses that give him that shifty look? Or his deferential politeness? If Fabius saw him, he would unhesitatingly classify him among the accomplices! Hasn't Laurent himself instinctively tried to unsettle him further by disconcerting questions? The poor wretch didn't need any such treatment though: the simplest words, in his mouth, assume an equivocal quality.

". . . My cooperation was so insignificant. . . ."

What was surprising if people talked about his professional activities? Perhaps, today, he is also affected by the death of one of his friends under his own scapel. Heart disease! Why not?

"Chance . . ."

Chance, for the second time, puts this little doctor in a rather curious situation. Laurent will not be completely satisfied until the capital sends on the coroner's conclusions. If Dupont has committed suicide, a specialist can tell that the shot was fired at close range: Juard has realized this and is trying, out of friendship, to convince Laurent that Dupont was murdered. He has come here to decide what effect his declarations have produced; he is afraid that the body—even after the operation—might betray the truth. He is apparently unaware that the police van has removed it to another destination.

He is a truly loyal friend. Didn't he, last night, "out of respect for the deceased," request that the press not make too much fuss over this "sensational incident!" Besides, he had nothing to fear: the morning papers could insert only a last minute brief account; as for the evening papers, they will have plenty of time to receive the group's orders. Although a professor and living quietly, Daniel Dupont belonged to that section of the industrial and mercantile bourgeoisie that does not like to see its life, or its death, discussed in the marketplace. Now no newspaper in the whole country could flatter itself that it was completely independent of this class; with all the more reason in this provincial city, where their omnipotent influence seemed to have no flaws. Shipowners, paper manufacturers, wood exporters, spinning-mill owners, all join hands to protect identical interests. Dupont—it was true—denounced the weaknesses of their system in his books, but that was more a question of advice than attack, and even the ones who did not listen to him respected the professor.

Political crime? Did this withdrawn figure exert the occult influence some attributed to him? Even if it were so, you would have to be a Roy-Dauzet to construct such absurd hypotheses: a murder every day at the same hour. . . . Luckily, this time he has not confided his hallucinations to the regular police. Laurent still has a bad memory of the minister's last whim: large quantities of arms and munitions were—he claimed—being landed daily in the harbor on behalf of some revolutionary organization; this traffic would have to be stopped at once and the guilty parties arrested! For almost three weeks the police have exhausted themselves: the depots minutely inspected, the holds searched from top to bottom, the crates opened one by one, the bales of cotton unpacked (then repacked) because their weight was over normal. They had picked up, as their entire prize, two undeclared revolvers and the hunting rifle an unfortunate passenger had concealed in a trunk to avoid paying customs duty. No one took the matter seriously, and the police, after a few days, were the laughingstock of the town.

The chief commissioner is not about to set off on a wild goose chase of that sort so quickly.

6

As he left the police station, Wallas was once again seized by that impression of empty-headedness which he had earlier attributed to the cold. He then decided that the long walk on an empty stomach—which too light a breakfast had not made up for afterward—also contributed something to this feeling. To be in a position to think to advantage about the commissioner's remarks and to put his own ideas in order, Wallas has decided it would be a good idea to eat a heavier meal. So he has gone into a restaurant he had noticed an hour before, where he has eaten with a good appetite two eggs and some ham with toast. At the same time, he has had the waitress explain the most convenient way to get to the Rue de Corinthe. Passing once more in front of the statue that decorates the Place de la Préfecture, he has approached it to read, on the west side of the pedestal, the inscription carved in the stone: "The Chariot of State—V. Daulis, sculptor."

He has found the clinic easily, but Doctor Juard has just left. The reception nurse has asked him the purpose of his visit; he has answered that he preferred to speak to the doctor in person; she has then asked him if he wished to speak with Madame Juard who—she said—was also a doctor and, besides, was in charge of the clinic. Wallas has explained that he had not come for medical reasons. This explanation made the nurse smile—for no apparent reason—but she has asked nothing further. She did not know when the doctor would be back; it would be best to come back later, or telephone. While she closes the door behind him, she has murmured, loud enough so Wallas could hear her:

"They're all the same!"

Wallas has returned to the square and walked around the prefecture on the right side, intending to come out onto the Boulevard Circulaire near the Rue des Arpenteurs; but he has lost his way in a labyrinth of tiny streets where the sudden turns and detours have forced him to walk much longer than was necessary. After crossing a canal, he has finally reached a familiar neighborhood: the Rue de Brabant and the imitation brick buildings of the wood exporters. During this entire course his attention has been completely absorbed by his concern to proceed in the right direction; and when, after crossing the parkway, he has found himself standing in front of the little house surrounded by spindle trees, the latter has suddenly looked sinister to him, whereas this morning he had been struck, on the contrary by its attractive appearance. He has tried to dismiss such unreasonable ideas, setting them down to fatigue, and he has decided to take the streetcar to move around the city from now on.

It is at this moment that he has realized that, for almost a half-hour, his mind had been exclusively preoccupied by the nurse's expression and tone: polite but apparently full of double meanings. She almost looked as though she supposed he wanted a shady doctor—for God knows what reason.

Wallas follows the hedge, behind the iron fence, and stops at the gate, where he stares for a minute at the front of the house. There are two windows on the ground floor, three upstairs, one of which (on the left) is partly open.

Contrary to his expectation, no bell sounds when he opens the gate and walks into the garden. He closes the gate, follows the gravel path, and walks up the four steps to the door. He presses the bell; a distant ring answers. In the center of the varnished oak door is a rectangular window protected by an elaborate grillwork: something like intertwined flower stems, with long, supple leaves . . . it might also represent wisps of smoke. . . .

After a few seconds, Wallas rings again. Since no one comes to open the door, he glances through the little window—but without being able to make out anything inside. Then he looks up toward the second-story windows. An old woman is leaning just far enough out of the left one to catch sight of him.

"Who do you want?" she cries when she realizes she has been seen. "No one's here. You'd better leave, young man."

Her tone is suspicious and cold, but nevertheless something about it hints at the possibility of getting around her. Wallas assumes his most agreeable manner:

"You're Madame Smite, aren't you?"

"What did you say?"

"You're Madame Smite, aren't you?" he repeats, somewhat louder.

This time she answers as if she had understood long before:

"Yes, of course! What do you want Madame Smite for!" And without waiting she adds in her shrill voice: "If it's for the telephone, I can tell you now that you've come too late, young man: there's no one here any more!"

"No, Madame, that's not what it's about. I'd like to talk to you."

"I don't have time to stay and talk. I'm packing my things."

Wallas is shouting now, by contagion and almost as loudly as the old woman. He insists:

"Listen, Madame Smite, I only want to ask you for a little information."

The old woman still does not seem to have made up her mind to let him in. He has stepped back so that she can see him more easily: his respectable clothes certainly count in his favor. And finally the housekeeper declares, before disappearing into the room: "I can't understand a word you're saying, young man. I'll come down."

But quite a while passes, and nothing at all happens. Wallas is on the point of calling, fearing she has forgotten all about him, when suddenly the window in the front door opens without his having heard the slightest noise in the hall, and the old woman's face presses up against the grill.

"So you're here for the telephone, are you?" she shrieks stubbornly (and just as loudly, though she is now six inches from her interlocutor). "That makes a week we've been waiting for you, young man! You're not coming from an asylum, at least, like the one last night?"

Wallas is somewhat baffled.

"Well, I . . ." he begins, supposing she's referring to the clinic, "I stopped by there but . . ."

The old housekeeper interrupts him at once, outraged:

"What? Does the company hire only lunatics? And you've probably stopped in every café on the way too, before you got here, haven't you?"

Wallas remains calm. Laurent has suggested that the woman sometimes said funny things; still, he did not think she was

82

this crazy. He will have to explain the matter to her carefully, articulating each word so she can understand what he is saying:

"No, listen, Madame, you're making a mistake. . . ."

But Wallas suddenly remembers the two cafés he was in this morning—and the one he has slept in as well; these are facts he cannot deny, although he does not see why he should be blamed for them. Besides, why should he bother himself about these grotesque accusations?

"It's a misunderstanding. It's not the company that's sending me." (That, at least, he can state without any ambiguity whatever.)

"Then what's this all about, young man?" the suspicious face replies.

An interrogation is not going to be easy under these conditions! Probably her employer's murder has unsettled the housekeeper's mind.

"I told you I'm not here for the telephone," Wallas repeats, forcing himself to be patient.

"Well," she exclaims, "you don't have to shout so loud, you know. I'm not deaf!" She reads lips, obviously. "And if you're not here for the telephone, there's no use talking."

Preferring not to bring up the subject again, Wallas quickly explains the purpose of his visit. To his great surprise, he makes himself understood without the slightest difficulty: Madame Smite agrees to let him come in. But instead of opening the door, she remains staring at him, behind the grill that half conceals her face. Through the opening in the window which she is about to close again, she remarks, finally, with a touch of reproach (shouldn't he have known about it long since?):

"Not through this door, young man. It's too hard to open. You can walk around to the back."

And the window closes with a click. As he walks down the

steps to the gravel path, Wallas feels her eyes fixed on him from the darkness of the hall.

Nevertheless old Anna hurries toward the kitchen. This gentleman has a nicer look about him than the two who came last night, with their red faces and their big boots. They went all over the place to do their dirty work and did not even listen to what they were told. She had to keep a close watch over them, for fear they might take something; their looks did not inspire much confidence. What if they were accomplices who had come to look for what the thief had not been able to steal when he ran away? This one looks less shrewd—and keeps getting mixed up in a lot of nonsense before coming to the point—but certainly he is better brought up. Monsieur Dupont always wanted her to let people in through the front door. The locks are too complicated. Now that he is dead, they can just as well walk around.

Wallas arrives at the little glass door the commissioner has mentioned to him. He knocks on a pane with his forefinger doubled up. Since the old housekeeper has disappeared again, he tries to turn the handle; the door is not locked. He pushes it open, it creaks on its hinges, like the door in an abandoned house—haunted maybe—where each movement provokes a flight of owls and bats. But once the door is closed, no rustle of wings disturbs the silence. Wallas takes a few hesitant steps; his eyes, growing used to the dimness, glances around the woodwork, the complicated moldings, the brass column at the foot of the staircase, the carpets, everything that constituted the ornaments of a bourgeois residence early in the century.

Wallas starts, suddenly hearing Madame Smite's voice calling him from the end of the hallway. He turns around and sees

the figure silhouetted against the glass door. For a second he
has the impression that he has just been caught in a trap.

It is the kitchen she has asked him to come into, a lifeless
kitchen that looks like a model: the stove perfectly polished,
the paint spotless, a row of copper pots fastened to the wall,
and so well scrubbed no one would dare use them. There is no
suggestion of the daily preparation of meals; the few objects
that are not shut away in the cupboards seem fixed forever in
their places on the shelves.

The old lady, dressed in black, is almost elegant despite her
felt slippers; besides, this is the only detail that indicates she is
at home here and not visiting an empty house. She tells Wallas
to sit down opposite her and begins immediately:

"Well, it's some story!"

But her loud voice, instead of sounding distressed, seems to
Wallas like a clumsy exclamation in a play. He would swear,
now, that the row of pots is painted on the wall in *trompe-l'oeil*.
The death of Daniel Dupont is no more than an abstract event
being discussed by dummies.

"He's dead, isn't he?" the housekeeper shrieks, so loudly that
Wallas moves his chair back a few inches. He is already preparing a sentence expressing his condolences, but without
leaving him time to get it out, she continues, leaning a little
closer to him: "Well, I'm going to tell you, my boy, I'm going
to tell you who killed him, so listen to me!"

"You know who killed Dupont?" Wallas asks, flabbergasted.

"It's that Doctor Juard. The one with the sly face. I went
to call him myself because—it's true—I was forgetting to tell
you: they cut the telephone wires here. Yes! Since the day
before yesterday . . . no, even before that: I'm losing track now.
What is it today . . . Monday . . ."

"Tuesday," Wallas corrects timidly.

"What did you say?"

"Today is Tuesday," Wallas repeats.

She moves her lips as she watches him talk, then squints incredulously. But she continues: you have to make such concessions to stubborn children.

"All right, say Tuesday. Well, as I was saying, the telephone hasn't been working since . . . Sunday, Saturday, Friday . . ."

"Madame, are you saying it was Doctor Juard who murdered Daniel Dupont?" Wallas interrupts.

"Of course that's what I'm saying, young man! Besides, everyone knows he's a murderer; go out and ask anyone in the street. Oh, I'm sorry now I ever listened to Monsieur Dupont; he insisted on Doctor Juard—he had his notions, you know, and he never paid any attention to whatever I might think of them. Well, people are what they are; I'm not going to start speaking ill of him now. . . . I was here, washing the dishes after dinner, when I heard him call me from upstairs; when I passed, I noticed the door had been opened—the one you just came in. Monsieur Dupont was on the landing—and as alive as you or I, you know—only he had his left arm against his chest and a little blood on his hand. He was holding his revolver in the other hand. I had a terrible time getting rid of the little bloodstains he made on my carpet, and it took me at least two hours to clean the bedspread where I found him lying when I came back—when I came back from telephoning. It's not easy to get off, you know; luckily, he wasn't bleeding much. He told me: 'It's just a flesh wound in my arm; don't worry, it's nothing serious.' I wanted to take care of him myself, but he didn't let me, stubborn as he was—I told you—and I had to go call that miserable doctor who took him away in a car. He didn't even want me to hold him up, coming down the stairs! But when I got to the clinic early this morning to take him a change of linen, they suddenly told me he was dead.

'Heart failure,' that murderer told me! And he wasn't any prouder than that, no indeed, young man. I didn't make a fuss; still, I'd like to know who killed him if it wasn't that Doctor Juard! For once in his life, Monsieur Dupont would have done better to listen to me. . . ."

It is almost a note of triumph that sounds in the old woman's voice. Most likely her master kept her from talking, so as not to be deafened by that terrible voice; now she's trying to make up for it. Wallas attempts to put some order in this flood of words. Madame Smite, apparently, has been more disturbed by the bloodstains she had to wash off than by her employer's wound. She has not checked whether it was really his arm that had been hit: moreover, Dupont had not let her get too close a look; and the blood on his hand does not prove much. He was wounded in the chest and did not want to terrify his house-keeper by admitting it. In order to deceive her, he even managed to stand up and walk to the ambulance; it may even have been this effort that finished him off. The doctor, in any case, should not have let him do it. Obviously it is the doctor who must be questioned.

"Juard Clinic. Gynecology. Maternity Home." The nurse who opened the door did not even tell him to come in; she was standing in the opening of the door, ready to close it again: like a guardian afraid that some stranger would try to force his way in, but at the same time she insisted on keeping him:

"And what is it you wish, Monsieur?"

"I wanted to speak to the doctor."

"Madame Juard is in her office—it's always Madame Juard who receives our clients."

"But I'm not a client. I must see the doctor in person."

"Madame Juard is a doctor too, Monsieur. She is in charge of the clinic, so of course she's in touch with all the . . ."

When he finally told her that he had no need of the clinic's services, she stopped talking, as though she had found out what she wanted; and she looked at him with the vaguely superior smile of someone who knew perfectly well what he wanted from the start. Her politeness assumed a nuance of impertinence:

"No, Monsieur, he didn't say when he was coming back. Don't you want to leave your name?"

"It's no use, my name won't mean anything to him."

He had distinctly heard: "They're all the same!"

". . . that murderer told me . . ."

On the hallway carpet downstairs, the old woman shows him the scarcely perceptible traces of five or six spots of something. Wallas asks if the inspectors who came the evening before took the victim's revolver with them.

"Certainly not!" Madame Smite exclaims. "You don't suppose I let those two loot the house? I put it back in his drawer. He might have needed it again."

Wallas would like to see it. She leads him into the bedroom: rather a large room, of the same impersonal and old-fashioned comfort as the rest of the house, stuffed with hangings, curtains, and carpets. A complete silence must have reigned in this house, where everything is arranged to muffle the slightest sound. Did Dupont wear felt slippers too? How did he manage to speak to his deaf servant without raising his voice? Habit probably. Wallas notices that the bedspread has been changed—it could not have been cleaned so perfectly. Everything is as neat and orderly as if nothing had ever happened.

Madame Smite opens the night table drawer and hands Wallas a pistol he recognizes at first glance: it is the same model as his own, a serious weapon for self-defense, not a plaything. He takes out the clip and notices that one bullet has already been fired.

"Did Monsieur Dupont shoot at the man running away?"

he asks, although he knows the answer in advance: when Dupont came back with his revolver, the murderer had disappeared. Wallas would like to show the gun to Commissioner Laurent, but the housekeeper hesitates about letting him take it, then she gives in with a shrug:

"Take it with you, young man. What use is it here now?"

"I'm not asking you for a present. This pistol is a piece of evidence, you understand?"

"Take it, I tell you, since you want it so much."

"And you don't know if your employer had used it before, for something else?"

"What do you think he would use it for, young man? Monsieur Dupont was not a man to shoot off his revolver in the house to amuse himself. No, thank God. He had his faults, but . . ."

Wallas puts the pistol in his overcoat pocket.

The housekeeper leaves her visitor; she has nothing else to tell him: her late employer's difficult character, the strenuous washing of the bloodstains, the criminal doctor, the continuing negligence of the telephone company. . . . She has already repeated all this several times; now she has to finish packing her suitcases in order not to miss the two o'clock train that will take her to her daughter's. It is not a very nice time of the year to be going to the country; still, she has to hurry. Wallas looks at his watch: it still shows seven-thirty. In Dupont's bedroom, the bronze clock on the mantelpiece, between the empty candlesticks, had also stopped.

Yielding to the special agent's urging, Madame Smite finally admits that she is supposed to give the house keys to the police; somewhat reluctantly she gives him the key to the back door. He will close it himself when he leaves. The housekeeper will leave by the front door, for she also has the keys for it. As for the garden gate, the lock has not been working for a long time.

Wallas remains alone in the study. Dupont lived in this tiny room, he left it only to sleep and to take his meals, at noon and at seven at night. Wallas approaches the desk; the inspectors appear to have left everything as it was: on the blotter is lying the sheet of paper on which Dupont had written only four words so far: "which can not prevent . . ."—". . . death . . ." obviously. That is the word he was looking for when he went downstairs to eat.

CHAPTER TWO

1

It is certainly the sound of footsteps; footsteps on the stairs, coming closer. Someone is coming up. Someone is coming up slowly—no: carefully; perhaps cautiously? Holding on to the banister, judging from the sound. Someone who becomes breathless from a climb which is too stiff for him or who is tired from having come a long distance. They are a man's footsteps, but deliberate, muffled by the carpet—which gives them, at moments, something of a timorous or clandestine quality.

But this impression does not last. At closer range, the footsteps sound spontaneous, uninhibited: the footsteps of a relaxed man peacefully climbing the stairs.

The last three steps are taken more vigorously, probably in haste to reach the landing. The man is in front of the door now; he stops a moment to catch his breath . . .

(. . . one knock, three short quick knocks . . .)

But he does not remain there more than a few seconds and begins to climb the next flight. The steps die away toward the top of the building.

It was not Garinati.

It is ten o'clock, though: Garinati should be coming. He should even have been here over a minute ago; he's late already. Those footsteps on the stairs should have been his.

He walks upstairs somewhat in that way, but he makes even

93

less noise, though setting his feet down more firmly, step after step without any particular attention, without the least . . .

No! It's impossible to involve Garinati in this business any longer: after tonight, someone else will have to replace him at his job. For a few days at least he will have to be kept under cover and watched; afterward, maybe, he could be given some new job, but one without any serious risks.

For several days he has seemed somewhat tired. He complained of headaches; and once or twice, he said peculiar things. During the last meeting he even went so far as to be downright difficult: uneasy, hypersensitive, constantly asking about details long since settled, and more than once raising unreasonable objections and turning sullen if they were rejected too quickly.

His work has suffered from it: Daniel Dupont did not die immediately—every report confirms this. It does not matter really, since he died all the same and, what's more, "without regaining consciousness"; but from the point of view of the plan, there is something irregular about it: Dupont did not actually die at the time his death was scheduled for. Without any doubt, it is Garinati's exaggerated nervousness that is responsible. Afterward he did not come to the prescribed meeting place. Finally, this morning, despite the written order, he is late. No question about it, he is not the same man any more.

Jean Bonaventure—called "Bona"—is sitting on a garden chair, in the middle of an empty room. Beside him, a leather briefcase is lying on the floor—a pine floor distinguished by no particular quality save an obvious lack of care. The walls, on the other hand, are covered with a paper in good condition, if not new: tiny multicolored bouquets uniformly decorating a pearl-gray background. The ceiling too has obviously been whitewashed recently; in the center, a wire hangs down with an electric light bulb at the end.

A square window without curtains provides what light there is. Two doors, both wide open, lead into a darker room on one side, and on the other into a little hall to the entrance door of the apartment. There is not a stick of furniture in this room except for two wrought-iron chairs painted the usual dark green. Bona is sitting on one; the other, facing him, about six feet away, remains empty.

Bona is not dressed for sitting indoors. His overcoat is tightly buttoned up to the collar, his hands are gloved, and he keeps his hat on.

He is waiting, motionless on this uncomfortable chair, bolt upright, his hands crossed on his knees, his feet riveted to the floor, betraying no impatience. He is looking straight ahead at the little spots left by the raindrops on the windowpanes and, beyond, over the huge blue-glazed window of the factories on the other side of the street, at the irregular buildings of the suburbs, rising in waves toward a grayish horizon bristling with chimneys and pylons.

Usually this landscape has little relief and looks rather unattractive, but this morning the grayish yellow sky of snowy days gives it unaccustomed dimensions. Certain outlines are emphasized, others are blurred; here and there distances open out, unsuspected masses appear; the whole view is organized into a series of planes silhouetted against one another, so that the depth, suddenly illuminated, seems to lose its natural look—and perhaps its reality—as if this overexactitude were possible only in a painting. Distances are so affected that they become virtually unrecognizable, without it being possible to say in just what way they are transformed: extended or telescoped—or both at once—unless they have acquired a new quality that has more to do with geometry. . . . Sometimes this happens to lost cities, petrified by some cataclysm for centuries—or only for a few seconds before their collapse, a wink of hesitation between life and what already bears another name: after, before, eternity.

Bona watches. Eyes calm, he contemplates his work. He is waiting. He has just astounded the city. Daniel Dupont died, yesterday, murdered. Tonight, at the same hour, an identical crime will echo this scandal, finally wrenching the police from their routine, the papers from their silence. In a week, the organization has already sown anxiety in every corner of the country, but the powers that be still pretend to regard these acts as unconnected accidents of no importance. It will take this highly unlikely coincidence that is being prepared to set off the panic.

Bona cocks his ears. The footsteps have stopped in front of his door.

A pause. No one.

Lightly, but distinctly, the agreed-upon signal is given . . . a faint knock, three quick, almost imperceptible knocks, a faint knock. . . .

"We won't talk about it any more, now that it's settled."

But Garinati does not quite understand the meaning of these words; he insists: he will begin again, and this time he will not make any mistakes. Finally the admission escapes him: he will put out the light, if this precaution is indispensable, although from another point of view . . ."

"You didn't put it out?" Bona asks.

"I couldn't. Dupont came back upstairs too soon. I barely had time to recognize things around me."

"But you saw him come down, and you went up right after that?"

"I had to wait until the old woman left the kitchen too."

96

Bona says nothing. Garinati is even guiltier than he thought. It is fear that made him confuse his actions, as it is making him confuse his words now:

"I went up right away. He probably wasn't hungry. I couldn't see in the dark either, could I? But I'll start over, and this time . . ."

He stops, seeking encouragement from his chief's stern face. Why has Bona suddenly abandoned the friendly tone he had been using the last few days? That stupid detail of the light switch is only an excuse. . . .

"You should have turned out the light," Bona says.

"I'll go back, I'll turn out the light. I'll go tonight."

"Tonight is someone else's job."

"No, it's my job: it's my job to finish the job I started."

"You don't know what you're saying, Garinati. What are you talking about?"

"I'll go back to the house. Or I'll go find him wherever he's hiding. I'll find him and I'll kill him."

Bona stops examining the horizon to stare at his interlocutor.

"You said you'll kill Daniel Dupont *now*?"

"I swear I will!"

"Don't swear anything, Garinati: it's too late."

"It's never . . ."

It's never too late. The failure automatically goes back to the starting point for the second try. . . . The hands go once around the dial and the condemned man makes his theatrical gestures again, pointing to his chest once more: "Aim for the heart, soldiers!" And again . . .

"Don't you read the papers?" Bona asks.

He leans over to look for something in his briefcase. Garinati takes the folded newspapers that is handed to him and reads the first paragraph his eyes focus on:

97

"A daring burglar made his way at nightfall yesterday . . ."
He reads slowly, carefully; when he reaches the end, he starts
over to be sure he has not missed anything: "A daring burglar . . ." He looks up at Bona, who is staring over his head,
without smiling.

Garinati reads the article through once again. He says in a
low voice:

"He's dead. Of course. I had turned out the light."

All right, this man is crazy.

"It must be a mistake," Garinati says. "I only wounded
him."

"He died of it. You're lucky."

"Maybe this newspaper's made a mistake?"

"Don't worry: I have my own informants. Daniel Dupont is
dead—a little late, that's all."

After a pause, Bona adds less severely:

"After all, you did kill him."

The way you throw a dog a bone.

Garinati tries to make Bona explain; he is not convinced; he
wants to tell about his reservations. But his chief soon wearies
of this weak man's "probablys" and "maybes":

"All right, that's enough. We won't talk about it any more,
now that it's settled."

"Did you find the man named Wallas?"

"I know where he spent the night."

"What is he doing this morning?"

"This morning, I had to . . ."

"You've let him get away. And you haven't picked up his
trail?"

"I had to come here and . . ."

"You were late. Anyway you had several hours to do it in. Where do you expect to find him now? And when?"

Garinati does not know what to answer any more.

Bona stares at him sternly:

"You were supposed to report to me last night. Why didn't I see you?"

He would like to explain his failure, the light, the fact that he did not have time enough. . . . But Bona does not give him a chance; he interrupts him harshly:

"Why didn't you come?"

That is just what Garinati was going to talk about, but how can you make someone understand things if he does not want to listen to you? Still, he will have to start with that light, it is the cause of everything: Dupont turned it on again too soon and saw him before he could shoot, so that he did not . . .

"Now about this Wallas they've sent us, what's he done since he's been here?"

Garinati tells what he knows: the room in the Café des Alliés, Rue des Arpenteurs; his departure very early this morning. . . .

"You've let him escape. And you haven't picked up his trail?"

Of course that's unfair: how could he know Wallas would be leaving so early, and it is not easy to find someone you have never seen, in a city this size.

Besides, why bother spying on this policeman who cannot do anything more than anyone else? Wouldn't it be better to get ready for tonight's job? But Bona seems reserved; he pretends not to hear. Garinati goes on nevertheless: he wants to make up for his mistake, go back to Daniel Dupont's house and kill him.

Bona seems surprised. He stops staring at the horizon to look at his interlocutor. Then he leans over toward his brief-case, opens it, and takes out a folded newspaper:

"Don't you read the papers?"

Garinati holds out his hand without understanding.

Even his footsteps have changed: they are slow, almost sluggish; they have lost their vitality. They gradually fade away down the staircase.

Far away, the same bluish-gray color as the chimneys and the roofs, blending into them despite slight movements whose direction, moreover, is difficult to determine because of the distance, two men—chimneysweeps maybe, or roofers—are preparing for the early approach of winter.

Downstairs the door to the building can be heard closing.

2

The latch clicks as it falls back into place; at the same time the door has just slammed against the jamb and vibrates noisily, producing unexpected echoes in the frame as well. But no sooner has it started than this tumult suddenly stops; in the calm of the street a faint whistle can then be heard—something like a jet of steam, thin and continuous—which probably comes from the factories opposite, but so dissolved in the air that no precise source could accurately be attributed to it—so faint, in fact, that it might be, after all, just a buzzing in the ears.

Garinati hestitates in front of the door he has just shut behind him. He does not know in which direction he will follow this street he is standing in the middle of, where on one side as on the other. . . . How can Bona be so sure of Daniel Dupont's death? There was not even any question of arguing about it. Yet the mistake—or the lie—in the morning papers is easily explained, and in any of several ways. Besides, no one, in so serious a matter, would be satisfied with that kind of information, and it is obvious that Bona either found out for himself or used some informant. Garinati, moreover, knows that his victim did not seem seriously hurt—that he had not, in any case, lost consciousness right away, and that it is unlikely he did so before help arrived. So then? Did the informants make a mistake? Maybe Bona does not always pay enough. . . .

Garinati raises his hand to his right ear which he covers and releases several times; then he does the same thing to the other ear. . . . His chief's conviction still bothers him; he himself is not absolutely certain he only hit the professor on the arm; if the professor was seriously hurt, he might have been able to take a few steps to get away, guided by the instinct of self-preservation, and then collapsed later on. . . .

Again Garinati covers his ears to get rid of that irritating noise. This time he uses both hands, which he keeps pressed close to each side of his head for a minute.

When he takes them away, the whistling noise has stopped. He begins walking, carefully, as if he were afraid of making the noise start again by some excessively lively movement. Maybe Wallas will give him a clue to the riddle. Doesn't he have to find him anyway? He has been ordered to. That's what he has to do.

But where to find him? And how to recognize him? He does not have any clues, and the city is a big one. Nevertheless he

decides to head toward the center of town, which means he
has to turn around.

After a few steps he again finds himself in front of the
building he has just left. He raises his hand to his ear with
irritation: will that damned machine never stop?

3

Wallas, already half turned around, hears the latch fall back
into place; he lets go of the doorknob and looks up at the house
opposite. He immediately recognizes, at a third-story window,
that same net curtain he has noticed several times during his
morning walk. It probably is not very healthy to make a baby
drink from the ewe's teats that way: certainly not very sani-
tary. Behind the wide mesh of the netting, Wallas glimpses a
movement, discerns a figure; someone is watching him and,
realizing he has been seen, gradually moves into the dark room
to keep out of sight. A few seconds later there is nothing left,
in the window frame, but the two shepherds carefully bending
over the body of the newborn baby.

Wallas walks along the garden fence toward the bridge,
wondering if, in an apartment building of that size and inhabited by middle-class people, one can calculate that there is
always at least one tenant watching the street. Five floors, two
apartments per floor on the south side, then, on the main
floor . . . In order to estimate the probable number of tenants,
he glances back; he sees the embroidered net curtain fall back
—someone had shoved it aside to watch him more easily. If
this person had remained watching all day long yesterday, he
could be a useful witness. But who would carry curiosity so
far as to watch the comings and goings of some hypothetical
passer-by after dark? There would have to be some specific

reason—suppose his attention had been attracted by a scream, or some unusual sound . . . or in any way at all.

Fabius, having closed the garden gate behind him, inspects the premises; but he does not look as if that is what he is doing: he is an ordinary insurance agent leaving his client's house and looking up at the sky to the right and to the left to see from what direction the wind is coming. . . . Suddenly he notices someone odd watching him behind the curtains at a third-story window. He immediately looks away, to avoid arousing any suspicion that he has noticed, and walks at an ordinary pace toward the parkway. But once he has crossed the bridge, he veers right, taking a winding course that brings him back, in about an hour, to the Boulevard Circulaire; without wasting any time he crosses the canal, taking the footbridge at this point. Then, furtively keeping to the base of the houses, he returns to his point of departure, in front of the apartment building at the corner of the Rue des Arpenteurs.

He walks into it boldly, through the door that opens onto the canal side, and knocks at the concierge's window. He is representing a shade and blind establishment; he'd like to have the list of tenants whose windows look south, exposing them to the excessive ravages of the sun: faded rugs, pictures, draperies, or even worse—everyone has heard about those masterpieces that suddenly explode with a terrible noise, those ancestral portraits that suddenly begin to run, creating in the bosom of a family that disturbing impression whose fatal consequences are dissatisfaction, bad humor, quarrels, sickness, death. . . .

"But winter's coming now," the concierge observes judiciously.

That doesn't matter: Fabius knows that perfectly well, but he is preparing his spring campaign, and, besides, the winter sun that people worry about least is all the more to be feared!

Wallas smiles at this thought. He crosses the street and turns into the parkway. In front of the main entrance of the apartment building, a fat man in a blue apron, his face calm and cheerful, is polishing the brass doorknob—the concierge probably. He turns his head toward Wallas, who nods politely in reply. With a sly wink, the man says:

"If you're cold, there's still the bell to do!"

Wallas laughs pleasantly:

"I'll leave you that for tomorrow: the good weather seems to be over."

"The winter's coming now," the concierge answers.

And he begins polishing vigorously.

But Wallas wants to take advantage of the man's good mood to engage in conversation:

"By the way, do you take care of the other wing of this building too?"

"Yes, of course! You think I'm not big enough to take care of two bells?"

"It's not that, but I thought I recognized the face of an old friend of my mother's up there, behind the window. I'd like to go say hello to her if I was sure I wasn't mistaken. On the third floor, the apartment at the end . . ."

"Madame Bax?" the concierge asks.

"Yes, that's right, Madame Bax! So it was Madame Bax. Funny how things happen: yesterday we were talking at dinner and we were just wondering what had become of her."

"But Madame Bax isn't old. . . ."

"No, of course not! She's not at all old. I said 'an old friend' but I didn't mean her age. I think I'll go up. You don't suppose she's too busy?"

"Madame Bax? She's always glued to the window watching the street! No, I'm sure she'd be delighted to see you."

And without a moment's hesitation, the man opens his door wide, then steps aside with an agreeably ceremonious gesture:

"This way, Prince! It doesn't matter, the two staircases meet. Number twenty-four, on the third floor."

Wallas thanks him and walks in. The concierge follows him in, closes the door and goes into his room. He has finished his work. He'll polish the bell another day.

Wallas is received by a woman of uncertain age—perhaps still young, in fact—who, contrary to what he suspected, shows no surprise at this visit.

He simply tells her, showing her his police card, that the necessities of a difficult investigation oblige him to question, at random, all the people in the neighborhood who might provide any information at all. Without asking him any questions, she leads him into a room crowded with period furniture and indicates a tapestried chair. She herself sits down facing him, but some distance away, and waits, her hands clasped, looking at him earnestly.

Wallas begins speaking: a crime has been committed the evening before in the house opposite. . . .

Her face carefully composed, Madame Bax indicates a slightly surprised—and pained—interest.

"You don't read the newspapers?" Wallas asks.

"No, very rarely."

In saying this, she gives him an almost mournful half-smile, as if she did not often have the daily papers at her disposal or else did not have time to read them. Her voice is like her face, gentle and faded. Wallas is an old relative come to pay a call, on her visiting day, after a long absence: he is telling

her about the death of a mutual friend, whose loss she laments
with well-mannered indifference. It is five in the afternoon. In
a little while she will offer him a cup of tea.

"It's a very sad story," she says.

Wallas, who is not here to receive condolences, puts the
question in precise terms: the position of her window might
have allowed her to see or hear something.

"No," she says, "I didn't notice anything."

She is very sorry.

Hadn't she at least noticed some prowler, some suspicious-
looking types she could identify: a man in the street, for instance, who might have been paying abnormal attention to the
house?

"Oh, Monsieur, no one ever walks through this street."

Many people walk along the parkway, yes, at certain times:
they walk fast and disappear at once. No one comes along this
street.

"Still," Wallas says, "someone had to come last night."

"Last night . . ." It is obvious she is searching her memory.
"Yesterday was Monday?"

"It might just as well have been the day before too, or even
last week: apparently their work was carefully prepared in
advance. Even the telephone was out of order: it might have
been a case of sabotage."

"No," she says after a moment's thought, "I didn't notice
anything."

Last night a man in a raincoat tore something out at the
gate. It was hard to see because it was getting dark. He stopped
at the end of the spindle-tree hedge, took out of his pocket a
small object which might have been pliers or a file, and quickly
stuck his arm between the last two bars to reach the top of the
gate inside. . . . It only took half a minute: he pulled his hand

out immediately and went on his way, with the same casual gait.

Since this lady assures him she knows nothing, Wallas is ready to say good-bye. It would obviously have been surprising if she had happened to be at her window at just the right time. Besides, on thinking it over, did this "right time" ever exist? It is rather unlikely that the murderers have come here in broad daylight to plan their attack so calmly—to inspect the premises, make a false key, or dig trenches in the garden to cut the telephone lines.

The first thing he has to do is get in touch with that Doctor Juard. Afterward, if no clue turns up there and if the commissioner has not learned anything new, the other tenants in the building could be questioned. The slightest opportunity must not be neglected. Meanwhile, he will ask Madame Bax not to give away the little story he used as an excuse to the concierge.

To prolong this rest period before continuing his wanderings, Wallas asks two or three more questions; he suggests different noises that might have caught the young woman's attention, unconsciously; a revolver shot, footsteps running on the gravel, a slamming door, an automobile starting up suddenly. . . . But she shakes her head and says with her strange smile:

"Don't tell me too many details; you'll end up making me think I saw the whole thing."

Last night a man in a raincoat did something to the gate and since this morning you cannot hear the automatic buzzer when it opens. Yesterday, a man . . . No doubt she'll end up telling him her secret. Moreover, she does not exactly know what it is restraining her.

Wallas, who since the start of the conversation has been

107

wondering how to ask her politely if she has been watching much from her window recently, finally stands up. "May I?" He walks over to the window. It was in this room that he saw the curtain moving. Now he reconstitutes the image which, on the spot and from such close range, does not seem the same any more. He raises the material in order to see more clearly.

From this new angle, the house in the middle of its meticulous garden looks as though it were isolated by the lens of an optical instrument. His gaze shifts to the high chimneys, the slate roof—which in this part of the country strikes a note of preciosity—the brick front ornamentally framed by two fieldstone courses which are also echoed, above the windows, by projecting lintels, the arch over the door and the four steps of the stoop. From the street level one cannot appreciate so fully the harmony of the proportions, the rigor—the necessity, one might say—of the whole structure, whose simplicity is scarcely disturbed—or on the contrary, accentuated—by the complicated grillwork of the balconies. Wallas tries to decipher some pattern in these intertwining curves, when he hears the slightly bored voice behind him declaring, as though it were an insignificant thing without any relation to the subject:

"Last night, a man in a raincoat . . ."

At first, Wallas did not believe in the truthfulness of a recollection so belated. Somewhat confused, he turned around toward Madame Bax: her face was still as calm, with that expression of polite exhaustion. The conversation continued in the same mundane tone.

When he expressed a certain discreet surprise at her repeated assertions that she had noticed nothing, the young woman replied that one always hesitates before handing a man over to the police, but from the moment she learned it was a question of murder, she had dismissed her scruples.

There remained the more likely explanation: Madame Bax concealed, beneath her calm exterior, a little too much imagination. But she seemed to divine this impression, and to give more weight to her testimony she added that at least one other person had seen the malefactor: before the latter had reached the parkway a man who was obviously drunk came out of the little café—about twenty yards to the left—and took the same direction, staggering slightly; he was singing or talking to himself in a loud voice. The malefactor turned around and the drunk man shouted something to him, trying to walk faster to catch up with him; but the other man, without paying any more attention to him, went on his way toward the harbor.

Unfortunately Madame Bax was unable to furnish a more detailed description: a man in a raincoat with a light gray hat. As for his impromptu traveling companion, she thought she had passed him frequently in the neighborhood; in her opinion, he was probably well known in all the bars in the vicinity.

Leaving the building by the second exit, the one to the Rue des Arpenteurs, Wallas crossed the street to examine the gate: he was able to verify the fact that the automatic buzzer had been twisted to prevent contact when the gate was opened; this job, executed at arm's length, seemed to him to have been the work of uncommon muscular strength.

Looking up, he glimpsed, once again, behind the mesh of embroidered net, the figure of Madame Bax.

"Hello," Wallas says as he closes the door behind him.

The manager does not answer.

He is motionless, at his post. His massive body is leaning on his arms, spread wide on the counter where his hands grip the edge, as though to keep the body from springing forward— or from falling. The neck, already short, vanishes completely

109

between the raised shoulders; the head hangs, almost threatening, the mouth slightly twisted, the gaze blank.

"Cold enough for you this morning?" Wallas says—to say something.

He walks over to the cast-iron stove that looks less disagreeable than this mastiff confined, for safety's sake, behind his bar. He holds out his hands toward the glowing metal. For the information he needs, he would probably do better to look elsewhere.

"Hello," a voice says behind him—a drunken voice, but full of good intentions.

The room is rather dim and the wood-burning stove, which draws badly in cold weather, thickens the air with a bluish haze. Wallas has not noticed the man before. He is slumped over the rear table, the only customer in the café, happy to find someone to talk to at last. He probably knows that other drunkard Madame Bax referred to as a witness. But now he is staring at Wallas, opening his mouth and saying with a kind of thick-tongued resentment:

"Why didn't you want to talk, yesterday?"

"Me?" Wallas asks, surprised.

"You think I don't recognize you?" the man exclaims, his face lighting up with a cheerful grimace.

He turns around toward the bar and repeats:

"He thinks I don't recognize him!"

The manager, his eyes blank, has not moved.

"You know me?" Wallas asks.

"Of course I do, my friend! Even though I didn't think you were very polite. . . ." He counts carefully on his fingers. . . . "It was yesterday."

"No," Wallas says, "you must be making some mistake."

"He says it was a mistake!" the drunk shrieks toward the manager. "Me, a mistake!"

And he bursts into the thunderous laughter.

When he has quieted down a little, Wallas asks—to get into the spirit of the thing:

"Where was it then? And what time?"

"What time, don't ask me! I never know what time it is. . . . It was still dark. And it was here, going out . . . here . . . here . . . here . . ."

With each new "here" his voice gets louder; at the same time, the man makes a series of huge vague gestures toward the door with his right arm. Then, suddenly calmer, he adds in almost a whisper, and as though to himself:

"Where else would it be?"

Wallas despairs of getting anything out of him. Still the pleasant temperature of the room keeps him from leaving. He sits down at the next table.

"At this time yesterday I was over a hundred kilometers from here. . . ."

Slowly the commissioner begins rubbing his palms together again:

"Of course! Don't good murderers always have an alibi?"

A satisfied smile. The two plump hands come to rest on the desk, fingers wide apart. . . .

"What time was it?" the drunk asks.

"When you said."

"That's just it, I didn't say!" the drunk exclaims triumphantly. "You pay for the round."

Funny joke, Wallas thinks. But he does not budge. The manager now looks at him reproachfully.

"It's all a lie," the drunk concludes after a pause for laborious reflection. He examines Wallas and adds scornfully: "You don't even have a car."

"I came by train," Wallas says.

"Oh," the drunk says.

His good humor has vanished; he seems worn out by the

discussion. Nevertheless he translates for the manager, but in a completely gloomy tone:

"He says he came by train."

The manager does not answer. He has changed position; his head up, his arms dangling, it is apparent he is preparing to take some action. As a matter of fact he grasps his rag and wipes it back and forth across the top of the bar.

"What's the difference," the drunk begins with difficulty . . . "what's the difference between a railroad and a bottle of wine?"

He is talking to his glass. Wallas automatically tries to think of the difference.

"Well?" his neighbor suddenly asks, cheered by the prospect of a victory.

"I don't know," Wallas says.

"So there's no difference for you? You hear that, bartender, he doesn't see any difference!"

"I didn't say that."

"Yes you did!" the drunk shouts. "The bartender's here to back me up. You said it. You pay for the round!"

"I'll pay for the round," Wallas admits. "Bartender, give us two glasses of white wine."

"Two glasses of white wine!" repeats his companion, who has recovered his good humor.

"Don't wear yourself out," the manager says. "I'm not deaf."

The drunk has emptied his glass in one gulp. Wallas is just starting to drink his. He is surprised to feel so comfortable in this filthy bar; is it only because it's warm in here? After the sharp air of the street, a somewhat numbing sense of well-being penetrates his body. He feels full of kindness toward this drunken bum, and even toward the manager who scarcely encourages sympathy. As a matter of fact the latter keeps his

eyes on his latest customer; and his expression is so deliberately suspicious that Wallas ends up, in spite of everything, by
being somewhat disturbed. He turns back toward the riddle-
lover, but the wine the latter has just drunk seems to have
plunged him back into his gloomy thoughts. In the hope of
cheering him up, Wallas asks:

"Well, what was the difference?"

"The difference?" The drunk seems completely in the dark
this time. "The difference between what?"

"You know, between the railroad and the bottle!"

"Oh . . . the bottle . . ." the other man says slowly, as if he
were coming back from a great distance away. "The difference.
. . . Well, it's a big one, the difference . . . the railroad! . . . It's
not at all the same thing. . . ."

It would certainly have been better to question him before
giving him more to drink. Mouth open, the man is staring into
space, one elbow on the table propping up his bloated head.
He stammers incoherent words; then, with an obvious effort
to make himself clear, he manages to say, with several halts
and repetitions:

"You make me laugh with your railroad. . . . If you think
I didn't recognize . . . didn't recognize . . . just leaving here.
. . . We walked the whole way together . . . the whole way. . . .
That's too easy! It's not enough to change your coat. . . ."

After that, the monologue becomes more obscure. A word
that sounds like *foundling* keeps recurring, without any apparent reason.

Half asleep on his table, he stammers incomprehensible
phrases, broken by exclamations and attempted gestures that
fall back heavily or dissolve in the fog of his memories. . . .

In front of him a tall man in a raincoat is walking along
the fence.

"Hey! Aren't you waiting for me? Hey, you!"

The man is deaf!

"Hey, you! Hey!"

Good, this time he heard.

"Wait up! Hey! I've got a riddle for you!"

Pretty rude, that man. Funny how no one likes riddles.

"Hey, wait up! You'll see: it's not hard!"

Not hard! They never guess them.

"Hey, you!"

" . . ."

"All right, you made me run to catch up!"

With a sudden movement, the man brushes off his arm.

"All right, if you won't let me take your arm . . . Hey, not so fast! Let me catch my breath until I can remember my riddle. . . ."

But the other man turns around threateningly, and the drunk steps back.

"What's the animal . . ."

He chokes when he catches sight of the man's furious expression; he is obviously about to beat the drunk to a pulp. The latter retreats, stammering some pacifying words; but as soon as the other man, who decides he produced his effect, starts walking again, the drunk begins following, trotting after him and whining:

"Hey, don't walk so fast. . . . Hey! Wait up! Hey!"

People stop as they pass, turn around and step aside to make room for this surprising couple; a tall, powerful man wearing a raincoat too tight for him and a pale gray felt hat whose brim conceals the upper part of his face is walking fast, head down, hands in his pockets; he walks without rushing and seems to pay no attention whatever to the creature—strange as he is— who accompanies him, sometimes on his right, sometimes on his left, most often behind him, where he makes a series of unexpected swerves with the sole purpose, it seems, of keeping

114

up with him. He manages to, more or less, but at the cost of a considerable amount of gymnastics, covering a course twice or three times as long as the one which would be necessary, with spurts of speed and stops so sudden that he looks as if he's going to fall down at any moment. Despite these continual difficulties, he still manages to keep talking, in fragments, it's true, but so that certain elements remain intelligible: "Hey! Wait up! . . . ask a riddle . . ." and something that sounds like "foundling." Obviously he has had too much to drink. He is short and potbellied, wrapped in odd clothes, mostly in tatters.

But from time to time the man walking ahead turns around without any warning and the drunk, terrified, steps back to keep out of reach; then as soon as the danger seems less, he starts walking again, stubbornly trying to catch up with his companion and sometimes even hanging onto his arm to hold him back—or else getting a step ahead of him only to find himself, an instant later, trotting along far behind—as if he were trying to make up for lost time.

Night has almost fallen now. The light from the rare street lamps and a few shops does not manage to create anything but a dim, fragmentary illumination—interrupted by gaps, more or less widely fringed with vague areas where the mind hesitates to venture.

Still the staggering little man persists in his chase, though perhaps he has undertaken it somewhat at random, and has not even figured out what its origin is.

Ahead of him, the wide, inaccessible back has gradually assumed terrifying dimensions. The tiny L-shaped rip on the left shoulder of the raincoat has grown so large that a whole flap of the garment has been detached and floats in his wake, like a flag, beating furiously against his legs. As for the hat, which was already drawn exaggeratedly far down over the face, it now forms a tremendous bell from which escapes, like the tentacles of some giant octopus, the vortex of intertwined ribbons to which, finally, the rest of the coat has been reduced.

The little man, in a supreme effort, manages to grasp one of these arms; he hangs onto it with all his might, determined not to let go; hard as Wallas shakes him, he can no longer disengage himself. The drunk clings to him with an energy he seemed quite incapable of; but when his head bumps the floor in a convulsion, he suddenly releases his grip, his hands open and the body rolls to the ground, limp, inanimate. . . .

The manager does not seem very affected by this scene. The drunk has probably had such fits before. With a strong grip he picks him up and sets him on his chair, while a wet rag restores him to consciousness at once. The man is cured as though by magic; he rubs his hand over his face, stares around, smiling, and declares to the manager, who is already back behind his counter:

"He wanted to kill me too!"

Nevertheless, since he does not seem to be holding this attempted murder against him, Wallas, who is beginning to be interested in this character, takes advantage of his mood to ask for information. The drunk, fortunately, has a much clearer mind than before his fall; he listens carefully and answers questions readily: yes, he met Wallas yesterday at nightfall, leaving this very café; he followed him, caught up with and accompanied him, despite Wallas' unfriendliness; the latter was wearing a pale gray felt hat slightly too big for him and a tight raincoat with a small L-shaped rip on the right shoulder.

"Last night, a man in a raincoat . . ." So this man was the drunken bum Madame Bax noticed from her window, and the malefactor himself would be none other than . . . Wallas cannot help smiling at the absurdity of his conclusion. If it could only be determined that the suspect resembles himself! It is difficult to rely on the judgment of such a witness.

116

The latter, in any case, persists in confusing them, despite Wallas' new denials. The other man walked along with him long enough—he says—for him to recognize him the next day. According to the rather vague indications he gives as to their route, it seems that they followed the Rue de Brabant, then the Rue Joseph-Janeck for its whole length, to the parkway, where Wallas' hypothetical double went into a post office.

Then the drunk came back to drink at the Café des Alliés.

The manager feels the story has something funny about it: why doesn't this man want to admit that he was seen the day before? He must have something to hide. . . . Last night? He's the one who pulled the job. He came out of the little house when the drunk surprised him; he managed to lose him on the other side of town and then he came back to spend the night in peace here. Now he would like to know what the drunk remembers about his escapade. He probably thinks his memory is too good, since he has just tried to knock him out: bumped his head . . . that's it. He must be the one who pulled the job.

Unfortunately the hours do not coincide: when the old housekeeper ran in to call the ambulance, he was . . . Still, he'd better be careful and tell the police about this shady customer; after noon, there is the risk of a fine if he is not reported, and if anything happened . . .

The manager picks up the telephone book which he leafs through for a long time, glancing suspiciously over the counter at the tables. Finally he dials a number.

"Hello, is this the registration service?"

At the same time he glares accusingly at Wallas.

"This is the Café des Alliés, ten Rue des Arpenteurs . . . a lodger to declare."

A long silence. The drunk opens his mouth wide. From be-

117

hind the counter comes the sound of a faucet dripping regularly into the sink.

"Yes, a room rented by the day."

" . . ."

"Sometimes."

" . . ."

"I'll send the form, but I prefer being registered as soon as possible. . . . Especially in dealing with certain kinds of people . . ."

The offhandedness with which this man talks about him in his presence has something so shocking about it that Wallas is on the point of protesting—when he hears, once again, the chief commissioner's ironic voice:

"If you're not registered, what proof is there?"

In short, if he is trying to get him in trouble, the manager is making a mistake: by neglecting to register him, he was, on the contrary, permitting Laurent to continue his little joke. And with that strange man you never know where a joke is going to stop—or where it starts. Wallas, though deciding that it is scarcely reasonable to pay attention to such trifles, feels a kind of contentment in finding himself justified on this point.

"Name is Wallas. W-a-double l-a-s. Wallas. At least that's what he says."

The phrase is deliberately insulting—libelous even—and the way the manager stares at his customer while pronouncing it finally obliges the latter to intervene. He takes out his wallet to get at his police card, intending to thrust it under the manager's nose but he has barely started his gesture when he remembers the photograph attached to the official card: the photograph of a man obviously older than himself, whose heavy brown mustache makes him look like a music-hall Turk.

Of course this too-noticeable "identifying mark" was incompatible with Fabius' theories as to the outer aspect of special agents. Wallas had to shave off his mustache and his face was transformed, rejuvenated, almost unrecognizable to a stranger. He still has not had time to have his old papers changed; as for the pink card—the ministerial pass—he must, of course, avoid using that.

After having pretended to check something on a ticket taken out of his wallet at random—the return coupon of his train ticket—he puts the whole thing back in his pocket, as naturally as possible. After all, he is not supposed to hear what is being said on the telephone.

Moreover, the manager finds his insinuations turning against him, and the questions being asked at the other end of the wire are already making him lose his patience:

"Of course not, I tell you he arrived last night!"

. . .

"Yes, only last night! You'll have to ask him about the night before that."

. . .

"In any case, I would have notified you!"

The drunk would like to add a word; he half stands up from his chair:

"And then he tried to kill me! . . . Hey! You better tell them he tried to kill me too!"

But the manager does not bother to answer. He hangs up the receiver and goes back behind his bar, to rummage through a drawer full of papers. He is looking for his police forms, but it has been too long since he has needed them and he has difficulty finding them again. When he finally gets hold of an old and flyspecked form, Wallas will have to fill it out, show his *carte d'identité,* explain his transformation. Then he will be able to leave—to inquire at the police station if a man in a raincoat was seen last night. . . .

The drunk will go back to sleep in his chair, the manager will wipe off the tables and start washing the glasses in the sink. This time, he will turn off the faucet more carefully, and the little drops that strike the surface of the water with metronomic regularity will stop.

The scene will be over.

His heavy body resting on his widespread arms, his hands gripping the edge of the bar, his head hanging forward, his mouth somewhat twisted, the manager will go on staring into space.

5

In the murky water of the aquarium, furtive shadows pass—an undulation whose vague existence dissolves of its own accord . . . and afterward it is questionable whether there had been anything to begin with. But the dark patch reappears and makes two or three circles in broad daylight, soon coming back to melt, behind a curtain of algae, deep in the protoplasmic depths. A last eddy, quickly dying away, makes the mass tremble for a second. Again everything is calm. . . . Until, suddenly, a new form emerges and presses its dream face against the glass . . . Pauline, sweet Pauline . . . and no sooner does it appear than it vanishes in its turn, to make way for other specters and phantoms. The drunk is making up a riddle. A man with thin lips, in an overcoat buttoned up to his neck is waiting on his chair in the middle of an empty room. His motionless face, his gloved hands clasped on his knees, betray no impatience. He has plenty of time. Nothing can keep his plan from being carried out. He is preparing to receive a visit—not the one from a disturbed, evasive person without any strength of character—but a visit, on the contrary, from someone who can be counted on: it is to this person that tonight's execution, the second, will be entrusted. In the first murder, he had been kept in the background, but his work was flawless;

while Garinati, for whom everything had been so meticulously prepared, had not even been capable of turning out the light. And now, this morning, he had let his man get away:

"What time this morning?"

"I don't have any idea," the manager says.

"You didn't see him leave?"

"If I had seen him leave, I'd know what time it was!"

Leaning on his bar, the manager wonders if he should tell Wallas about this visit. No. They'll have to manage by themselves: no one told him to say anything.

Besides, Wallas has already left the little café to return to the scene. . . .

6

Once again Wallas is walking toward the bridge. Ahead of him, under a snowy sky, extends the Rue de Brabant—and its grim housefronts. The employees are now all at work, in front of their ledgers and their adding machines: the figures form columns, the tree trunks are piled on the docks; mechanical arms maneuver the controls of the cranes, the windlasses, the keys of the adding machines, without wasting a second, without a slip, without an error; the wood export business is in full swing.

The street is as deserted and silent as it was the first time. Only a few cars parked in front of the doors, under the black plaques with their gold letters, testify to the activity now reigning behind these brick walls. The other modifications—if there are any—are imperceptible: there is no change in the varnished wood doors, recessed above their five steps, nor in the curtainless windows—two to the left, one to the right, and, above, four floors of identical rectangular openings. There is not much daylight for working in these offices where the electric lights—for economy—have not been turned on—and the near-sighted faces lean their bespectacled eyes toward the big ledgers.

Wallas feels overcome by a great weariness.

But having crossed the canal that divides the Boulevard Circulaire, he stops to let a streetcar pass.

Ahead of him, the plaque indicating the number of the line shows the number 6 in yellow on a vermilion disk. The car, its new paint shiny, looks exactly like the one that had appeared this morning in the same spot. And like this morning, it comes to a stop in front of Wallas.

The latter, who was not looking forward to the long, tiresome walk along the Rue de Brabant and the Rue Janeck, climbs up the iron step and goes to sit down inside: this streetcar can only take him closer to his goal. With a ring of its bell the car starts up, its machinery groaning. Wallas watches the houses along the canal's edge slide by.

But once the conductor has passed through, Wallas realizes his mistake: the number 6 line does not continue along the parkway as he had thought; instead it turns off at the first stop and heads south, through the suburbs. And since no line follows this unfrequented portion of the parkway that leads to the other end of the Rue Janeck—where the post office mentioned by the drunk must be—Wallas remains rather confused. It is the conductor who explains matters to him, showing him a plan of the transportation network throughout the city: instead of heading directly for this post office, Wallas will first stop at Doctor Juard's clinic—which is preferable from every point of view. Line number 4, which this one crosses at the next stop, will take him there.

He thanks the conductor, pays his fare, and gets off.

Around him, the scene is still the same: the parkway, the canal, the irregular buildings.

"Then she told him that since that was how things were, he might as well leave!"

"And he left?"

"No, he didn't. He wanted to know if it was all true, what she had just told him. At first he said it was silly, that he didn't believe her and that they'd see about it; but when he realized that the others were going to come back, he was afraid it would turn against him and he remembered he had things to do. Things to do! We know what kind of things. So you know what she said? 'Don't do too many things,' she said, 'or you'll wear yourself out!'"

"Oh . . . what did that mean?"

"Oh, you know, that meant that he might still run into him: she meant the car and everything else."

"No!"

Wallas is sitting facing the front of the car, next to the window; there is an empty seat to his right. The two voices—woman's voices, with uneducated intonations—come from the seats behind him.

"She wished him 'Good luck!' when he left."

"And did he run into him?"

"No one knows yet. Anyway, if he met him, there must have been a rumpus!"

"I'll say."

"Well, we'll find out tomorrow, I hope."

Neither woman seems to have any special interest in the outcome of this matter. The people in question are neither relatives nor friends. It is even apparent that the existence of the two women is unrelated to this kind of story, but such people enjoy discussing the glorious events in the lives of great criminals and kings. Unless it is simply a story in the serial published by some paper.

The streetcar, after following a winding route along the somber buildings, reaches the central part of the city whose relative prosperity Wallas has already noticed. He recognizes the Rue de Berlin, in passing, that leads to the prefecture. He turns around toward the ticket taker, who is supposed to tell him when it is time to get off.

The first thing he notices is a bright red sign with a huge red arrow over the words:

> For drawing
> For school
> For the office

VICTOR HUGO STATIONERY SHOP
2, Rue Victor Hugo
(One Hundred Yards to Your Left)
Quality Supplies

This detour takes him away from the clinic; but since he is not in any particular hurry, he turns in the direction indicated by the arrow. After having turned—following the instructions of a second sign—he discovers a shop whose ultra-modern exterior and elaborate advertising indicate a recent opening. Its elegance and its great size are surprising, moreover, in this small, rather isolated street which is located, nevertheless, not far from the main boulevards. The shopfront—plastic and aluminum—is brand new and if the left-hand window contains only a rather ordinary display of pens, note paper, and school notebooks, the one on the right is designed to attract the attention of pedestrians: it represents an "artist" drawing "from nature." A dummy, dressed in a paint-spotted smock and whose face is hidden under a huge "bohemian" beard, is hard at work in front of his easel; stepping back slightly to see both his work and the model at the same time, he is putting the finishing touches on a carefully drawn landscape—which must actually be a copy of some master. It is a hill with the ruins of a Greek temple among cypress trees; in the foreground, fragments of columns lie scattered here and there; in the distance, in the valley, appears a whole city with its triumphal arches and palaces —rendered, despite the distance and the accumulation of buildings, with a scrupulous concern for detail. But in front of the man, instead of the Greek countryside, stands instead of the setting a huge photographic reproduction of a modern city intersection. The nature of this image and its skillful arrangement give the panorama a reality all the more striking in that it is the negation of the drawing supposed to represent it; and suddenly Wallas recognizes the place: that house surrounded by huge apartment buildings, that iron fence, that spindle-tree hedge, is the corner of the Rue des Arpenteurs. Obviously.

Wallas walks in.

"Well," he exclaims, "you certainly have a strange window!"

"It's interesting, isn't it?"

The young woman greets him with a low, throaty laugh.

"It certainly is strange," Wallas admits.

"Did you recognize it? Those are the ruins of Thebes."

"The photograph is particularly surprising. Don't you think so?"

"Oh yes. It's a very fine photo."

Her expression actually indicates that she sees nothing remarkable about it. But Wallas would like to know more:

"Yes, indeed," he says, "you can tell it's the work of an expert."

"Yes, of course. I had the enlargement made by a laboratory that specializes in such things."

"And the shot had to be extremely clear too."

"Yes, probably."

Already the saleswoman is looking at him with a profession-
ally friendly expression of interrogation. "Can I help you?"

"I'd like an eraser," Wallas says.

"Yes. What kind of eraser?"

That's just the whole point, and Wallas once again begins de-
scribing what he is looking for: a soft, crumbly gum eraser that
friction does not twist but reduces to dust; an eraser that cuts
easily and whose cut surface is shiny and smooth, like mother-
of-pearl. He has seen one such, a few months ago, at a friend's
but the friend could not tell him where it came from. He
thought he could find himself one of the same kind without difficulty, but he's been searching in vain ever since. It looked like
a yellowish cube, about an inch or two long, with the corners
slightly rounded—maybe by use. The manufacturer's brand
was printed on one side, but was too worn to be legible any more:
only two of the middle letters were still clear: "di"; there must
have been at least two letters before and perhaps two or three
others after.

The young woman tries to complete the name, but without
success. She shows him, with mounting discouragement, all the
erasers in the shop—and she has, in fact, a splendid stock—
whose respective merits she warmly extols. But they are all
either too soft or too hard: "breadcrumb" erasers, as easily
kneaded as modeling clay, or else dry and grayish substances
which abrade the paper—good at best for getting rid of ink
blots; the rest are pencil erasers of the usual kind, more or less
elongated rectangles of more or less white rubber.

Wallas hesitates to return to the subject that is plaguing him:
he might seem to have come in for the sole purpose of obtaining
God knows what information about the photograph of the
house, without even being willing to spend the money for a
little eraser—preferring to turn the whole shop upside down

over an imaginary object attributed to a lengendary brand whose name he could not even remember—and with good reason! His strategy would soon appear for the foolish thing it was, since by giving only the middle syllable of this name he kept his victim from questioning the existence of the brand.

He is therefore going to be obliged, once again, to buy an eraser he will not know what to do with, since it is not, apparently, the one he is looking for and since he does not need any other—despite certain resemblances—than *that one.*

"I'll take this one," he says. "It may do the trick."

"You'll see, it's a good one. All our customers are satisfied with it."

What's the use of explaining further? Now he must bring the conversation back to . . . But the farce goes so fast that he scarcely has time to think: "How much do I owe you?" the bill taken out of his wallet, the change ringing on the marble. . . . The ruins of Thebes . . . Wallas asks:

"Do you sell reproductions of pictures?"

"No, for the time being I have only post cards." She points to two revolving stands. "If you'd like to look: there are a few museum paintings; all the rest are views of the city and its environs. But if you're interested, there are a few that I took myself. Here, I made this one from the shot we were talking about just now."

She takes out a glossy-print post card and hands it to him. It is the one that was used for the window. Besides, it shows in the foreground the paving stones that form the edge of the quay and the end of the railing at the end of the little drawbridge. Wallas assumes an admiring tone:

"It's a pretty little house, isn't it?"

"Yes it is, if you like it," she answers with a laugh.

And he leaves the shop, taking the post card with him—whose acquisition was inevitable after all his praises when he

127

first came in—and the little eraser which has already joined the
one purchased this morning—as useless as the first.

Wallas is in a hurry; it must be almost noon. He still has
time to speak to Doctor Juard before lunch. He will have to
bear left to reach the Rue de Corinthe, but the first street he
come to on that side leads only to a cross street where he might
lose his way; he prefers to go on to the next main intersection.
After his visit to the clinic, he will look for that post office at the
end of the Rue Janeck; he might walk there, for it cannot be
very far away. Above all, find out the exact time.

A policeman is on duty in the middle of the street, probably
to control traffic in front of a school (otherwise, there are not
enough cars to justify his presence at this unimportant crossing). Wallas turns back and walks over to him. The policeman
salutes.

"Can you tell me what time it is, please?" Wallas asks.

"Twelve-fifteen," the man answers without hesitating.

He has probably just looked at his watch.

"Is the Rue Joseph-Janeck far from here?"

"That depends on what number you want."

"I want to go to the end, near the Boulevard Circulaire."

"Then it's easy: you go straight ahead to the first intersection and turn right, and then just afterward you turn left;
after that it's straight ahead. It won't take you long."

"There's a post office there, isn't there?"

"Yes . . . On the parkway at the corner of the Rue Jonas.
But you don't need to go that far to find a post office . . ."

"No, I know, but . . . I have to go to that one . . . for the
poste restante."

"Well, the first right, the first left, and then straight ahead.
You can't miss it."

Wallas thanks him and continues on his way, but once he

reaches the intersection and is about to turn left—toward the clinic—he realizes that, having omitted to inform the policeman of this detail, the latter will suppose he is taking the wrong turn despite his clear and repeated explanations. Wallas turns back to see if he is being watched: the man is making wide gestures with his arm to remind him that he should turn to the right first. If he goes in the other direction now, he will look like a lunatic, an idiot, or a practical joker. Maybe the policeman will run after him to set him right. As for going back to reassure the policeman, that would be really ridiculous. Wallas has already begun walking toward the right.

Since he is so near this post office, wouldn't it be better to go straight there? Besides, it is after noon and Doctor Juard is eating his lunch; while the post office does not close and he will not be disturbing anyone.

Before getting out of sight, he glimpses the policeman making a gesture of approval—to reassure him: he is going the right way.

It's silly to put a traffic policeman in a place like that, where there is no traffic to control. At this hour, the schoolchildren have already gone home for lunch. Is there even a school there?

As the policeman had said, Wallas immediately reaches another intersection. If he turned right into the Rue Berna-dotte, it would take him straight back and allow him to reach the Rue de Corinthe, after a slight detour; but now he can not be any closer to the clinic than to the post office, and besides, he does not know the neighborhood well enough: he might find himself face to face with that policeman again. His invention of the *poste restante* was not very satisfactory: if he had had mail sent to him there, he would have known the address, instead of knowing its location only approximately.

What kind of spell is it that is forcing him to give explanations wherever he goes today? Is it a particular arrangement of the streets in this city that obliges him to be always asking his way, so that at each reply he finds himself led into new detours? Once before he has wandered among these unexpected bifurcations and blind alleys, where you got lost even more certainly when you happened to walk straight ahead. Only his mother was worried about it. Finally they had reached that dead end of a canal; the low houses, in the sun, reflected their old façades in the green water. That must have been in summer, during the school vacation; they had stopped (on their way to the seashore, farther south, where they went every year) to visit some relative. He thought he remembered that she was annoyed, that there was something about a legacy or something of the kind. But did he ever know just what it was? He does not even remember now if they had ever found the woman, or if they had left empty-handed (they had only a few hours between trains). Besides, are these real memories? That day might have been described to him often: "You remember when we went . . ."

No. The dead end of the canal he had seen himself, and the houses reflected in the still water, and the low bridge that closed off the end . . . and the abandoned hull of the old boat. . . . But it is possible that this happened on another day, in another place—or even in a dream.

Here is the Rue Janeck and the wall of the recreation courtyard where the Indian chestnuts are shedding their leaves. "Citizens Awake." And here is the plaque ordering drivers to slow down.

At the end of the drawbridge, the workman in the dark blue pea jacket and the visored cap makes a gesture of recognition.

CHAPTER THREE

1

As usual, the big house is silent.

On the ground floor, the old deaf housekeeper is almost finished preparing dinner. She is wearing felt slippers that muffle the sound of her comings and goings along the hallway between the kitchen and the dining room, where she sets a single, unalterable place at the enormous table.

It is Monday: Monday's dinner is never very complicated: a vegetable soup, probably ham, and a cream dessert of some vague flavor—or else caramel rice pudding . . .

But Daniel Dupont is not much concerned with gastronomy.

Sitting at his desk, he is examining his revolver. It must not fall out of order—though it has been so many years since any-one has used it. Dupont handles it carefully; he opens it, takes out the bullets, carefully cleans the mechanism, checks its op-eration; finally he returns the clip and puts his rag away in a drawer.

He is a meticulous man who likes every task to be executed correctly. A bullet in the heart is what makes the least mess. If it is fired properly—he has talked it over extensively with Doctor Juard—death is immediate and the loss of blood quite slight. So old Anna will have less trouble getting rid of the stains; for her, that is what matters. He is well aware that she does not like him.

On the whole, people have not liked him much, Evelyne. . . . But that is not why he is killing himself. It does not matter to him whether people have liked him or not. He is killing himself for nothing—out of exhaustion.

Dupont takes a few steps on the water-green carpet that muffles every noise. There is not much room to walk in the little study. Books hem him in on all sides: law, social legislation, political economy. . . . Down below, to the left, at the end of the long shelves, stands the row of books he himself has added to the series. Not much. There were two or three ideas there, even so. Who has understood them? Too bad for them.

He stops in front of his desk and glances at the letters he has just written: one to Roy-Dauzet, one to Juard . . . to whom else? One to his wife, maybe? No; and the one he is addressing to the minister has no doubt been mailed the day before. . . .

He stops in front of the desk and glances one last time at this letter he has just written to Doctor Juard. It is clear and persuasive; it furnishes all the explanations necessary for camouflaging his suicide as a murder.

At first Dupont had thought of making it look like an accident: "Professor kills himself while cleaning old revolver." But everybody would have known.

A crime is less suspicious. And he could count on Juard and Roy-Dauzet to keep his secret. The wood exporters will not have to turn their faces into masks when his name comes up in conversation. As for the doctor, he shouldn't be surprised after their conversation last week; he had probably understood. He cannot, in any case, refuse to do this favor for a dead friend. What is asked of him is not very complicated: transferring the body to the clinic and immediately informing Roy-Dauzet by telephone; afterward the report to the municipal police and the release to the local papers. A minister's friendship is very useful at times: there will be neither coroner nor inquest of any kind. And later (who knows?) this complicity may be useful to the doctor as well.

Everything is in order Dupont need only go down to dinner.

He must seem in his usual mood, so that old Anna will suspect nothing. He gives orders for the next day; with his habitual precision, he settles several details henceforth without importance.

At seven-thirty he goes back upstairs and, without a moment's hesitation, fires a bullet through his heart.

Here Laurent stops; there is still something that is not clear: did Dupont die immediately, or not?

Suppose he merely wounded himself: he still had strength enough to fire a second bullet, since the doctor declares he was able to get down the stairs and walk to the ambulance. And supposing the revolver was out of the question, the professor had other means at his disposal: slitting his wrists, for instance; he was the kind of man to have a razor blade handy in case the revolver failed him. It takes great courage to kill yourself, they say, but such courage is more characteristic of Dupont than this sudden renunciation.

On the other hand, if he had succeeded in killing himself outright, why should the doctor and the old housekeeper have invented this story: Dupont, wounded, calling for help from the top of the stairs and, though his life till then did not seem to be threatened, his sudden death on reaching the clinic. It might be supposed that Juard preferred this version, so that he would not be censured for having taken away the body: Dupont would have had to be still alive for him to be entitled to move him; and he would have also had to be capable of standing, so that the stretcher-bearers would not be needed; lastly, this brief survival permitted the victim to explain the circumstances of the murder *viva voce*. It is possible that Dupont himself recommended this precaution in his letter. But what is strange is that this morning the doctor virtually insisted that the wound had seemed insignificant to him at first—this, in spite of everything, makes Dupont's death a little surprising. As for the housekeeper, she didn't seem to have imagined even that the victim could have perished. If it is already surprising that Dupont, or Juard, adopted a solution that necessitated taking the old woman into their confidence, it is even more so that the latter played her role so skillfully with the inspectors only a few hours after the tragedy.

There is, of course, another hypothesis: Dupont might have shot himself the second time once he had reached the clinic—in this way, Madame Smite would have known nothing and her possible testimony would have to be taken into consideration by the doctor in concocting his own. Unfortunately, if it is likely that the doctor agreed to disguise his friend's suicide, it is scarcely conceivable that he provided him the opportunity to carry it out.

To recapitulate: it must be taken as certain that Dupont killed himself without the help of either the doctor or the house-keeper; consequently he did it when he was alone—that is: either in his study at seven-thirty, or in his bedroom, while the housekeeper was calling the clinic from the telephone in a nearby café. After the old woman's return, Dupont remained with someone at all times—the housekeeper first, later the doctor—and either one would have kept him from making a second attempt. He might also have fired a first shot in the study and a second in the bedroom, but this complication would not settle anything, for in any case he didn't seem seriously wounded at the time of the doctor's arrival. As a matter of fact, it is not plausible to question the housekeeper's good faith (only the doctor is an accomplice in the distortion of the truth). When he left his house, Dupont wasn't dead, he could even walk, more or less—the doctor was forced to indicate this, in order not to be contradicted by the housekeeper. All of which, moreover, could be calculated ahead of time: the housekeeper not being in on the secret, it was necessary to avoid having her find the body holding a revolver—which would give her more opportunities to suspect suicide and would also permit her to call in any doctor—or even the police.

Consequently the solution is as follows: Dupont shoots himself in the chest, knowing the wound to be mortal but giving him time enough to shout that he has been attacked. He takes advantage of the housekeeper's deafness to get her to admit to a murderer's hasty flight through the house. Then he waits for his friend the doctor to arrive and explains to the latter what he must do after his death. Juard takes the wounded man away and then attempts to save him in spite of himself. . . .

There is still something that does not fit: if he seemed in such good condition, Dupont could not be so certain that his wound was mortal.

Which leads back to the hypothesis of the apparent failure followed by a last-minute retreat when faced with death. Dupont aimed badly; he gave himself an apparently harmless wound which nevertheless frightened him enough to make him abandon his plan. He then called for help, but being unwilling to admit the truth, he invented the preposterous story of an attack. As soon as the doctor arrived, Dupont had himself taken to the clinic and operated on, without waiting for a stretcher. But his wound was more serious than was supposed, and an hour later he was dead. Hence not only are the housekeeper's declarations sincere (she could even have seen some door open that wasn't supposed to be), but it remains possible that the doctor's are, too: the gynecologist need not have discovered that the bullet was fired at point-blank range. The minister, who knows the ins and outs of the case because of a letter from Dupont sent just before, has had the inquest stopped and the body removed.

Commissioner Laurent knows that he will now recapitulate all his hypotheses once again, for it is precisely this last solution he finds the most unsatisfactory. Though at each new attempt since this morning he has come out at the same point, he refuses to accept this conclusion. He would prefer any unlikelihood to that banal reversal generally attributed to the instinct of self-preservation, but which fits in so badly with the professor's character, the courage he has shown in many circumstances, his behavior at the front during the war, his refusal to compromise in civil life, his unquestioned force of character. He could decide to kill himself; he could have reasons for wanting to disguise this death; but he could not abandon his plan so suddenly, once he had embarked upon it.

Yet aside from this, there remains only one explanation: murder; and since there is no possible murderer, it is Wallas' theory that has to be adopted: the phantom "gang" with their mysterious purposes and inscrutable conspiracies. . . . Commissioner Laurent laughs to himself over this, so preposterous does he find the minister's latest notion. This case is mixed up enough already, without looking for such nonsense to add to it.

Then too, it is really too absurd to go on wracking his brains over a riddle from which he has been so opportunely excused. Besides, it is time for lunch.

But the rubicund little man cannot make up his mind to leave his office. He expected to have some word from Wallas during the morning, but he has received neither a second visit nor a phone call. Has the special agent also been assassinated by the gangsters? Vanished for ever, swallowed up by the shadows?

Actually, he knows nothing about this Wallas, nor about the exact nature of his job. Why, for instance, did he need to visit Laurent before starting his work? The commissioner possesses nothing but the testimony of the doctor and the old housekeeper; the agent sent from the capital could question both of the latter directly. And he had no particular need to ask permission to enter the dead man's residence—open henceforth to anyone at all, under the protection of a half mad old woman.

In this respect, one might say that the minister's behavior is at the least frivolous: in a criminal case you don't . . . But isn't this offhandedness the best evidence that the case is one of suicide, and that they are well aware of this in the capital? All the same, it may cause them some difficulties later on, with the heirs.

And Wallas, if this is so—what is he doing here? Is it by an error of transmission in Roy-Dauzet's orders that the illustrious Fabius has started this counterinvestigation? Or does the special agent also know that Dupont committed suicide? His job could be merely to pick up important papers in the house in the Rue des Arpenteurs, and his visit to the police was then only a sign of courtesy. If you can call it courtesy to come and make fun of a high official by telling him old wives' tales. . . .

No, that's not it! It's obvious that Wallas is sincere: he believes strongly in what he says; as for his unexpected visit, wouldn't it be one more sign that Laurent is respected in the capital?

The chief commissioner has reached this point in his reflections, when he is interrupted by the arrival of a strange character.

Without any announcement from the officer on duty, without even a knock, the door opens slowly and a head appears in the aperture, glancing around the room with an anxious expression.

"What is it?" the commissioner asks, ready to throw the intruder out.

But the latter turns his long face toward Laurent and, placing his index finger vertically across his lips as though to ask for silence, he begins making a series of clownish gestures, both imperative and suppliant. At the same time he enters completely and closes the door behind him with a thousand precautions.

"Now, Monsieur, what do you want?" the commissioner asks.

He no longer knows whether to be annoyed, amused, or disturbed. But his loud voice seems to terrify his visitor. In fact, the latter, who is trying to make as little noise as possible, stretches his arm out toward him in a pathetic exhortation to be still, while approaching the desk on tiptoe. Laurent, who has stood up, instinctively steps back toward the wall.

"Don't worry," the stranger murmurs, "and please don't call any one or you'll ruin me."

He is a man in late middle age, tall and thin, dressed in black. His measured tone and the middle-class dignity of his clothes somewhat reassure the commissioner.

"To whom have I the honor of speaking, Monsieur?"

"Marchat, Adolphe Marchat, wood exporter. I apologize for this intrusion, Commissioner, but I have something extremely important to tell you, and since I wanted no one to know I am here, I thought that the gravity of the circumstances would authorize me to . . ."

Laurent interrupts him with a gesture that means "In that case, of course!" but he is irritated: he has already noticed that the rotation of the floor men was not efficient between service hours; he must have that taken care of.

"Sit down, Monsieur," he says.

Returning to his desk and his familiar position, he spreads out his hands on top of the papers.

The visitor sits down in the chair indicated but, finding it too far away, he remains on the edge of it and leans forward as far as he can, so as to make himself heard without raising his voice.

"I'm here about the death of poor Dupont. . . ."

Laurent is not at all surprised. Without having quite realized it, he was waiting for this sentence. He recognizes it as if he had heard it ahead of time. It is what is coming next that interests him:

"I was present during our unfortunate friend's last moments. . . ."

"Oh, you were Daniel Dupont's friend . . ."

"Let's not exaggerate, Commissioner; we knew each other for a long time, that's all. And I find, in fact, that our relations . . ."

Marchat stops talking. Then, suddenly making up his mind, he declares in a dramatic tone of voice—but still just as softly:

"Commissioner, I'm supposed to be killed tonight!"

This time Laurent raises his arms to the ceiling. This was all he needed!

"What kind of joke is that?"

"Don't shout, Commissioner. Do I look like I'm joking?"

He doesn't certainly. Laurent drops his hands on the desk.

"Tonight," Marchat continues, "I'm supposed to go to a certain place where the murderers will be waiting for me—the ones who shot Dupont yesterday—and then it'll be my turn. . . ."

He climbs the stairs—slowly.

This house has always looked sinister to him. The ceilings that are too high, the dark woodwork, the corners harboring shadows which the electric light never manages to dispel—everything seems to reinforce the anxiety that has seized him since he came in.

Tonight, Marchat notices details that had never struck him before: creaking doors, disturbing hallways, inexplicable shadows. At the end of the banister grimaces a jester's head.

141

From step to step the ascent grows slower. In front of the little painting of the blasted tower, the condemned man stops. He would like to know, now, what this painting means.

In a minute it will be too late—for there are only five more steps before he reaches the place where he will die.

His interlocutor's lugubrious tone does not impress the commissioner. He asks for details: who is to kill Marchat? Where? Why? And how does he know? Besides, Doctor Juard hasn't made any reference to his presence in the clinic; why not? Laurent has difficulty concealing his thoughts; he is almost convinced he is dealing with a lunatic who may not even have known the professor and in whom the mere delusion of persecution may have inspired notions so senseless. If he weren't apprehensive about this lunatic's possible violence, Laurent would show him the door at once.

However, Marchat speaks vehemently. What he has to say is extremely serious. There are unfortunately certain things which he cannot reveal, but he begs the commissioner's help: he can't let an innocent man be killed in this way! Laurent grows impatient:

"How do you expect me to help you if you can't tell me anything?"

Marchat finally tells how he happened to be in front of Juard's clinic in the Rue de Corinthe just when the doctor was bringing in a wounded man. He came closer out of curiosity and recognized Daniel Dupont, whom he had met, in other circumstances, at the home of mutual friends. He offered his services to help carry him, for the doctor was alone. If the latter has not mentioned his intervention, it is by Marchat's express request: the latter was particularly anxious that his name not be connected with this crime in any way. Nevertheless the turn events are taking obliges him to put himself under police protection.

Laurent is astonished: would Doctor Juard have accepted the help of a passer-by, when he had specialized personnel at his disposal?

"No, Commissioner, there was no one there at that hour."

"There wasn't? What time was it?"

Marchat hesitates a few second before answering:

"It must have been around eight—eight-thirty; I couldn't say exactly."

It was at nine that Juard telephoned the police to announce Dupont's death. Laurent asks:

"Wasn't it probably after nine?"

"No, it wasn't: by nine poor Dupont was already dead."

So Marchat has been to the operating room. The doctor declared he needed no assistant for the operation, whose extreme seriousness had, in fact, not yet become apparent to him. Yet Dupont, fearing the worst, has taken advantage of the few minutes he had before he was put under the anesthetic to reveal the circumstances of the attack. Marchat must have promised not to divulge them, though he doesn't understand why secrecy must be kept with regard to the police. In any case, he doesn't think he's breaking his word by revealing to the chief commissioner the task the professor has entrusted him with—though nothing, he repeats, would indicate himself as a candidate for such an adventure. He is supposed to go this very day to the little house in the Rue des Arpenteurs and take certain files which he will then hand over to a prominent political figure to whom these papers are of the greatest importance.

There are two things Laurent doesn't understand. Why, first of all, must this operation be kept secret? (Is it on account of the heirs?) And on the other hand, what is so dangerous about it? As for the "circumstances of the attack," Marchat can rest easy: it is easy to reconstitute them!

In adding this, the commissioner—who still suspects suicide —winks meaningfully at his interlocutor. He is no longer sure what to make of this Marchat: according to the details the latter is furnishing about his friend's death, one must admit that he certainly was at the clinic last evening; yet the rest of his remarks are so irrational and confused that it seems difficult to dismiss the hypothesis of madness, even so.

Emboldened by what he interprets as signs of complicity, the businessman is now speaking—ambiguously—of the terrorist organization and its opposition to a political group that . . . of which . . . Laurent, who finally sees what the other man is trying to say, helps him out of his difficulty:

"A political group whose members have systematically been assassinated, one by one, every evening at seven-thirty."

And Marchat, who has not noticed the ironic smile which has accompanied this sentence, seems enormously relieved by it.

"Aha," he says, "I suspected you knew all about it. That simplifies things a lot. Keeping the police in ignorance of the truth, as Dupont wanted to do, could only have unfortunate consequences. No matter how often I repeated my conviction to him that it was precisely the police's business—and not mine!—there was no way of making him give up his ridiculous mystery. That's why I started by playing this farce; and since you answered me in the same tone, we have had some difficulty putting a stop to it. Now we'll be able to talk."

Laurent decides to take him up on it. He is rather curious to see what will come out of all this.

"You were saying that Daniel Dupont, before dying, had given you a secret mission which endangered your life?"

Marchat opens his eyes wide. "Before dying?" He no longer knows what he can say and what he must conceal.

"Well," Laurent insists, "what makes you think that someone's lying in wait for you in that house?"

144

"The doctor, Commissioner! Doctor Juard! He heard everything!"

Doctor Juard was present when Dupont explained the importance of the files in question and what must be done with them. Once he understood that Marchat was to go for them, he slipped away on some pretext or other and telephoned the leader of the gang to warn him. Marchat had taken the precaution of repeating loudly that he didn't belong to the group, but he noticed that the doctor had not believed a word he said; so that the gangsters have decided to make the businessman their victim this very evening. And the police simply must stop them, for it is *a mistake,* a tragic mistake: he has never had any relation with the group, he isn't even an advocate of their policy, and he doesn't want . . ."

"All right," Laurent says, "calm down. Did you hear what the doctor said on the telephone?"

"No . . . I mean: not exactly, but . . . Just from the look on his face, it was easy to see what he was going to do."

Obviously this man is every bit as mad as Roy-Dauzet. But what is the source of this collective hysteria? As for Dupont, it is understandable that he has found it convenient to accuse the mysterious anarchists: he would have been wiser to have sent his papers off before killing himself. Still other points are not extremely clear. Unfortunately, there is not much hope of having them explained by questioning this man.

To get rid of him, the commissioner suggests a good way of escaping his murderers: since the latter can strike only at seven-thirty sharp, he need only go for the files at some other time.

The businessman has already thought of this, but it is not so easy to escape an organization this powerful: the murderers will keep him prisoner and kill him at the appointed hour; they're outside, waiting for him; for the doctor—being ignorant of it—didn't specify exactly when Marchat would go to the professor's house. . . .

"You heard what the doctor said on the telephone?"

"I didn't actually hear what he said, except for a word from time to time. . . . But from what I did hear, I could reconstruct the whole conversation."

Laurent is beginning to get tired of this and makes his visitor increasingly aware of his fatigue. The latter, for his part, grows more and more nervous; at times, he almost abandons his whispering and his discretion:

" 'Calm down, calm down!' It's easy for you to say that, Commissioner! If you had been in my shoes since this morning, counting the hours you had left to live . . ."

"Ah," Laurent says, "why only since this morning?"

It was 'since last night' that the businessman meant. He quickly corrects himself: he hasn't slept a wink all night.

In that case, the commissioner informs him, he was making a mistake. He could have slept as soundly as usual: there *are* no murderers, and there *is* no conspiracy. Daniel Dupont committed suicide!

Marchat remains somewhat flabbergasted. But he immediately continues:

"No, that's impossible! I can assure you there was no question of suicide."

"You can? How do you know?"

"He told me himself. . . ."

"He said whatever he wanted to say. . . ."

"If he had meant to kill himself, he would have made another attempt."

"There was no need for that, since he died anyway."

"Yes . . . of course. . . . No, it's really impossible! I saw Doctor Juard go to the telephone. . . ."

"Did you hear what the doctor said on the telephone?"

"Yes, I did, I heard everything. You can imagine I didn't

miss a word. The red files, the study cabinet, the designated victim would walk into the trap of his own accord . . ."

"Well then, go there now: it isn't the 'hour of the crime'!"

"I told you they're waiting for me already!"

"Did you hear what the doctor . . ."

. . . .

2

The businessman leaves. Now his mind is made up. It is Dupont who was right: the chief commissioner is in the murderers' pay. His behavior cannot be explained in any other way. He wanted to allay Marchat's suspicions by persuading him that there was no conspiracy at all and that Dupont has committed suicide. Suicide! Luckily Marchat stopped in time before he spilled everything he knew. . . .

No, there was nothing to fear there: the commissioner knows perfectly well that Dupont isn't dead, since Doctor Juard is keeping them informed. They are pretending to believe he is dead to achieve their purposes in a few days. What they want now is to get Marchat into the little house to kill him in place of the professor.

Well, it's simple: he will not go to pick up the files—not at seven-thirty, or at any other time (for he isn't stupid enough to fall into the commissioner's trap: the killers, no doubt about it, will remain on the alert all afternoon). Even Dupont, when he finds out just what the situation is, will no longer insist. Roy-Dauzet will just have to send another commissioner.

Marchat is not going to be satisfied with these purely negative measures; the murderers would have no difficulty finding an opportunity to take revenge for their failure. He must protect himself against any new attempt. The best way to do it is to leave the city as soon as possible, and to go into hiding somewhere in the country. It might even be wiser to take the first boat and get across the ocean altogether.

But Marchat cannot make up his mind. Since early in the day he has wavered between one plan and the next, convinced, each time, that the last idea that has occurred to him is the best:

Take the police into his confidence—or deceive them; escape without delay—or wait here in the city; inform the professor of this decision—or say nothing; go get the files right away from the house in the Rue des Arpenteurs—or not go there at all. . . .

He has, in fact, not given up all thought of doing this favor for his friend. And he keeps seeing himself in front of the house surrounded by spindle trees. . . . He pushes open the heavy oak door, to which Dupont has given him the keys. He climbs the stairs—slowly. . . .

But from step to step he walks more and more slowly. He never reaches the top.

This time, he is certain of what is waiting for him if he goes all the way to the study. He won't go. He will inform the professor and give him back his keys.

On the way, however, he ponders the difficulties of the undertaking: Dupont—he knows him—will not be willing to admit his reasons. And if Doctor Juard, who will certainly listen at the door, manages to overhear their discussion and consequently learns that Marchat is not going for the files, the latter will also lose his last chance of escaping the murderers; for instead of waiting for him until seven-thirty in the trap where he is supposed to appear, they will shadow him from now on, so that he will not even have the subsequent freedom to hide or run away.

It would be better to get out of the country immediately, while the others may not have begun watching him.

He climbs the stairs. As usual, the big house is silent. . . .

3

Before coming to a complete halt, the drawbridge platform quivers slightly. Paying no attention to this almost imperceptible movement, the bicyclist has already passed through the gate to continue on his way:

"Good morning, Monsieur."

Jumping on his vehicle, he has shouted, "Good morning" instead of "Good-bye." They had exchanged two or three remarks about the weather, waiting until passage was re-established.

The drawbridge has a single platform; the system's axis of rotation is on the other side of the canal. Heads raised, they watch the girders and cables under the platform gradually vanish from sight.

Then the free end of the bridge, showing a cross section of the roadway, passes in front of their eyes; and then, all at once, they see the entire surface of smooth asphalt stretching toward the other bank between the two sidewalks with their railings on the outer sides.

Their glances have continued to move slowly downward, following the movement of the bridge, until the two corner plates of iron—polished by the car wheels—have come exactly opposite the other pair on the bank. Suddenly the noise of the motor has stopped, and in the silence, the electric bell has rung,

announcing to the pedestrians that they may cross the bridge
again.

"I wouldn't be surprised!" the bicyclist has repeated.

"Maybe you're right! Good luck!"

"Good morning, Monsieur."

But on the other side of the barrier, it was apparent that
everything was not yet over; because of a certain elasticity in
the materials, the platform's descent had not stopped when the
machinery did; it had continued for several seconds, moving a
fraction of an inch perhaps, creating a tiny gap in the continuity of the roadway which brought the metal rim slightly
above its position of equilibrium; and the oscillations—growing fainter and fainter, less and less noticeable, but whose
cessation it was difficult to be certain of—consequently approxi-
mated—by a series of successive prolongations and regressions
on either side of a quite illusory fixity—a phenomenon completed, nevertheless, some time before.

This time, the bridge is open to traffic. No barge is seeking
passage. The workman in the navy blue pea jacket, idle, stares
blankly at the sky. He glances toward the man walking toward
him, recognizes Wallas and nods to him, as he might to someone
he was accustomed to see every day.

On either side of the gap that marks the end of the movable
part of the bridge, the metal corner plates look motionless and
appear to be on the same level.

At the end of the Rue Joseph-Janeck, Wallas turns right onto
the Boulevard Circulaire. Some twenty yards farther on, the
Rue Jonas begins, and there is a small post office at the corner.

A neighborhood post office: only six windows and three telephone booths; between the main door and the booths: a large

ground-glass window, and beneath it the long, slightly tilted writing desk where people can fill out forms.

At this hour, the room is empty and, on the employees' side of the counter, only two elderly ladies can be seen, nibbling their sandwiches over immaculate napkins. Wallas decides it is better to wait to begin his investigation until the entire staff is present. He will come back at one-thirty. In any case, he will have to eat lunch sooner or later.

He heads toward a NOTICE that looks as if it had been posted recently, and to justify his entrance he pretends to examine it with interest.

It is a series of paragraphs announcing certain modifications made by the minister in the organization of details in the postal system—nothing, in short, of interest to the public, aside from a few hypothetical specialists. For an outsider, the precise nature of these modifications does not seem clear, so that Wallas finds himself wondering if there is any real difference between the new state of affairs and the one that existed previously.

As he leaves, he has the impression that the two women are staring at him in perplexity.

Retracing his steps, Wallas notices, on the other side of the Rue Janeck, an automat of modest size but equipped with the most recent machinery. The chromium-plated dispensers are lined up along the walls; at the rear sits the cashier from whom the diners obtain special tokens. The entire length of the room is occupied by two rows of small round plastic tables attached to the floor. Standing in front of these tables, some fifteen people—continually changing—are eating with quick, precise gestures. Girls in white laboratory smocks clear the tables and wipe them off once the diners leave. On the white walls, a sign reproduced many times:

151

"Please Hurry. Thank You."

Wallas examines all the machines. Each of them contains—
placed on a series of glass trays, equidistant and superposed—
a column of earthenware plates with precisely the same culinary
preparation on each one reproduced down to the last lettuce
leaf. When a column is emptied, anonymous hands fill up the
blanks from behind.

Having reached the last dispenser, Wallas has not yet made
up his mind. Besides, his selection is of slight importance, for
the various dishes differ only by the arrangement of articles on
the plate; the basic element is marinated herring.

Behind this last pane of glass, Wallas glimpses, one on top of
the other, six replicas of the following composition: on a bed of
toast, spread with margarine, is arranged a broad filet of herring with silvery-blue skin; to the right, five quarters of tomato,
to the left, three slices of hard-boiled egg; set on top, at specific
points; three black olives. Each tray also contains a fork and a
knife. The circular slices of toast are certainly made for this
purpose.

Wallas drops his token into the slot and presses a button.
With a pleasant hum of its electric motor, the entire column of
plates begins to descend; in the empty compartment at the
bottom appears, then halts, the plate whose owner he has become. He removes it and the napkin that accompanies it and
sets them both down on a free table. After having performed
the same operation to obtain a slice of the same toast, accompanied this time by cheese, and once again for a glass of beer,
he begins to cut up his meal into little cubes.

A quarter of tomato that is quite faultless, cut up by the
machine into a perfectly symmetrical fruit.

The peripheral flesh, compact, homogeneous, and a splendid
chemical red, is of an even thickness between a strip of gleam-

ing skin and the hollow where the yellow, graduated seeds appear in a row, kept in place by a thin layer of greenish jelly along a swelling of the heart. This heart, of a slightly grainy, faint pink, begins—toward the inner hollow—with a cluster of white veins, one of which extends toward the seeds—somewhat uncertainly.

Above, a scarcely perceptible accident has occurred: a corner of the skin, stripped back from the flesh for a fraction of an inch, is slightly raised.

At the next table, three men are standing, three railroad workmen. In front of them, the entire table top is covered by six plates and three glasses of beer.

All three are cutting little cubes out of three disks of toast with cheese on them. The other three plates each contain an example of the herring-tomato-hard-boiled egg-olives arrangement of which Wallas also possesses a replica. The three men, aside from their identical uniforms, are the same height and are equally heavy; they also have more or less similar faces.

They eat in silence, with quick, precise gestures.

When they have finished their cheese, they each drink half of their glass of beer. A short conversation begins:

"What time did you say it happened?"

"It must have been around eight, eight-thirty."

"And there was no one there then? That can't be—he told me himself . . ."

"He said what he wanted you to believe."

After having redistributed the plates on the table, they begin the second dish. But after a moment's pause, the man who has spoken first stops eating to conclude:

"It's as unlikely in the one case as in the other."

After this, they stop talking, absorbed by their arduous problem of cutting.

Wallas feels a disagreeable sensation in the region of his stomach. He has eaten too fast. He now forces himself to continue more slowly. He must take something hot to drink, otherwise he might have pains in his stomach all afternoon. When he leaves this place, he will drink a cup of coffee somewhere where he can sit down.

When the railroad workmen have finished their second plateful of food, the man who has said what time it was resumes the discussion:

"In any case, it was last night."

"It was? How do you know?"

"Don't you read the papers?"

"Oh, you know, the newspapers!"

This remark is accompanied by a cynical gesture. All three have serious, but dispassionate faces; they are speaking in neutral, even tones, as if they were not paying too much attention to their words. Probably they are talking about something of slight interest—or about something already repeated over and over again.

"And what do you make of the letter?"

"In my opinion, that letter proves nothing at all."

"Then nothing ever proves anything."

With simultaneous gestures, they finish their glasses of beer. Then, in single file, they head for the door. Wallas can still hear:

"Well, we'll see tomorrow, I hope."

In a café that is the image of the one in the Rue des Arpenteurs—not very clean, but well heated—Wallas is drinking a cup of coffee.

He is vainly struggling to get rid of this cottony discomfort that keeps him from thinking about his case seriously. He must be catching some kind of grippe. Though he usually escapes minor ailments of this kind, it would have to be today that he doesn't feel "up to snuff." Yet he awoke feeling fine, as usual; it was during the morning that a kind of generalized discomfort gradually invaded his system. At first he ascribed it to hunger, then to the cold. But, even so, he has eaten and warmed himself with this coffee without managing to overcome his torpor.

Yet he needs all his wits about him if he wants to come to any conclusion; for up to now, though luck has been with him to a certain extent, he hasn't made much progress. Yet it is of the greatest importance to his future that he give evidence at this time of lucidity and skill.

When he started to work at the Bureau of Investigation, some months ago, his chiefs did not conceal from him that he was being hired on probation, and that the job he would ultimately be given would depend in particular on the successes he achieved. This crime is the first important case he has been given. Of course he is not the only man to be concerned with it: other people, other services too, whose very existence he doesn't know a thing about, are working on the same case; but since he has been given his opportunity, he should expend all his zeal upon it.

The first contact with Fabius was not very encouraging. Wallas came from another division of the ministry, where he was very well thought of; he had been offered this transfer to replace a man who had fallen critically ill.

"So you want to work in the Bureau of Investigation . . ."

Fabius is talking. He examines the new recruit dubiously, obviously apprehensive that he will not be equal to his job.

"It's difficult work," he begins, his tone severe.

"I know it is, Monsieur," Wallas answers, "but I'll do . . ."

"Difficult and disappointing."

He speaks slowly and hesitantly, without letting himself be distracted by Wallas' answers, which he seems, moreover, not to hear.

"Come over here, we'll have a look."

Out of his desk drawer, he takes a curious instrument that looks like a combination of calipers and a protractor. Wallas approaches and bends his head forward, to permit Fabius to take the customary measurements of his forehead. This is a regulation formality. Wallas knows that; he has already taken his own approximate measurements with a tape-measure: he is slightly over the compulsory square centimeters.

"One hundred-fourteen. . . . Forty-three."

Fabius takes a slip of paper to make the calculation.

"Now let's see. One hundred-fourteen multiplied by forty-three. Three times four, twelve; three times one, three, and one makes four; three times one, three. Four times four, sixteen; four times one, four and one makes five; four times one, four. Two; six and four, ten: zero; five and three, eight, and one makes nine; four. Four thousand nine hundred and two. . . . That's not so good, young man."

Fabius stares at him mournfully, shaking his head.

"But Monsieur," Wallas protests politely, "I made the calculation myself and . . ."

"Four thousand nine hundred and two. Forty-nine square centimeters of frontal surface; you have to have at least fifty, you know."

"But Monsieur, I . . ."

"Well, since you've come recommended, I'm going to hire you—on probation. . . . Maybe some good hard work will help you gain a few millimeters. We'll decide about that after your first important case."

Suddenly in a hurry, Fabius takes from his desk a rubber stamp which he first presses on an ink pad, and afterward nervously taps on his new man's transfer sheet; then, with the same automatic gesture, he vigorously adds a second stamp right in the middle of Wallas' forehead, shouting:

"Ready for service!"

Wallas wakes up with a start. His forehead has just bumped against the edge of the table. He straightens up and drinks the rest of his cold coffee with disgust.

Having examined the check stuck under the saucer by the waiter, he stands up and tosses a coin on the counter as he passes. He goes out without waiting for his change. "For service" as he was told by . . .

"Well, Monsieur, did you find your post office?"

Wallas turns around. Still under the effect of his brief somnolence, he has not noticed the woman in an apron who is washing the window.

"Yes, I did; thank you."

It is the woman with the broom who was washing the sidewalk this morning—in this very place.

"And it was open?"

"No, not until eight."

"Then you should have listened to me! The one in the Rue Jonas was just as good."

"Yes, I suppose so. I didn't mind the walk, though," Wallas answers as he leaves.

On his way to the Rue Jonas, he considers the best way to obtain information about the man in the torn raincoat. Despite his reluctance and Fabius' advice, it will be necessary for him to reveal his profession: it is impossible to start up a conversation with all six employees, one after the other, on some ordinary excuse as though by chance. It would therefore be best to ask the postmaster to call his staff together for a brief conference. Wallas will give the description of the man, who must have come in last night between five-thirty and six—unfortunately a busy time. (According to the statements—which agree on this point—of Madame Bax and the drunk, the scene at the fence occurred at nightfall, that is, around five o'clock.)

The hat, the raincoat, the approximate height, the general manner . . . He does not know much that's very exact. Should he add that the man looks like himself? This may disturb the witnesses to no purpose, for this resemblance is quite problematical—and, in any case, subjective.

The employees are all in their places now, though the electric clock indicates only one-thirty. Wallas assumes a preoccupied expression and walks past the windows while examining the signs above them:

"Postage Prepaid. Stamps in Sheets. Surcharges. Parcel Post. Air Mail."

"Parcel Post. Stamps. Registered Letters. Special Delivery. Registered Letters and Packages."

"Stamps. Money Orders: Postal Orders, Checks, International Money Orders."

"Savings Bank. Pension Coupons. Pensions and Retirement. Stamps. Money Orders Cashed."

"Telegrams. Telegraph Money Orders Sent and Cashed. Telephone Payments and Surcharges."

"Telegrams. Pneumatic Correspondence. Poste Restante. Stamps."

Behind the window, the girl raises her head and looks at him. She smiles and says as she turns around toward a set of pigeonholes on the wall:

"There's a letter for you."

As she looks through the packet of envelopes she has just taken out of one of the pigeonholes, she adds: "I didn't recognize you right away with that overcoat."

"It's because it's not as warm today," Wallas says.

"Winter's coming now," the young woman answers.

Just as she is about to give him the letter, she asks with a sudden and satirical respect for the regulations:

"Do you have your card, Monsieur?"

Wallas thrusts his hand into the inside pocket of his overcoat. The registration card is not there, of course; he will explain forgetting it by the fact that he has changed his clothes. But he does not have time to act out this little comedy.

"You know you gave it in last night," she says. "I shouldn't be giving you any mail any more, since you aren't registered here any more; but since the box hasn't been bought by anyone else yet, it doesn't matter."

She hands him a crumpled envelope: "Monsieur André WS. Post Office 5, 2 Rue Jonas. No. 326 D." The word "Pneumatic" is written in the left corner.

"Has it been here long?" Wallas asks.

"Just after you came in, this morning. It must have been quarter to twelve, or twelve. You see, you were right to come back, in spite of what you told me. There isn't even any address on the back to forward it to. I wouldn't have known what to do with it."

"It was sent at ten-forty," Wallas remarks, examining the postmarks.

"Ten-forty? . . . You should have had it this morning. There was probably some delay in sending it. You were right to stop by again."

"Oh," Wallas says, "it can't be very important."

4

"In my opinion, this letter proves nothing at all."

Laurent flattens the sheet out on his desk with his open hand.

"Then nothing ever proves anything."

"But," the commissioner remarks, "that's what I just finished telling you."

As though to console Wallas, he adds:

"Let's put it this way: with this letter, you can prove anything you want—you can always prove whatever you want—for instance, that *you* are the murderer: the post office employee recognized you, and your name has a certain resemblance to this discreet 'WS' that indicates it. You don't happen to be named André, do you?"

Wallas finds himself faced again with the commissioner's jokes. He nevertheless answers, out of civility:

"Anyone can have letters sent to him under any name. All you need to do is buy a postal number; no one asks for the purchaser's real identity. The latter could just as well get himself called 'Daniel Dupont' or 'Chief Commissioner Laurent.' It's only unfortunate that we haven't discovered the place where he received his mail sooner; we would have picked it up this morning too. I repeat that you have to send a man to the Rue Jonas right away, to wait for his possible return; however, since he himself told them he wouldn't be back, this precaution will probably be of no use. All we can do is send for that girl and question her. Maybe she'll give us some clue."

"Don't get excited," Laurent begins, "keep calm. Actually, I don't see any reason why this Monsieur WS should be the murderer. What do you really know, when you come down to facts? With the help of a fanciful woman and a drunk man, you've been induced to accept mail, some mail that didn't belong to you from a *poste restante* window. (Please note, by the way, that this is absolutely irregular: in this country, the police have no right to force the postal authorities to hand over private correspondence; you must have a court order for that.) All right. Who was this letter addressed to? To a man who looks like you. On the other hand, you also happen to resemble (though the testimony is more suspect) someone who is supposed to have walked past the little house and "stuck his arm between the bars of the fence" at around five o'clock. You have

decided, consequently, that this person then went into this same
post office. All right. That would certainly be a coincidence—
which the letter in question should explain. But just what does
this letter say? That the sender (who signs himself J.B.) will
expect this 'André WS' sooner than they had previously arranged ("after quarter to twelve")—unfortunately the location
of their rendezvous is not specified; that, because of the defec-
tion of a third person designated by the letter G, this same WS
will need the whole afternoon to do some job, concerning which
we are given no clues except that part of it was already completed yesterday (besides, you have to admit that one wonders
what could still be done as regards Dupont's murder). Aside
from that, I can find only a little phrase whose meaning neither
you nor I can figure out, but which we can probably dismiss as
secondary—you agree with me on that. Finally, to finish up, we
find that one word is illegible in one of the sentences you
consider indicative—a word of seven or eight letters that looks
like 'ellipse' or 'eclipse' or that could be 'align' or 'idem' or a
lot of other things."

Laurent then declares that the possession of a postal box does
not indicate necessarily criminal intentions any more than the
use of a pseudonym. The city's six post offices have a total of
several thousand addressees of this nature. Some of the latter—
less than a quarter, it appears—carry on a purely sentimental
or parasentimental correspondence. One must also include
about the same number of more or less fictional commercial-
philanthropic enterprises such as marriage agencies, employ-
ment offices, Hindu fakirs, astrologists, spiritual mentors, . . .
etc. The rest, say more than half, consists of businessmen of
whom only a tiny proportion are actually crooks.

The pneumatic message has been sent from post office number 3, the one serving the inner harbor and the northeast sub-

urbs. It is, as always, a matter of a sale of wood, or of some operation relating to it: adjudication, transportation, cargo or some such thing. Since the market suffers extremely variable daily fluctuations, it is essential for the middle men to know how to take advantage of it quickly; a delay of twenty-four hours in a transaction can sometimes ruin a man.

J.B. is a commission-merchant (perhaps unlicensed—it isn't necessarily so). G and André WS are two of his agents. They cooperated yesterday on a deal which is to be closed tonight. Without G's cooperation, the second agent must be on hand sooner than usual in order not to be left behind.

5

Wallas is alone again, walking through the streets.

This time he is going to see Doctor Juard; as Laurent has just repeated to him: that is the first thing to do. He has managed to obtain the cooperation of the municipal police in the surveillance of the little post office and the questioning of the young woman working there. But he could see that the commissioner's mind was henceforth made up: there is no terrorist organization, Daniel Dupont has killed himself. This is the only explanation Laurent regards as reasonable; he admits that "minor details" are temporarily at variance with this notion, yet each new element that is brought to his attention immediately becomes an additional proof of suicide.

This is the case, for instance, with regard to the revolver which Wallas has found in the professor's house. The caliber of the weapon corresponds to that of the bullet turned in by the doctor; and this bullet just happens to be missing from the clip. Finally, and most significant to the commissioner's way of thinking, the revolver was jammed. This fact, determined in the police laboratories, would be a capital one: it explains why Dupont, merely wounded by his first bullet, did not fire a second shot. Instead of being ejected normally, the shell has remained jammed inside; this is why it has not been found on the floor in the study. As for the rather blurred fingerprints taken from the grip, their arrangement is not incompatible with the gesture the commissioner has imagined: the index finger on the trigger as though to fire straight ahead, but the elbow stuck out and the wrist twisted in such a way that the muzzle of the gun is pressed, at only a slight angle, between the two ribs. Despite this inconvenient position, the weapon must be held firmly so that it remains in place. . . .

A deafening shock in the chest, immediately followed by an extremely sharp pain in the right arm; then nothing more— then nausea, which is certainly not death. Dupont stares at his revolver with astonishment.

His right arm moves without difficulty, his head is clear, the rest of his body would also respond if he called upon it to do so. He is nevertheless certain of having felt the detonation and the rending of his flesh in the region of his heart. He should be dead; now he finds himself sitting at his desk as if nothing had happened. The bullet must have swerved. He must finish the job as soon as possible.

He turns the muzzle toward himself again; he presses it against the material of his vest, in the place where the first hole must already be. Fearing he might weaken, he puts all his strength into contracting his finger. . . . But this time nothing happens, absolutely nothing. However hard he tightens his finger on the trigger, the weapon remains inert.

He lays it on the desk and puts his hand through several exercises to prove to himself that it is functioning normally. It is the revolver that is jammed.

Although hard of hearing, old Anna, who was clearing off the table in the dining room, has obviously heard the explosion. What is she doing? Has she gone out to call for help? Or is she coming upstairs? She never makes any noise with her felt slippers. Something must be done before she reaches him. He must get out of this absurd situation.

The professor tries to get up; he succeeds easily. He can even walk. He goes to the mantelpiece to look at himself in the mirror; he moves a pile of books aside. Now he sees the hole, a little too high; the material of his vest, torn, is faintly stained with blood; almost nothing. He need only button his jacket and it won't show any more. A glance at his face: no, he doesn't look so bad. He turns back to his desk, tears up the letter he has written to his friend Juard before dinner, and throws it in the wastebasket. . . .

Daniel Dupont is sitting in his study. He is cleaning his revolver.

He manipulates it with care.

After having checked the proper functioning of the mechanism, he puts the clip back in place. Then he puts his rag away in a drawer. He is a meticulous man, who likes every task to be executed properly.

He stands up and takes a few steps on the water-green carpet that muffles every sound. There is scarcely any room to walk in the little study. On every side books surround him: law, social legislation, political economy. . . . Down below, to the left, at the end of the long shelves, stands the row of books he himself has added to the series. Not much. There were two or three ideas nevertheless. Who has understood them? Too bad for them; that's no reason to kill oneself in despair! The professor smiles faintly, rather contemptuously, thinking again of the preposterous notions that had suddenly passed through his mind just now, while he was holding the revolver. . . . People would have thought it was an accident.

He stops in front of his desk and glances one last time at this letter he has just written, to a Belgian colleague interested in his theories. It is a clear, dry letter; it gives all the explanations necessary. Perhaps, when he has eaten dinner, he will add a warmer word at the end.

Before going downstairs he must put the revolver back in the night table drawer. He wraps it up carefully in the piece of rag he has just put away absent-mindedly. Then he turns out the large lamp on his desk. It is seven o'clock. . . .

When he came back upstairs to finish his letter, he found the murderer waiting for him. It would have been better if he had kept the revolver in his pocket. . . . But who said that he had examined it just that day? He would have removed the old shell that jammed the mechanism. The laboratory only indicated that the weapon was "well cared for" and that the missing bullet had been "recently" fired, that is, after the last cleaning —which could, after all, date from several weeks ago, even several months. Laurent translated this as follows: Dupont cleaned it yesterday, in order to use it that very evening.

Wallas is now thinking that he should have been able to convince the commissioner. The latter's arguments often seemed worthless, and it was certainly possible to prove it to him. Instead of which, Wallas has let himself get involved in futile arguments over secondary points—or even discussions having no relation to the crime whatever—and when he wanted to make the broad outlines of the case clear, he did so with phrases so clumsy that this whole story of the secret society and the timed murders assumed an unreal, gratuitous, "badly put together" quality in his mouth.

As he talked, he grew more and more aware of the unbeliev-

able character of his account. Moreover, maybe this was not a
matter of the words he was using: others chosen with more care
might have suffered the same fate; it was enough for him to
pronounce them for them to cease to inspire confidence. Wallas
consequently reached the point of no longer trying to react
against the ready-made formulas that naturally occurred to
him; they were the ones that were easiest.

To top it off, opposite him was the commissioner's cynical
face, whose all too obvious incredulity completely annihilated
the plausibility of Wallas' constructions.

Laurent has begun asking himself precise questions. Who
are the victims? What, exactly, was their role in the state?
Hasn't their sudden and collective disappearance already
caused an appreciable void? How does it happen that no one
speaks of it in society, in the newspapers, in the street?

In reality, this is easily explained. It is a matter of a rather
numerous group of men scattered throughout the country. For
the most part, they occupy no official positions; they are not
supposed to belong to the government; their influence is nevertheless direct and considerable. Economists, financiers, heads
of industrial corporations, men in charge of union councils,
jurists, engineers, technicians of all kinds, they prefer remain-
ing in the background and leading quite obscure lives; their
names are meaningless to the public, their faces completely
unknown. Yet the conspirators make no mistake about them:
they know how to reach, through them, the very core of the
nation's politico-economic system. Up to now, everything possible has been done in high places to conceal the gravity of the
situation; no publicity has been given to the nine murders
already committed, several have even been treated as accidents;
the newspapers are keeping quiet; public life continues as
usual, to all appearances. Since leaks are likely in a service as
enormous and as ramified as that of the police, Roy-Dauzet has
decided that the latter should not be directly assigned to com-

bating the terrorists. The minister has more confidence in the
various information services he controls and whose personnel,
at least, is personally committed to him.

Wallas has answered the chief commissioner's questions as
well as he could, without betraying any essential secrets. But
he realizes the weaknesses of his position. These background
characters who clandestinely run the country, these crimes no
one mentions, these secret services marginal to the actual police,
and lastly, these terrorists, more mysterious than all the rest—
there is enough here to disturb a self-confident official who is
hearing about them for the first time. . . . And probably the
story could be invented entirely and would still leave everyone the possibility of believing it—or not—and these successive
deviations, in one direction or another, would only modify its
nature in exactly the same way.

Laurent, pink and plump, sitting comfortably in his official
armchair among his salaried informers and his files, contradicted the special agent so categorically that the latter has suddenly felt his very existence threatened: himself a member of
one of these vague organizations, Wallas himself could just as
well be, like the conspiracy, a pure invention of an overly
imaginative minister; it is to this status, in any case, that his
interlocutor seems to relegate him. For the commissioner now
declared his opinion without bothering about appearances or
discretion: they were dealing, once again, with one of Roy-
Dauzet's whims; the fact that people like Fabius had any confidence in it was not enough to make it hold water. Moreover,
other disciples went still further in their extravagance, like that
Marchat—who, unfortunately, might even go so far as to die at
seven-thirty tonight by suggestion. . . .

The businessman's intervention has obviously been of no
help at all.

Wallas has left, taking with him the dead man's revolver.
Laurent did not want it: he had nothing to do with it; since

Wallas was in charge of the investigation, he should hold on to the "items of evidence." At the commissioner's request, the laboratory had returned the weapon in the state in which it had been found, that is, with the empty shell that kept it from functioning.

Wallas walks on. The arrangement of the streets constantly surprises him in this city. He has followed the same route as this morning ever since he left the prefecture, and yet he has the impression of walking much longer than he had to the first time, to cover the distance from the police station to Doctor Juard's clinic. But since all the streets in the neighborhood look alike, he could not swear that he has always taken precisely the same ones. He is afraid of having veered too far to the left and hence passed the street he was looking for.

He decides to go into a shop to ask the way to the Rue de Corinthe. It is a small bookstore that also sells stationery, pencils, and paints for children. The saleswoman stands up to wait on him:

"Monsieur?"

"I'd like a very soft gum eraser, for drawing."

"Yes of course, Monsieur."

The ruins of Thebes.

On a hill above the city, a Sunday painter has set up his easel in the shade of cypress trees, between the scattered shafts of columns. He paints carefully, his eyes shifting back to his subject every few seconds; with a fine brush he points up many details that are scarcely noticeable to the naked eye, but which assume a surprising intensity once they are reproduced in the picture. He must have very sharp eyes. One could count the stones that form the edge of the quay, the bricks of the gable-end, and even the slates in the roof. At the corner of the fence, the leaves of the spindle trees gleam in the sun, which emphasizes their outlines. Behind, a bush rises above the hedge, a bare bush whose every twig is lined with a bright streak where the light hits it, and a dark one on the shadow side. The snapshot has been taken in winter, on an exceptionally clear day. What reason could the young woman have for photographing this house?

"It's a pretty house, isn't it?"

"Well yes, if you like it."

She cannot have been the tenant who preceded Dupont; the latter took up residence there some twenty-five years ago, and inherited it from an uncle. Has she been the servant there? Wallas sees again the gay, slightly provocative face of the saleswoman; thirty to thirty-five years old at the most, prepossessing maturity with full, rounded form; warm complexion, shining eyes, dark hair, an uncommon physical type in this country —actually reminiscent of the women of southern Europe or the Balkans.

"Well yes, if you like it."

With a throaty little laugh, as if he had just indulged in some flattering compliment. His wife? That would be strange. Didn't Laurent say she was running a shop now? Around fifteen years younger than her husband . . . dark, with black eyes . . . that's who it is!

Wallas leaves the bookstore. A few yards farther on, he reaches a crossroad. Opposite him stands the red placard: "For drawing, for school, for the office . . ."

It is here that he got off the streetcar, before lunch. Again he follows the arrow toward the Victor-Hugo stationery shop.

CHAPTER FOUR

1

Down below, directly beneath his eyes, a cable runs along the surface of the water.

Leaning over the parapet, he sees it rising from under the arch, straight and taut, apparently no thicker than his thumb; but distance is deceptive when there is no object of comparison. The coiled strands follow each other smoothly, giving the impression of great speed. A hundred spirals a second, perhaps? . . . Actually, that would still be no great rate of speed, that of a man walking briskly—that of the tug pulling a train of barges along a canal.

Beneath the metal cable is the water, greenish, opaque, chopping slightly in the wake of the already distant tug.

The first barge has not yet appeared under the bridge; the cable still runs along the water, without anything to suggest that it must soon be interrupted. Yet the tug is now reaching the next footbridge and, in order to pass under it, begins lowering its smokestack.

2

"Daniel was a melancholy man . . . melancholy and solitary. . . . But he wasn't the kind of man to commit suicide—anything but. We lived together almost two years in that house in the

Rue des Arpenteurs (the young woman stretches out her arm and points east—unless she is merely indicating the big photograph on the other side of the partition, in the shopwindow) and not once during those two years did he ever reveal the slightest sign of discouragement or doubt. It wasn't just a front: that serenity was the true expression of his nature."

"You were saying, just now, that he was melancholy."

"Yes. That probably isn't the right word. He wasn't melancholy. . . . He certainly wasn't gay: gaiety didn't mean anything once you got through the garden gate. But melancholy didn't either. I don't know how to tell you. . . . Boring? That isn't right either. I enjoyed listening to him, when he was explaining something to me. . . . No, what made it impossible to live with Daniel was that you felt he was alone, definitively alone. He was alone, and it didn't bother him. He wasn't made for marriage, or for any other kind of attachment. He had no friends. At the School of Law, his courses were popular, but he didn't even know his students' faces. . . . Why did he marry me? . . . I was very young, and I felt a kind of admiration for this older man; everyone I knew admired him. I had been brought up by an uncle, and Daniel came to his house for dinner now and then. I don't know why I'm telling you all this, it can't be interesting for you."

"Yes, yes it is," Wallas protests. "On the contrary, we need to know if Dupont's suicide is plausible, if he might have had reasons to kill himself—or if he was capable of doing it without any reason."

"Oh, not that! There was always a reason—for his least action. When it didn't appear at the moment, you found out later that there had been one all the same, a precise, long deliberated reason that left no aspect of the question in doubt. Daniel did nothing without having decided to do it in advance, and his decisions were always rational; unchangeable too, of course.

. . . A lack of imagination, if you like, but to an extraordinary degree. . . . I had nothing but virtues to reproach him for, really: never doing anything without thinking first, never changing his mind, never being wrong."

"But you said his marriage was a mistake?"

"Well yes, of course, in his relations with human beings he risked making mistakes. You could even say that he did nothing but make mistakes. Yet in the long run he was right anyway: his only mistake was in supposing the rest of the world was as reasonable as he was."

"Do you think he might have been somewhat bitter about this incomprehension?"

"You don't understand the kind of man he was. Absolutely unshakable. He was sure of being right, and that was enough for him. If other people enjoyed themselves over chimeras, too bad for them."

"He might have changed as he grew older; you hadn't seen him since . . ."

"Oh yes, we've seen each other several times: he was still the same. He talked to me about his work, about how he spent his time, the few people he still saw. He was happy, in his way; a thousand miles from any thought of suicide, anyway; satisfied with his monk's life between his old deaf housekeeper and his books. . . . His books . . . his work . . . that was all he lived for! You know the house, gloomy and silent, muffled with rugs, full of old-fashioned ornaments no one is allowed to touch. Once inside you felt uncomfortable, as if you were choking in the gloom that took away any desire to joke, to laugh, to sing. . . . I was twenty. . . . Daniel seemed comfortable there and didn't understand that someone else might feel differently. Besides, he rarely left his study where no one was allowed to move anything. Even at the beginning of our marriage, he only left the house to do his errands, three times a week; the minute he came

175

back he went upstairs and shut himself in; and he often spent
some of the night there. I only saw him during meals, when he
came down to the dining room, punctually at noon and at seven.

"When you told me he was dead, just now, it gave me a funny
feeling. I don't know how to describe it to you. . . . What difference could there be between Daniel living and Daniel dead?
He wasn't ever alive. . . . Not that he lacked personality, or
character. . . . But he was never *alive*."

"No, I haven't seen him yet. I plan on going there when I
leave here."
"What's his name?"
"Doctor Juard."
"Oh. . . . He's the one who performed the operation?"
"Yes."
"That's funny."
"He's not a good surgeon?"
"Oh yes . . . I think he is."
"You know him?"
"Just by name . . . I thought he was a gynecologist."

"And that happened a long time ago?"
"Everyone began talking about it just before the beginning
of . . ."

Wallas suddenly has the disagreeable sensation that he is
wasting his time. At the moment it occurred to him that the
stationery seller in the Rue Victor-Hugo was perhaps the
former Madame Dupont, this coincidence seemed miraculous

to him; he hurried back toward the shop, where from the
woman's first words he discovered that he had guessed right. He
felt tremendously pleased, as if an unhoped-for piece of luck
had just helped his investigation along considerably. Yet the
fact of having met this woman by chance, on his way, changed
nothing about the importance of the information he was entitled to expect from her: if Wallas had seriously supposed she
could furnish anything important he would immediately have
looked up the address of the divorced wife whose existence
Commissioner Laurent had indicated to him this morning. At
the time, he had decided it was more important to proceed to
other interrogations first—that of Doctor Juard, for instance,
whom he has not yet been able to contact.

Wallas now realizes how unreasonable his recent hope was.
He is left somewhat dazed by it—not only from realizing this
hope was vain, but disturbed, above all, by not having realized
it sooner. Sitting in the back room of the shop, facing this attractive young woman, he wonders what he came here for—
perhaps something he doesn't know himself.

At the same time, he is suddenly afraid of no longer finding
the doctor at the clinic. And as he stands up, apologizing for
being unable to stay and chat any longer, he is once again surprised by the little throaty laugh that seems to suggest some
complicity. Yet the banal phrase he has just spoken offered no
possibility of a double meaning. . . . In his uncertainty, Wallas
tries to reconstitute it; but he doesn't manage to: "I'm going to
have to . . . I'm going to . . ."

The buzzer at the door brings his attempts to an end, like a
bell trying to remind him of the time. But instead of freeing
him, this intervention delays his departure still longer; the
saleswoman has disappeared into her shop, leaving him alone
after a few cheerful words:

"Just a minute, please. I have to wait on a customer."

"I'm sorry, Madame, to have to . . . Just a minute, please, I

have to go. . . . I'm going to have to go. . . . I'm going to . . . I'm
going to have to . . ."

There was nothing to laugh about that way.

Wallas sits down again, not knowing what to do while waiting
for the woman to come back. Through the half open door he has
heard her receiving her visitor with a brief professional phrase
—hard to make out, moreover, for the room Wallas is in is
separated from the shop by a winding series of hallways and
anterooms. Afterward, he has heard no further words. The customer, no doubt, has a lower voice, and the young woman herself is not speaking—or else has lowered her voice. But why
would she lower her voice?

His ears involuntarily straining, Wallas tries to imagine the
scene. A series of possibilities quickly flashes before his eyes,
mostly silent, or whispered so low that the words are completely
lost—which further emphasizes their mimed, caricatural, even
grotesque quality. Besides, almost all these suppositions are
characterized by so flagrant an improbability that their own
creator is obliged to recognize them as relating more to delirium
than to reasonable conjecture. He worries over this for a moment: does not his job, in fact, consist of precisely . . . "It's
difficult work. . . . Difficult and disappointing . . . Well, since
you've come recommended, I'm going to hire you—on probation. . . ."

All that is obviously not very serious; if it were something
important—relating to his case—he would not let his mind
wander this way. He has no reason to be interested in what is
being said out there.

Yet he listens despite himself—he tries to listen, rather, for
he can hear nothing but extremely vague noises whose prove-
nance is as little characterized as their nature. . . . Nothing, in
any case, that resembles a little throaty laugh . . . warm and
provocative . . .

It is evening. Daniel Dupont returns from his errands. His eyes on the floor, he climbs the stairs with that determined gait of his in which only a slight fatigue can be detected. Having reached the second floor, he walks without a second's hesitation toward the study door. . . . He starts as he hears, just behind him, the little throaty laugh that greets his arrival. In the dimness of the landing, where he neglected to turn on the light, he has not noticed the attractive young woman who is waiting for him in front of the open bedroom door . . . with her little throaty laugh that seems to emanate from her whole body . . . provocative and suggestive. . . . His wife.

Wallas dismisses this image in its turn. The bedroom door shuts the overly carnal wife inside. The ghost of Daniel Dupont continues on its way toward the study, eyes the floor, hand already extended toward the doorknob it is about to turn. . . .

From the shop side, the situation is still just as vague. Wallas, who is growing impatient, mechanically pushes up his cuff to look at his wrist watch. He remembers at the same moment that it has stopped: it still shows seven-thirty. There is no use setting it as long as it won't work.

On the chest opposite him, on either side of a porcelain figurine of stylized gallantry, is a pair of portraits. The one on the left shows the stern face of a middle-aged man; he is seen in three-quarters, almost in profile, and seems to be observing the statuette out of the corner of his eye—unless he is looking at the second photograph, older than the first, as the yellowing of the paper and the old-fashioned clothes of the people shown in it indicate. A little boy in a communion suit is looking up toward a tall woman wearing the ruffled dress and plumed hat fashionable in the last century. It is probably his mother, an extremely young mother whom the child looks up at with rather perplexed admiration—as far as can be judged from this faded snapshot, where the features have lost a good deal of their actuality. This lady must also be the mother of the stationery seller; the severe gentleman may be Dupont. Wallas does not even know what the dead man looks like.

Seen at close range, the photograph reveals an almost imperceptible smile, without its being possible to tell whether it comes from the mouth or from the eyes. . . . From another angle, the man assumes an almost coarse expression that has something vulgar, self-satisfied, rather repugnant about it. Daniel Dupont returns from his errands. He climbs the stairs with a heavy tread in which his haste can nevertheless be detected. When he reaches the top, he turns left toward the bedroom, whose door he pushes open without bothering to knock. . . . But the figure of a young man has appeared from the study just behind him. Two revolver shots ring out. Dupont collapses without a sound on the hall carpet.

The young woman appears in the doorway: "I haven't kept you waiting too long, have I?" she asks in her throaty voice.

"No, not at all," Wallas answers; "but I'll have to be running along now."

She stops him with a gesture:

"Wait just a minute! You know what he bought? Guess!"

"Who?"

The customer, of course. And he has bought an eraser, of course. What does she think is so surprising about that?

"You know, the customer who just left!"

"I don't know," Wallas says.

"The postcard!" the young woman exclaims. "He bought the post card showing the house, the one you bought from me yourself this morning!"

This time the throaty laugh continues indefinitely

When she came into the shop, there was a short, sickly looking man there, wearing a long greenish coat and a dirty hat. He did not say what he wanted right away, merely murmuring "Good morning" vaguely between his teeth. He glanced around the room, and after a pause slightly too long to seem natural he decided on the rack of post cards, which he calmly went over to examine. He said something like:

". . . choose a card . . ."

"Take your time," the saleswoman replied.

But the man's manner had something so unusual about it that she was going to call Wallas in, on some excuse, to show that she was not alone, when the man stopped in front of one of the cards; he took it out of the stand and examined it carefully. Then, without saying another word, he put a coin down on the counter (the price of the card was indicated on the rack) and left the shop, taking his find with him. It was the little house in the Rue des Arpenteurs, the "scene of the crime!" Wasn't that a funny customer?

When Wallas is finally able to leave, there is no longer any chance of finding the strange collector of photographs. The Rue Victor-Hugo is empty in both directions. It is impossible to know which way the stranger turned.

Wallas therefore heads for the Juard Clinic—or at least where he imagines it to be, for he has forgotten to ask directions from the young woman, and he prefers—without any real reason, moreover—not to go back to her shop again.

He has just turned into the next street, when he sees in front of him, at the next intersection, the little man in the green coat staring at his post card, standing in the middle of the sidewalk. Wallas walks toward him without having exactly decided what he is going to do; having no doubt noticed him, the other man begins walking again and immediately disappears around the corner to the right. A few seconds later, Wallas, walking faster, reaches the intersection. To the right extends a long,

straight street without shops or any kind of doorway in which
a man could be concealed; it is completely empty, aside from a
tall pedestrian far in the distance, who is quickly disappearing
down the street.

Wallas continues to the first crossing and looks in all directions. Still no one. The little man has vanished.

3

Wallas has continued his pursuit. He has systematically ex-
plored all the neighboring streets. Afterward, still unwilling to
give up, although the chances of finding any trace of the unknown man are henceforth very slight, he has retraced his
steps, turning, turning back, passing the same places two or
three times, unable to tear himself away from the intersection
where he had seen the man for the last time.

Discouraged by this incident, he could make up his mind to
leave only when he saw what time it was in a jewelry store
window: he had just time enough to get to the police station,
where in his presence Laurent was to question the post office
employees summoned at Wallas' request.

But on the way, Wallas once again reviews the circumstances
of the appearance and the subsequent disappearance of the
purchaser of the post card—the little man standing in the
middle of the sidewalk, his eyes fixed on the photograph he is
holding in both hands, quite close to his face, as if he expected
to discover some secret in it—and then the empty streets in
every direction.

Already irritated by his own obstinacy in pursuing a shadow,
Wallas vainly tries to relegate this incident to its proper place
—a minor one, after all. It is most likely a case of some lunatic

who collects criminal documents; he doesn't have much to occupy him in this sleepy little town: the murder described by the morning papers is a windfall for him; after lunch, he went to look at the "scene of the crime" and on the way home he was struck by the stationery shopwindow, where he recognized the house; he immediately went in, but didn't know what to ask the saleswoman; in order to put a good face on the matter, he looked through the rack of post cards that happened to contain the object of his desire; he immediately bought the card and couldn't keep from examining it on the way home. As for his disappearance, it is even more easily explicable: after having turned at the intersection, he went into one of the first houses —he had reached his own residence.

This reconstruction is very plausible—the most plausible, in fact—but Wallas keeps going back to the sight of the little man in the green coat standing in the middle of the sidewalk, as if this presence had something irreducible about it which no explanation—however plausible—could account for.

At the police station, Laurent and Wallas begin by deciding on the questions to ask the post office employees: what do they know about the so-called André WS? Is he known in the neighborhood? Does anyone know where he lives? How long has he had a *poste restante* number in the Rue Jonas post office? Does he come for his mail often? Does he receive a lot? Where are his letters sent from? Lastly, why is he not coming back any more? Has he given any reason? When did he come for the last time? . . . etc. It is also a question of establishing as accurate a description as possible of the man in the torn raincoat.

The employees, who were waiting in an adjoining room, are shown in. There are three; the girl from the sixth window is named Juliette Dexter, her serious and thoughtful expression

183

inspires confidence; afterward come Lebermann, Emilie, fifty-
one, unmarried, who works at the next window and is always
interested in what is happening around her; also a woman who
no longer belongs to the post office staff, a Madame Jean, has
been summoned.

Madame Jean, because she once obtained a graduation
certificate, performed, during the summer, the functions of temporary clerk at the Rue Jonas post office; and for the month
of September, during Mademoiselle Dexter's vacation, she replaced the latter at her window. Apparently her work was not
regarded as entirely satisfactory, since the administration has
preferred not to continue the experiment and to do without her
service. Madame Jean, who at present is a simple domestic in
the house of a businessman on the Boulevard Circulaire, is not
at all bitter about this unfortunate effort. She prefers manual
work. The attraction of a higher salary had led her to give it
up; she has returned to it, after three months, with a kind of
relief: the various tasks she was assigned during her stay at the
post office all appeared somewhat odd to her, both complicated
and futile, something like a game of cards, for instance; the
internal operations, even more than those carried on at the windows, were subject to certain secret regulations and engendered
a number of rituals that were generally incomprehensible.
Madame Jean, who had always slept very well up to the time
she worked in the post office, had begun, after a few weeks of
this new job, to suffer from obsessive nightmares in which she
had to reproduce whole volumes of sibylline writings which
she transcribed, for lack of time, quite incorrectly, distorting
the signs and confusing their order, so that the work had to be
done over and over again.

Now she had recovered her old calm and the post office had
almost returned for her to the status of an ordinary shop where
stamps and letter-cards were sold, when suddenly a police in-

spector came to question her about her previous month's activities. Immediately her suspicions returned, her mistrust, her fears: so something really wrong was going on in the Rue Jonas post office after all. Unlike her former colleague, Emilie Lebermann, whom the promise of scandal hugely excited, Madame Jean was quite reluctant about coming to the police station, determined to open her mouth only enough to avoid any personal difficulties. Besides, there would be no problem: she has seen nothing, she knows nothing.

Nevertheless she is not too surprised to find in the commissioner's office the well-dressed (but suspiciously reticent) gentleman who asked her, this very morning, the way to the "main post office" in order to send, he said, a telegram. So he's mixed up in this business! He doesn't need to worry, in any case, that she'll say anything to the police about his comings and goings this morning.

This is the third time she has seen him today, but he has not recognized her; since he has only seen her up to now in an apron and without a hat, there is nothing surprising about that.

Madame Jean notices with some satisfaction that the commissioner is questioning Juliette Dexter first—quite pleasantly, moreover.

"You know," he says to her, "the man receiving *poste restante* mail under the name of André WS . . ."

The girl opens her eyes wide and turns toward the telegram clerk. She opens her mouth to speak . . . but says nothing and sits bolt upright on her chair, staring back and forth at the two men.

Then Wallas has to begin by explaining that he is not André WS, which plunges the girl into still greater astonishment:

"But . . . the letter . . . just now? . . ."

Yes, he was the one who took the letter, but it was the first time he had ever been seen in the Rue Jonas. He has taken advantage of his resemblance to the man in question.

"Well well . . . Well well . . ." the old maid keeps saying, flabbergasted.

Madame Jean, however, shows nothing and continues to stare at the floor straight ahead of her.

The girl's testimony is explicit: the man who calls himself André WS resembles Wallas almost exactly. She did not hesitate when she saw the latter present himself at the window—despite the change of clothes.

The other man was wearing quite modest and rather shabby clothes. He almost always wore a beige raincoat that was too tight for his powerful frame; on reflection, he must have been heavier than Wallas.

"And he had glasses."

It is the old maid who adds this detail. But Mademoiselle Dexter protests: André WS has never worn glasses. Her colleague insists on her point: she remembers distinctly, she even pointed out, one day, that it made him look like a doctor.

"What kind of glasses?" Laurent asks.

They were thick-rimmed tortoise-shell glasses with slightly tinted lenses.

"What color were they tinted?"

"A kind of smoky gray."

"Were the two lenses exactly the same color, or was one of them a little darker than the other?"

She hadn't noticed this detail, but it's quite possible, as a matter of fact, that one of the lenses was darker. It's hard to tell about the visitors—who come up to the windows with the light behind them—but she remembers now that . . .

Laurent asks Juliette Dexter the exact time of the last visit of the man with the *poste restante* number.

"It was around five-thirty or six," she answers; "he always came around then—a little later, maybe, at the beginning of the month, when it took longer to get dark. In any case, it was when we were busiest."

Wallas interrupts her: he had understood, from what the girl had told him when she gave him the letter, that the other man had come by shortly before, toward the end of the morning.

"Yes, that's right," she says after a moment's thought; "but that time it wasn't you yet. He came a little after eleven, as he did from time to time, as well as making his evening visits."

Did he come regularly every evening? And when did his visits start? No, he didn't come regularly: sometimes more than a week passed without him showing up, and then they would see him every evening for four or five days—and even mornings, too, sometimes. When he came, it was because he was expecting a message or a series of messages; mail never came for him during his periods of absence. He received mostly pneumatic messages and telegrams, rarely ordinary messages; the pneumatic messages came from within the city itself, obviously, the telegrams from the capital or elsewhere.

The girl stops talking, and since no one asks her anything further, she adds after a moment:

"He should have found his last pneumatic when he came by this morning. If he didn't, it's the fault of the central service."

But her reproach almost seems to be addressed to Wallas. And no one knows if the tinge of regret in her voice refers to that urgent letter which has not reached its addressee, or to the inefficient functioning of the post office system in general.

Mademoiselle Dexter saw the man in the tight raincoat for the first time when she returned from her vacation, early in

October; but the *poste restante* number had already been rented for some time since. When? She couldn't say exactly; it will be easy, of course, to find the date in the post office records. As for knowing if the man had already come during the month of September, they will have to ask her replacement about that.

Unfortunately, Madame Jean does not remember; she didn't notice, at the time, that name of André WS nor did she recall having ever seen this face—Wallas' face—with or without glasses.

Mademoiselle Lebermann thinks that he had come already, that he had even come long before, for that very remark she had made about his looking like a doctor must have dated from August, since it was in August that Doctor Gelin had taken on an assistant and she had thought at first that this was . . .

"Could you say," the commissioner asks her, "if it was the right lens that was darker, or the left?"

The old maid takes several minutes to answer.

"I think," she says finally, "that it was on the left side."

"That's strange," Laurent says thoughtfully. "Think carefully; wasn't it more likely the right eye?"

"Wait a minute, Commissioner, wait a minute: I said 'on the left side,' on *my* left side—for him that meant his right eye."

"Good, that sounds better," the commissioner says.

He would like to know, now, if the beige raincoat did not have a rip across the right shoulder last night. The girl didn't look up when the man turned around, and she hadn't seen any such rip from the front. Mademoiselle Lebermann, on the other hand, had looked up and watched him as he left: there had been an L-shaped tear across the right shoulder.

Lastly, they are not in agreement as to the contents of the telegrams either: the girl can remember extremely short and commonplace texts—confirmations, counter-orders, meetings—without any detail that suggests the nature of the business referred to; Mademoiselle Lebermann refers to long messages with obscure phrases that must have had a secret meaning.

"Telegrams are always short because of the price," Juliette Dexter adds, as though she had not heard what her colleague had just declared. "People don't repeat what the correspondent already knows if they don't have to."

Madame Jean has no opinion about what is or is not said in a telegram.

Alone again, Wallas and Laurent add up what they have just learned. The total is soon reached, for they have learned nothing at all. André WS never told the post office girl anything that could furnish a lead or suggest his activities; he was not talkative. On the other hand, he does not seem to have been someone from the neighborhood: at least, no one knows him there.

Mademoiselle Lebermann has given her personal opinion at the end of the questioning: a doctor specializing in illegal operations. "There are some funny doctors around here, you know," she has added knowingly.

There is no reason to reject this hypothesis *a priori*, but Laurent points out that his own, according to which it is merely the wood export market that is in question, has a better chance of being the right one after all; and besides, it would fit in better with the way the messages happened to be grouped.

Furthermore, it is still not certain that this André WS is the person Madame Bax saw from her window at nightfall, in front of the gate of the house in the Rue des Arpenteurs. The rip the drunk described in the back of the raincoat might have served to identify him, but the young post office employee has specified she saw nothing of the kind; now it is impossible, on this point, to take into account the affirmative testimony of the old maid, and the raincoat alone—without the rip—is not proof enough; any more—obviously—than the resemblance to Wallas which, if it were to be taken seriously, would just as well lead to accusing the latter.

Before leaving the commissioner, Wallas also examines a police report, the work of one of the two inspectors who, the evening before, made the first examinations of the dead man's residence.

"You'll see," Laurent remarked as he handed him the slender file of typed pages, "it's an interesting piece of work. This boy is a little young, of course: you can tell it's his first crime. For instance, he wrote this memoradum on his own, since our investigation has officially been interrupted. I even think he must have made additional investigations on his own account, after having been told to finish up. The enthusiasm of a neophyte, you understand."

While Wallas is reading the document, the commissioner makes a few further remarks—apparently ironic ones—as to the young inspector's conclusions and the naïveté with which he has received the suggestions of people who "obviously were taking him in."

The text begins as follows: "On Monday, October twenty-sixth, at eight minutes after nine . . ."

The first pages discuss in detail, but without digressions or commentary, the telephone call from Doctor Juard and the information furnished by the latter as to the professor's death and the attack itself. Then comes an extremely precise description of the house and its environs: the corner of the Rue des Arpenteurs, the little garden with its hedge of spindle trees and its fence, the two doors to the house—one in front, the other at the rear—the arrangement of the ground-floor rooms, the staircase, the carpet, the study on the second floor; the arrangement of the furniture in this last room is also analyzed in scrupulous detail. Then follow the police observations proper: bloodstains, fingerprints, objects apparently not in their normal place or position . . . "lastly the fingerprints number 3—right hand—also figure distinctly on a cubical paperweight weighing between seven and eight hundred grams, placed to the left of the manuscript page—about ten centimeters away."

Aside from these exaggeratedly detailed notations, the memorandum furnishes more or less the substance of the first reports made by the inspectors, to whom Laurent had introduced Wallas this morning. However, two new indications appear in it: the recent damaging of the buzzer system at the gate (which is no news to Wallas) and fresh tracks discovered on the narrow strip of lawn along the west end of the house; the measurements of these footprints are indicated, as well as the average length of the strides.

A little more attention is paid, this time, to the housekeeper's words. Wallas even recognizes, in the phrases quoted, the old woman's favorite expressions. In particular, the complete story of the damaged telephone line is given and Madame Smite's vain efforts to have it repaired.

After taking the housekeeper's testimony, the zealous inspector has interviewed the concierge from the apartment house across the street and the manager of a "small café located some twenty yards away, at nubmer 10"—the Café des Alliés. The concierge refers to the regular visitors to the house; he himself often sits—particularly in the spring and summer—on his doorstep in the afternoons, just opposite the garden gate; consequently he has been able to observe that very few people visited the victim: the postman, the employee from the public utilities system, occasionally a salesman of Venetian blinds or vacuum cleaners, as well as four or five gentlemen whom it is difficult at first glance to distinguish from salesmen—for they wear the same type of suit and carry the same briefcase—but who are businessmen from the city, professors, doctors, etc. It is apparent that the author only reproduces all these trifling remarks out of a concern for objectivity; and despite the care he takes to present what follows with the same detachment, he obviously regards it as much more important. It concerns a young man, apparently a student, extremely simply dressed, short, even somewhat puny; this boy had apparently come several times during the course of the summer, then after a lacuna of more than a month, three times in a row during the second week in October—the week when it was so warm; since the window of the room where Dupont was sitting was open then, the concierge could hear the tone of the conversation frequently rising during these visits; the last day, the visit ended in a violent quarrel. It was the young man who did most of the shouting, the concierge thinks; this boy seemed very nervous and may have been drinking a little too much—he sometimes went into the Café des Alliés when he left the professor's house. Lastly, the day before the murder, he walked along the canal with a friend—much taller and stronger than himself, and certainly older too. They stopped in front of the little house and the student pointed to one of the rooms on the second floor; he was obviously over-excited, he was explaining something to his companion with animation, making threatening gestures.

Although Madame Smite is extremely deaf (and "rather peculiar") and "seems to be completely ignorant of her employer's associates," it is possible that she can give the name of this young man and say what he was doing in the house.

It would be best to question the housekeeper once again; unfortunately she has left the city. In her absence, the inspector has attempted to question the manager of the Café des Alliés; he points out, by the way, that "members of this profession are generally quite well informed as to the private life of their customers." The manager had no desire to talk, and it required all the inspector's patience and diplomacy to get to the bottom of the affair:

Some twenty years ago, Dupont "had relations regularly" with a woman "in modest circumstances" who, subsequently gave birth to a son. The professor, who had "done everything to keep this regrettable event from occurring" (?) and whom the woman attempted to pressure into an alliance, persisted in his refusal to marry her. Finding no other way to bring to an end the "proceedings of which he was the object" he soon afterward married a young girl of his own circle. But the illegitimate child, having grown up, now returned with the intention of obtaining large sums of money, "which provoked stormy arguments whose echoes were heard by the neighbors."

In his conclusions, the inspector begins by proving that Daniel Dupont himself has, on a number of points, "distorted the truth."

"The mere examination of the material evidence," he writes, "proves, without there being any need to bring in the evidence of the witnesses, that:

"First, there were two aggressors, not just one: the man with the small hands (fingerprints number 3) and small feet (tracks on the lawn) who took such short strides, cannot be the one, necessarily tall and strong, who twisted the wire of the electric buzzer at the garden gate; furthermore, if the first man was obliged to walk on the lawn to avoid making the gravel crunch, it is because *there was already someone* walking beside him, on the brick rim of the path; had he been alone, he would have chosen this wide rim himself.

"Second, at least one of these two men was familiar with the house and not an anonymous malefactor: it is apparent that he was well acquainted with the premises and the household habits.

"Third, he was certainly recognized by the professor; the latter claimed to have been attacked before even having had time to open the door all the way, thereby explaining that he didn't see his murderer's face; actually, he went into the study and spoke to the two men: there was even a struggle between them, as is indicated by the disorder of the room (piles of books knocked over, chair moved, etc.) and the fingerprints (number 3) on the paperweight.

"Fourth, the motive of the crime is not theft: someone who knew the house so well would also know that there was nothing to steal in this room.

"Dupont was unwilling to reveal his murderer, for the latter was *too closely involved* with him. He even concealed as long as possible the seriousness of his wound, hoping that his friend Doctor Juard would take care of him, and that scandal would be avoided. It is for this reason that the housekeeper believed Dupont had only received a '*flesh wound in the arm.*' "

And the whole scene is reconstructed. The young man, after having vainly appealed to his rights, to filial love, to pity, and finally to blackmail, determined, as a last resort to attempt force. Since he is a weakling and afraid of his father, he has sought the services of a friend, stronger and older than himself, whom he will introduce as his attorney but who is actually his thug. They have decided to make their visit on Monday, October 26, at seven-thirty in the evening. . . .

Daniel Dupont reaches the study door, his eyes on the floor, his hand already stretched toward the doorknob that he is preparing to turn, when he is suddenly struck by this thought: "Jean is here waiting for me!" The professor stops and holds his breath. Perhaps Jean has not come alone: didn't he threaten him, the other day, with bringing his "lawyer" with him? Who knows what today's children are capable of?

Cautiously he turns around and tiptoes into the bedroom to

get the revolver he has kept, since the war, in the drawer of his night table. But just as he is slipping off the safety catch, he feels a sudden qualm: he is not going to fire at his own son, after all; it's only to frighten him.

Back in the hallway, the weight of the revolver in his hand seems unrelated to the fear that ran through him a minute earlier; by comparison this sudden fear vanishes altogether: why should his son have come tonight? Moreover, Dupont is not afraid of him. He puts the gun in his pocket. Starting tomorrow, he will have the house doors locked at nightfall.

He turns the doorknob and opens the study door. Jean is there waiting for him.

He is standing between the chair and the desk. He has been reading the papers there. Another man is standing in front of the bookcase, to one side, his hands in his pockets—obviously a bad type.

"Good evening," Jean says.

His eyes are bright, both arrogant and apprehensive; he must have been drinking again. His mouth grimaces in a parody of a smile.

"What are you doing here?" Dupont asks coldly.

"I came to talk to you," Jean says. "That's (gesture of his chin) Maurice . . . he's my attorney (another grimace)."

"Good evening," Maurice says.

"Who let you in?"

"No one," Jean says. "I know the house."

Which means: "I'm a member of the family!"

"Well, you can leave the way you came," the professor says calmly. "It's just as easy: you know the way."

"We're not leaving just yet," Jean says; "we came to talk— to talk business."

"We've already exhausted the subject, my boy. Now you're going to leave."

Dupont walks toward his son with a determined expression; he sees the boy's eyes fill with fear ... fear and hatred. ... He repeats:

"You're going to leave."

Jean picks up the first thing he finds within his reach: the heavy paperweight with sharp edges. He brandishes it, ready to strike. Dupont steps back and puts his hand on his revolver.

But Maurice has seen the gesture and is already in front of Dupont, quicker to take aim himself:

"Let go of that and take your hand out of your pocket."

After that no one speaks. With his dignity at stake, Dupont feels that he cannot obey this contemptuous treatment in front of his son.

"The police are coming," he says. "I knew you'd be here waiting for me. Before coming in I telephoned from the bedroom."

"The cops?" Maurice says. "I don't hear anything."

"It won't be long, don't worry."

"We have time enough to get things straight!"

"They'll be here any minute."

"The telephone's been cut for two days," Jean says.

This time, Dupont's anger is too much for him. Everything happens in a flash: the professor's sudden movement to take out his gun, the shot that hits him full in the chest, and the young man's shrill cry:

"Don't shoot, Maurice!"

4

But the chief does not seem convinced. He dares not reject his assistant's hypothesis out of hand, for you never know: suppose that happened to be what happened, what would he look like then? Then too, the obscurities and contradictions of the case have to be interpreted one way or another. . . . What bothers him about this theory is that it involves—accuses, actually—people too highly placed, whom it can only be dangerous to affront—whether they are innocent or guilty. He says:

"We aren't accustomed here . . . we aren't accustomed in the Executive Information Service to work on suspicions as vague as that. . . ."

He would like to add, by the way, some nasty joke about the Bureau of Investigation, and the "great Fabius," but he decides to restrain himself: this may not be the right moment.

In the hope of discouraging his assistant, at least temporarily, from the slippery path onto which the latter wants to lure him, he proposes to send him on an assignment to the scene of the crime: there he could deal with the local police functionaries and with the doctor who has received Professor Dupont's testimony along with his last breath; he could also discover whether the victim's residence furnishes any new clue; he could . . . But the assistant shakes his head. It is quite futile for him to waste his time in that gloomy provincial town, half asleep in the North Sea fog. He would find nothing there, absolutely nothing. It is here, in the capital, that the drama has been acted . . . that the drama *is being* acted.

"He thinks I'm afraid," the chief realizes; but he doesn't care. He says, quite casually:

"Sometimes you go through hell and high water to find a murderer . . ."

". . . far away," his assistant continues, "when all you need to do is stretch out your hand."

"Don't forget that the crime took place up there, even so . . ."

"It took place up there the way it could have taken place anywhere and, as a matter of fact, as it *takes place* anywhere, every day, now here, now there. What actually happened in Professor Dupont's house the evening of October twenty-sixth? A replica, a copy, a simple reproduction of an event whose original and whose key are elsewhere. And tonight, once again, as every evening . . ."

"That's still no reason for neglecting whatever clues we could find up there."

"What would I find up there, if I went? Nothing but reflections, shadows, ghosts. And tonight, once again . . ."

Tonight a new copy will be discreetly slipped under the door, a correct copy duly signed and notarized, with just what it needs in the way of misspellings and misplaced commas so that the blind, the cowardly, the stone deaf can go on waiting and reassuring each other: "It can't be really the same thing, can it?"

To try to persuade his chief, the assistant goes on:

"We're not the only ones concerned with this case. If we don't act fast enough, we run the risk of finding another service pulling the rug out from under us . . . maybe the great Fabius himself, who will pass himself off as his country's savior once again . . . and get us all arrested, if he finds out we knew the truth and concealed it. . . . You'll be accused of complicity, you can be sure of that."

But the chief does not seem convinced. He growls between his teeth, with an expression of suspicion and doubt:

". . . the truth . . . the truth . . . the truth . . ."

5

Madame Jean glances cautiously toward the post office. Everything is calm along the parkway.

But everything seemed just as calm before, and yet something happened, here, fifty yards away, at the corner of the Rue

Jonas. It had already begun in September—otherwise the commissioner would not have sent for her this afternoon. Probably she was taking part in their shady deals without even knowing it. In any case, she didn't get anything out of it.

She certainly gave the man letters, without thinking twice about it: she had enough trouble checking the numbers on the cards, without examining the faces of the people who handed them to her. He might even have come often: the little Dexter girl obviously knew him well. He said he wasn't the one, of course, and Madame Jean wasn't going to say anything different! They're big enough to get out of it by themselves. Yet she had proof of the fact that he really was the one: if he was so eager to find another post office this morning, it was because he couldn't go back to that one, where he would have been recognized right away.

When she saw him again, after lunch, he was so tired that he had fallen asleep over his table. What had he been doing all morning long? Something else besides sending a telegram, that was sure. And why was he loitering around here again?

A doctor, Emilie said—maybe. He's well dressed; he looks important. Madame Jean tries to imagine Wallas with the heavy glasses described by the old maid; actually it makes him into quite a likely doctor. Which obviously does not keep him from being a criminal.

"There are some funny doctors around here, you know." That's the truth. And who don't know much: the epidemic proved that. But this one's sly. He's even managed to put the commissioner in his pocket: a little more and he'd have been running the investigation! He sounded so cocky when he answered the little Dexter girl that the poor thing didn't dare say another word. They don't have much chance of finding the guilty man now.

Madame Jean thinks about this strange turn of events in

which the guilty man himself takes charge of the investigation. Since she cannot make any headway in so confusing a supposition, she deliberately turns her eyes away—and begins thinking about something else.

6

A tremendous voice fills the hall. Projected by invisible loudspeakers, it bounces back and forth against the walls covered with signs and advertisements, which amplify it still more, multiply it, reflect it, baffle it with a whole series of more or less conflicting echoes and resonances, in which the original message is lost—transformed into a gigantic oracle, magnificent, indecipherable, and terrifying.

As suddenly as it had begun, the uproar stops, again making way for the confused murmur of the crowd.

People are hurrying in all directions. They must have guessed —or imagined they guessed—the meaning of the announcement, for the agitation has redoubled. Among the curtailed movements—each of which affects only an extremely small section of the hall—between a timetable and a ticket window, from an information booth to a newsstand—or even within less defined areas, animated here and there with vague, hesitant, discontinuous, aleatory movements—in the middle of this swarming mass occasionally interrupted, up to now, by some less episodic trajectory, distinct currents now appear; in one corner a single file has started across the entire hall in a decisive diagonal; farther on, scattered impulses unite in a series of calls and quick steps whose impetus clears a wide passage until it comes to a halt against one of the exits; a woman slaps a little boy, a gentleman feverishly searches through his many pockets for the ticket he has just bought; on all sides people are shouting, dragging suitcases, hurrying.

Doctor Juard has neither suitcase nor ticket. He is not interested in the train schedules. He has not understood what the loudspeaker has said. Neither his movements nor his general attitude have undergone any important change since a moment ago: he takes five steps along the wall, between the snack bar and the telephones, turns around, takes two steps in the opposite direction, glances at his watch, looks up at the big clock, continues straight ahead to the first telephone booth, turns back, stops, stands still for a few seconds . . . and then starts slowly toward the snack bar. He is waiting for someone who has not come.

Again the warning buzzing can be heard and suddenly the whole hall echoes to the rumbling of the divine voice. It is a clear and strong voice; one must listen to it carefully to realize that what it is saying is incomprehensible.

This last message is shorter than the previous one. It is followed by no appreciable change among the crowd. Doctor Juard, who has stood stock still, begins walking toward the row of telephone booths again.

But these words that do not seem to have achieved their purpose leave him with a vague sensation of discomfort. If the announcement was not for the travelers, perhaps it concerned him: "Doctor Juard is wanted on the telephone." He did not imagine he could be summoned by so monstrous a voice. And upon reflection, it is indeed unlikely that the official station loudspeakers should bother to transmit personal messages between train departures.

Having reached the row of telephone booths once again, the little doctor realizes that the latter are not marked with numbers making it possible to distinguish them, and that consequently the voice could not have specified which telephone he should answer. Now he would have to pick up all the receivers, one after the other. . . . This presents no insurmountable difficulty, and if a station employee came to ask him to account for his behavior, he would explain that no one has told him which of these telephones he was wanted on. Nothing more natural, after all. Unfortunately, he risks intercepting other messages and consequently finding himself mixed up in some new drama, as if the situation in which he is struggling were not complicated enough already. He thinks back to the unlucky day when he made the other man's acquaintance, following an error of the same kind: he had dialed the wrong number, and immediately events had followed one another so quickly that he had not been able to disengage himself; one thing led to another and he ended up by agreeing to . . . Besides, the other man left him no choice.

Then was there only one surgeon in the whole town, so that Dupont too had to come to his clinic to hide out? To the clinic of Doctor Juard, the "gang doctor!" This title, though rather unsuitable in fact, corresponds none the less to the state of mind he himself has been in since that single encounter; he feels tied hand and foot; and since there is no question of his using what he knows against them, he can only see the other side of his position: he is in their hands, at their mercy. At the first slip they will get rid of this useless supernumerary. If they knew, for instance, that their latest victim has been hiding in his own clinic since last night . . .

Why doesn't that Wallas get here? Juard is growing impatient. He wasn't the one who asked for an interview; all he did was to arrange the meeting place, to keep the special agent's investigations away from the clinic. There are too many people sniffing around the phony dead man already.

Occasionally the little doctor is astonished that the catastrophe has not already occurred. Dupont is supposed to have been dead some twenty hours by now; Juard himself, who has given him asylum . . . He couldn't betray the professor's confidence either and hand him over to his enemies. Moreover, where would he find them? He'll use this excuse, he'll claim he didn't know where the bullet came from either, he'll say. . . . But what good would it all do? The other man isn't used to weighing the fate of his victims so long. Juard has realized from the start, without exactly admitting it to himself, that he was condemning himself by helping the professor—besides, he considered his help absurd: the other man doesn't let himself be fooled so easily as that.

Yet nothing has happened yet today. Time is passing quite normally. Dupont is calmly waiting for the car the minister promised. As the time set for Dupont's departure approaches, the little doctor's confidence increases despite himself.

But now he is afraid that this Wallas—who needed him?—might spoil everything at the last minute; he is anxious about this delay that nothing in the special agent's insistence a half-hour ago could have suggested. Juard could take advantage of it to get away without seeing him, particularly since his professional obligations do not allow him to stay here until tonight; but he cannot make up his mind to leave: the policeman might arrive from one minute to the next, and if he sees no one at the rendezvous he will go back to the Rue de Corinthe—which must be avoided at all costs.

The little doctor continues to walk back and forth between the snack bar and the telephones, five steps in one direction, five steps in the other. He does not know which side to take. . . . He stops a moment. He glances at his watch—although he had seen the time on the big clock scarcely twenty seconds before. He sets limits beyond which he will wait no longer; but he exceeds them, one after the other—and still does not leave.

To the left of the clock is posted a sign a foot and a half high in red capital letters:

DO NOT BLOCK EXIT

Symmetrically posted, a slogan in blue letters on a yellow background: "Don't Leave Without Taking *The Times*."

All at once Juard decides someone is playing tricks on him; this notion strikes him with such violence that it gives him an almost physical sensation, analogous to that afforded by a misstep that causes a sudden loss of balance.

The man named Wallas doesn't care about being on time at this absurd rendezvous: it's the clinic he's interested in! He is there at this very moment, busily rummaging through everything; since he has a search warrant, no one dares say a thing. By choosing this unexpected spot—the station—Juard has only reinforced the special agent's suspicions, while giving free rein to his curiosity.

Perhaps there is still time to keep Dupont from being discovered. Juard has not a minute to lose. While he is crossing the hall, he thinks of a way to arrange matters, when a new cause for alarm strikes him: this Wallas is a phony policeman, he's looking for the professor in order to kill him. . . .

The little doctor stops short in order to think.

He is in front of the newsstand, whose wares he pretends to be examining. Don't leave without taking *The Times*. He steps forward on the pretext of buying the evening edition.

A customer, bending over the counter, straightens up and steps back a little to make room for Juard in front of the tiny stand; then he exclaims:

"Oh, Doctor!" he says, "I was looking for you."

Doctor Juard has now described for the third time the discovery of the burglar in the study, the revolver shot, the "flesh wound," and death on the operating table. He knows his story by heart by this time; he is aware of repeating it more naturally than he did this morning in the commissioner's office; and when he is asked an additional question, he furnishes the requested detail without difficulty, even if he improvises. This fiction has gradually assumed enough weight in his mind to dictate the right answers to him automatically; it continues of its own accord to secrete its own details and hesitations—just as reality would, in such circumstances. Juard is not far, at moments, from being taken in himself.

His interlocutor is not trying, moreover, to complicate his task. He furnishes the next clue appropriately: it is obvious that he is already accustomed to this version of the facts and does not dream of contesting it.

"Could you suggest from approximately what distance the shot was fired?"

"About five or six yards; it's difficult to give an exact figure."

"The bullet penetrated the body from in front?"

"Yes, directly in front, between the fourth and fifth ribs. For a bullet fired by a man running away, it was skillfully aimed."

"There was no other wound, was there?"

"No, just the one."

The dialogue moves along easily—so easily that it becomes almost disturbing, like the overly cunning camouflage of a trap. Juard wonders if Wallas does not know more than he is admitting.

Isn't it obvious, in fact, that the special agent knows the whole truth? He wouldn't have been transferred from the capital for just a burglary. Then what is he trying to get out of the doctor? The latter cautiously asks a few indirect questions to try to find out if it is really necessary to continue this farce; but Wallas remains immured in their original conventions, either because he feels they are more certain or because he has not understood the signals of complicity Juard has made to him, or else for still other reasons.

The little doctor would especially like to know what kind of protection he can count on from the police. Despite the misunderstanding that burdens their conversation, he has a certain sympathy for Wallas; but he does not have the impression that his help could be very effective in dealing with so powerful an organization. He does not even wear a uniform. As for the men from the police station, though they have more apparent prestige, Juard is too close to them not to know how much he can expect from them and what he can count on there.

The relative confidence Wallas inspires in him still does not keep him from staying on the defensive: the so-called "special agent" may also be in the other man's pay.

On the other hand, it is not impossible that his sincerity is so complete that he doesn't even know what has really happened.

Juard returns to his clinic. He has been able to obtain neither information nor promises from Wallas. He has less and less hope of any possible help from the authorities, were things to go badly. They would be quicker to condemn him as an accomplice.

Whichever way he turns, he is just as guilty. The issue, as he sees it, is inevitably a fatal one.

Given these various dangers, the special agent, who at first inspired him with unexpected fears, now seems on reflection much less dangerous, if not exactly a savior. Juard is even about to reproach himself for his own suspicions: shouldn't he have told the truth—of which Wallas certainly seems, after all, basically ignorant. . . .

But the little doctor then remembers the last words he spoke as he was leaving: "Sometimes you go through hell and high water to find a murderer. . . ." He has immediately regretted

them, for they applied all too clearly—much more clearly than
he had planned—to the present situation. Now he is pleased at
having spoken them. Wallas, thanks to him, now possesses the
key to the riddle; if he considers it carefully and knows how to
deal with what he finds, he will not be following a false lead.
However, Juard has not felt that the special agent paid particularly close attention to his last words.

Back in the Rue de Corinthe, the doctor is going to rejoin
Daniel Dupont in the little white room. As is customary in the
clinic, he walks in without knocking. The professor, who has his
back to the door, starts when he hears him.

"You frightened me."

"I'm sorry," Juard says, "I came in as if this were my own
room. I don't know what I was thinking of."

Dupont must have been walking back and forth between the
bed and the window. He looks annoyed.

"How's the arm?" Juard asks.

"Fine, just fine."

"Any fever?"

"No, none. I'm all right."

"It would be better not to move around too much."

Dupont does not answer. He is thinking about something
else. He walks over to the window, pulls aside one of the curtains—only an inch or so—so as to look out into the street
without being seen.

"Marchat hasn't come back," he says.

"He'll be here soon," the doctor says.

"Yes . . . He'll have to hurry."

"You've still got plenty of time."

"Yes . . . not so much."

Dupont lets go of the curtain. The light material falls back,
letting the pattern of the embroidery appear again. Before be-

coming quite motionless, the curtain is still shaken by a few tiny oscillations—quickly dying away—a faint trembling.

The professor lowers his arm with a certain slowness, that of a man who has nothing else to do afterward—and therefore has no reason to move rapidly. He is waiting for someone who has not come; in order to conceal his nervousness—and to master it somewhat—he forces himself to observe this exaggerated moderation. He lowers his arm.

His hand, instead of hanging naturally, moves up his leg, hesitates at the bottom of his jacket, lifts it slightly, moves down again, rises again, passes underneath the bottom of the jacket and finally vanishes into the trouser pocket.

Dupont turns around to face the doctor.

7

He glimpses his face in the mirror over the fireplace and, beneath it, the double row of objects arranged on the marble: the statuette and its reflection, the brass candlestick and its reflection, the tobacco jar, the ashtray, the other statuette—a splendid wrestler about to crush a lizard.

The athlete with the lizard, the ashtray, the tobacco jar, the candlestick. . . . He takes his hand out of his pocket and extends it toward the first statuette, a blind old man led by a child. In the mirror, the hand's reflection advances to meet it. Both remain momentarily suspended over the brass candlestick—hesitating. Then the reflection and the hand come to rest, one opposite the other, calmly at equal distances from the mirror's surface, at the edge of the marble and at the edge of its reflection.

The blind man with the child, the brass candlestick, the tobacco jar, the ashtray, the athlete crushing a lizard.

The hand again advances toward the bronze blind man—the image of the hand toward that of the blind man. . . . The two hands, the two blind men, the two children, the two empty candlesticks, the two earthenware jars, the two ashtrays, the two Apollos, the two lizards . . .

He still remains hesitating for some time. Then he resolutely grasps the statuette on the left and replaces it by the terracotta jar; the candlestick replaces the jar, the blind man the candlestick.

The tobacco jar, the blind man with the child, the candlestick, the ashtray, the splendid athlete.

He examined his work. Something still disturbs him. The tobacco jar, the blind man, the candlestick. . . . He reverses the last two objects. The earthenware pot and its reflection, the blind man and his reflection, the candlestick, the athlete with the lizard, the ashtray.

Finally he pushes the little red ashtray about an inch toward the corner of the marble mantelpiece.

Garinati leaves his room, locks the door behind him, and begins walking down the long spiral of the staircase.

Along a canal. The blocks of granite that line the quay; under the dust gleam occasional crystals, black, white, and pinkish. To the right, a little farther down, is the water.

A rubber-coated electric wire makes a vertical line against the wall.

Below, to pass over a cornice, it makes a right angle, once, twice. But afterward, instead of following the inner surface, it stands away from the wall and hangs free for about a foot and a half.

Below, fastened again against the vertical wall, it describes another two or three sinusoidal arcs before finally resuming its straight descent.

The little glass door has creaked loudly. In his hurry to get away, Garinati has opened it a little more than he should have.

The cube of gray lava. The warning buzzer disconnected, the street that smells of cabbage soup. The muddy paths that fade away, far away, among the rusty corrugated iron.

The bicycles coming home from work. The wave of bicycles flows along the Boulevard Circulaire.

"Don't you read the papers?" Bona bends over toward his briefcase.

Garinati puts his hands over his ears to get rid of that irritating noise. This time he uses both hands, which he keeps pressed hard against each side of his head for a minute.

When he takes them away, the whistling sound has stopped. He begins walking, carefully, as though he were afraid of making it start all over again by movements that might be too sudden. After a few steps he is once again standing in front of the apartment house he has just left.

After a few steps more he sees, glancing up at a gleaming shop, the brick house at the corner of the Rue des Arpenteurs. It is not the house itself, but a huge photograph of it carefully arranged behind the glass.

He goes in.

There is no one in the shop. Through a door in the rear comes a dark young woman who smiles at him politely. He glances toward the shelves covering the walls.

One showcase entirely filled with candy, each piece wrapped in brightly colored paper and sorted out in large round or oval jars.

One showcase completely full of little spoons, in groups of twelve—in parallel rows, other rows fan-shaped, in squares, in circles . . .

Bona would go to the Rue des Arpenteurs, ring at the door of the little house. The old deaf servant would finally hear and come to the door.

"Monsieur Daniel Dupont, please."

"What did you say?"

Bona would repeat, louder:

"Monsieur Daniel Dupont!"

"Yes, this is the house. What do you want?"

"I came to find out how he was. . . . Find out how he was!"

"Oh, I see. Very kind. Monsieur Dupont is quite well."

Why should Bona go to find out how he was, since he knows the professor is dead?

Garinati stares, under the platform, at the girders and cables gradually disappearing from sight. On the other side of the canal, the huge drawbridge machinery hums smoothly.

It would be enough to insert some hard object—it could be of quite small size—into one of the essential gears in order to stop the whole system, with a shriek of wrenched machinery. A small, very hard object that would resist being crushed: the cube of gray lava . . .

What would be the use? The emergency crew would come at once. Tomorrow everything would be in operation as usual—as if nothing had happened.

"Monsieur Daniel Dupont, please."

"What did you say?"

Bona raises his voice:

"Monsieur Daniel Dupont."

"Yes, I hear you! You don't have to shout, you know. I'm not deaf! What do you want Monsieur Dupont for now?"

"I came to find out how he is."

"How he is? But he's dead, young man! Dead, you hear? There's no one else here, you've come too late."

The little glass door creaks loudly.

Something to say to that Wallas? What would he have to say to him? He takes the post card out of his pocket and stops to look at it. You could almost count the granite crystals in the curb of stone in the foreground.

A ball of crumpled paper—bluish and dirty. He kicks it, two or three times.

A plaque of black glass attached by four gilded screws. The one on the upper right has lost the decorative rosette that concealed its head.

A white step.

A brick, an ordinary brick, a brick among the thousands of bricks that constitute the wall.

That is all that remains of Garinati around five in the evening.

The tug has now reached the next footbridge and in order to pass under it begins lowering its smokestack.

Looking directly down, the cable still runs along the surface of the water, straight and taut, scarcely bigger around than a man's thumb. It rises imperceptibly above the glaucous wavelets.

And suddenly, preceded by a ripple of foam, appears from under the arch of the bridge the blunt bow of the barge, which moves slowly on toward the next bridge.

The little man in the long greenish coat who has been leaning over the parapet straightens up.

CHAPTER FIVE

1

And night is already falling—and the cold fog comes in from the North Sea; the city seems to fall asleep in it. There has been almost no day at all.

Walking along past the shopwindows that light up one after the other, Wallas tries to distinguish the usable elements of the report Laurent has given him to read. That the motive of the crime is not theft, he is—in the precise sense of the words— "paid to find out." But why go so far as to imagine this duplication of the murderer? It does not take anyone any further to have supposed that the man who fired the fatal shot is not the man who pointed out the familiar way across the garden and through the house. Moreover, the argument about the footsteps on the lawn is not very convincing. If someone were already walking on the brick rim of the path, the other man could have walked behind him or rather in front of him, since he was the only one supposed to know the way. This is the position it is easiest to imagine the two night prowlers adopting. In any case, no one needed to walk on the lawn; if anyone did, it must be for some other reason—or else for no reason at all.

Wallas feels the day's accumulated fatigue beginning to make his legs numb. He is not used to walking such long distances. These comings and goings from one end of the town to the other must ultimately add up to a good number of miles, most of which he has covered on foot. Leaving the police station, he headed for the Rue de Corinthe by way of the Rue de la

Charte, the prefecture, and the Rue Bergère; here he found himself at an intersection of three roads: the one he was on and two possible directions opposite him, forming a right angle between them. He remembered having already passed this place twice before: the first time he had gone the right way, the second time he had made a mistake; but he could no longer remember which of these two streets he had taken the first time—moreover, they looked very much alike.

He took the one to the left, and after a few detours made necessary by the arrangement of sidewalks, he came out—much sooner than he would have believed possible—on the courthouse square, just in front of the police station.

Laurent was just leaving; he has indicated his surprise at finding Wallas here, since he had left some fifteen minutes ago. Yet Laurent has not asked for any explanation and has offered to drive the special agent to Juard's clinic in his own car, for he was going that way himself.

Two minutes later, Wallas was ringing at Number 11. It is the same nurse who has opened the door before—the one who, this morning, had insisted so indiscreetly on keeping him there despite the doctor's absence. He could tell from her smile that she recognized him. "They're all the same!" He has told her he wanted to speak to Doctor Juard *in person;* he has emphasized the urgent nature of his visit and has given her a card on which were printed the words: "Bureau of Investigation of the Ministry of the Interior."

He has been asked to wait in a kind of dim parlor-library. Since no one has asked him to sit down, he has walked up and down in front of the shelves filled with books, now and then reading a few titles as he passed. One whole shelf was filled with books devoted to the plague—as many historical studies as medical ones.

A woman has walked through the room, then two others and a short, thin man wearing glasses, who seemed in a great hurry.

The nurse has finally come back and—as if she had forgotten him—asked him what he was waiting for. He has answered that he was waiting for Doctor Juard.

"But the doctor left a moment ago, didn't you see him just now?"

It was hard to believe that she was not making fun of him. How could he have guessed that the man he has just seen was Doctor Juard, since he did not know him. And why hadn't she announced his visit as he had asked her to?

"Don't be angry, Monsieur; I thought the doctor would have spoken to you before he went out. I had told him you were here. He's just been called on an emergency case, and it was impossible for him to stay—even a minute. Since the doctor has a very busy afternoon, he's asked if you could meet him at exactly four-thirty in the hall of the railway station, between the telephone booths and the snack bar; it's the only way you can meet him today: he won't be coming back here until late tonight. When I saw the doctor come in here, I assumed he was going to arrange the meeting himself."

On his way through the room, the little doctor had glanced at him out of the corner of his eye. "There are some funny doctors around here."

Since he had plenty of time, Wallas went around to Marchat's apartment building. But his ring at the door remained unanswered. That wasn't important, one way or the other, Laurent having repeated to him the essentials of his conversation with the man who believed himself doomed to die. Still, he would have liked to judge the man's mental equilibrium for himself. Laurent described him as raving mad, and the way he had behaved in the commissioner's office justified, at least in part, this opinion. But on certain points, Wallas is not so sure as the commissioner of the insanity of Marchat's fears: the execution of a new victim is in fact only too likely for this very evening.

Having walked back downstairs, Wallas has asked the concierge of the building if he knew when his tenant would be coming in. Monsieur Marchat had just left in his car for several days, with his entire family; he had probably heard of the death of a close relative: "The poor fellow was all worked up."

The businessman lives in the southern part of town, not far from the wood export offices. From here, Wallas proceeded toward the station, walking back along the Rue de Berlin and through the courthouse square. He then followed an endless canal bordered on the other side by a row of old houses whose narrow gables have been rotted away by the water for centuries, until they lean over the canal most alarmingly.

Walking into the station hall, he saw the little chromium-plated stand at once, where a man in a white apron was selling sandwiches and bottles of soda pop. About five yards to the right there was a telephone booth—just one. He began walking up and down, glancing frequently at the dial of the clock. The doctor was late.

The hall was full of people hurrying in all directions. Wallas did not budge an inch from the place indicated by the nurse, for the crowd was so thick that he was afraid he might miss the doctor when he arrived.

Wallas began to be worried. The hour agreed on had long since passed and the disagreeable impression his visit to the clinic had made on him was growing stronger minute by minute. There had certainly been a misunderstanding. The nurse had garbled the message, either in understanding or transmitting it —perhaps in both.

He would have to telephone to the clinic to ask for an explanation. Since there was no phone book in the one booth standing here, Wallas has asked the man behind the soda fountain where he might find one. While handing out bottles and counting change, the man indicated a place in the hall where Wallas, despite his efforts, could see nothing but a newsstand. It seemed to him that the boy had not understood what he wanted. He has nevertheless started toward the tiny stall where there was obviously no trace of a phone book. A few stationery articles were exhibited among the illustrated magazines and the brightly colored covers of the detective stories; Wallas has asked to see some erasers.

It was at this moment that Doctor Juard appeared. He had been waiting at the other end of the hall, where the real snack bar and a whole row of telephone booths are.

The doctor was unable to tell him anything new. Wallas did not want to speak of the conspiracy, out of discretion, and Juard merely repeated what he had said that morning to the chief commissioner.

Quite naturally Wallas has taken, from the station square, the same streetcar as the evening before—the one that had taken him near the Rue des Arpenteurs. He got off at the same stop, and now follows the Boulevard Circulaire that brings him back to the little brick house and the wretched room over the Café des Alliés. It is completely dark now. Wallas is no further along than when he arrived, the day before, by this same route.

He walks into the huge stone apartment building that stands at the corner of the street. He is going to be forced, for the counter-questioning of the concierge, to show his pink card and, most likely, to admit, at the same time, his little deception of this morning concerning his mother's supposed friendship with Madame Bax.

From the greeting of the heavy-set, jovial man, Wallas sees that the latter recognizes him. When he reveals the object of his visit to him, the concierge smiles and merely says:

"I knew this morning that you were from the police."

The man then explains that an inspector has already come by to question him, whom he has told that he knew nothing. Wallas then refers to the youth whose disturbing manners the concierge had mentioned. The other man raises his arms to heaven:

"Disturbing!" he repeats.

It had seemed to him, in fact, that the inspector was attaching to this young man an importance which he himself was far from . . . etc. Wallas discovers, as he expected, that Commissioner Laurent made no mistake in suspecting his subordinate of immoderate "zeal." Hence the concierge did not say that there had been quarreling during these encounters, but only that at moments "voices were raised." Nor did he say that the student often seemed to be drunk. Yes, he saw him point to the house as he walked by to a friend, but he did not say that his gesture was threatening; he only mentioned "sweeping gestures"—the kind all boys that age make, impassioned or nervous. Lastly the concierge adds that the professor had already received, in the past—though rarely, as a matter of fact —visits from students at the School of Law.

The café is warm and cheerful despite the heavy atmosphere —smoke, men's breath, and the vapors of white wine. There are a good many people—five or six drinkers laughing and talking in loud voices, all at once. Wallas has returned to this place as to a refuge; he would like to have told someone to meet him here; he would wait for hours, lost in the noise of these trifling discussions—drinking hot rum at this rather isolated table. . . .

"Greetings," the drunk says.

"Hello."

"You kept me waiting," the drunk says.

Wallas turns around. Here, too, there is no isolated table where he can be quiet.

He has no desire to go upstairs to his room, which he remembers is gloomy and which is probably quite cold as well. He walks over to the bar, where three men are standing.

"Well," the drunk shouts behind him, "aren't you going to sit down over here?"

The three men turn around at the same time and stare at Wallas without the slightest embarrassment. One is wearing a grease-stained mechanic's suit; the two others are in heavy navy blue pea jackets with big collars. It occurs to Wallas that his bourgeois clothes are betraying his profession. Fabius would have started by dressing up as a sailor.

. . . Fabius comes in. He is wearing a bargeman's uniform and rolls his hips when he walks—the token of imaginary pitching on stormy seas.

"Not much to catch today," he remarks to no one in particular. "Guess all the herring are already canned. . . ."

The three men stare at him with surprise and suspicion. Two other customers, standing in front of the stove, have broken off a conversation—though one they were deeply involved in—to stare at him too. The manager wipes a rag across the bar.

"All right, are you coming?" the drunk repeats during the silence. "I'll ask you the riddle."

The two sailors, the mechanic, the other two men next to the stove all go back to their previous conversations.

"Give me a hot rum, please," Wallas says to the manager.

And he goes to the first table and sits down, facing away from the drunk.

"Still polite as ever," the latter observes.

"I could still," someone says, "be walking obliquely to the canal and be walking in a straight line anyway."

The manager serves the three men at the bar another round. The other two have resumed their argument; it is the meaning of the word *oblique* that is in dispute. Each man is trying to prove he is right by shouting louder than the other.

"Are you going to let me talk?"

"That's all you do is talk!"

"You don't understand: I said I can go straight ahead while still taking a direction that's oblique—oblique in relation to the canal."

The other man thinks a moment and remarks calmly:

"You're going to fall into the canal."

"Then you refuse to answer?"

"Listen, Antoine, you can say whatever you want, I'm not changing what I said: if you walk obliquely, you don't go straight ahead! Even if it's in relation to a canal or anything else."

The man in the pharmacist's gray smock and cap considers the argument he has just given an irrefutable one. His adversary shrugs in disgust:

"I've never met anyone so stupid in my life."

He turns toward the sailors; but the latter are speaking among themselves, making exclamations in dialect and laughing loudly. Antoine comes over to the table where Wallas is drinking his hot rum; he calls on Wallas as his witness:

"You heard that, Monsieur? Here's a supposedly educated man who doesn't allow that a line can be both straight and oblique."

"Oh."

"Do you allow that?"

"No, I don't," Wallas quickly answers.

"What do you mean, you don't? An oblique line is a line . . ."

"Yes, of course. I said I don't allow that it isn't allowed."

"Oh, all right . . . fine."

Antoine does not seem quite satisfied with this position, which he considers too subtle. All the same he shouts to his companion:

"You hear that, pillpusher?"

"I don't hear anything," the pharmacist answers.

"This gentleman agrees with me!"

"That's not what he said."

Antoine grows more and more exasperated.

"All right, explain to him what 'oblique' means, will you?" he asks Wallas.

"Oblique," Wallas repeats evasively. "That can mean several things."

"That's my opinion too," the pharmacist says approvingly.

"All right," Antoine cries, at the end of his patience, "a line that's oblique in relation to another line, that means something, doesn't it?"

Wallas tries to formulate a precise answer:

"It means," he says, "that they form an angle, an angle between zero and ninety degrees."

The pharmacist chuckles.

"That's what I said," he concludes. "If there's an angle, it isn't straight."

"I never met anyone so stupid in my life," Antoine says.

"Well, I know one even better. . . . Listen to this . . ."

The drunk has stood up from his table to get into the conversation. Since it is difficult for him to stand, he immediately sits down again beside Wallas. He speaks slowly, so as not to get his words confused:

"Tell me what animal is a parricide in the morning . . ."

"That's all we needed was this goon here," Antoine objects.
"You don't even know what an oblique line is, I'll bet. . . ."

"You look pretty oblique to me," the drunk says mildly. "I'm
the one around here who asks riddles. I have one here just for
my old pal. . . ."

The two adversaries move away toward the bar, seeking new
partisans. Wallas turns his back on the drunk, who goes on
nevertheless, his voice jubilant and deliberate:

"What animal is parricide in the morning, incestuous at noon,
and blind at night?"

At the bar the discussion has become a general one, but the
five men are all talking at once and Wallas can hear only
snatches of their remarks.

"Well," the drunk insists, "can't you guess? It's not so hard:
parricide in the morning, blind at noon. . . . No . . . blind in the
morning, incestuous at noon, parricide at night. Well? What
animal is it?"

Fortunately the manager comes over to take away the empty
glasses.

"I'll be keeping the room tonight," Wallas informs him.

"And he'll pay the next round," the drunk adds.

But no one pays any attention to this suggestion.

"Well, are you deaf?" the drunk asks. "Hey! Buddy! Deaf
at noon and blind at night?"

"Let him alone," the manager says.

"And limps in the morning," the drunk concludes with sudden seriousness.

"I told you to let him alone."

"All right, I wasn't doing anything. I'm asking a riddle."

The manager wipes his rag across the table.

"Let us alone with your riddles."

Wallas leaves. More than any specific task to be accom-
plished, it is the man with the riddles who is chasing him out of
the little café.

226

He prefers to walk, despite the cold and the night, despite his fatigue. He tries to organize the various elements he has been able to pick up here and there during the course of the day. Passing in front of the garden fence, he glances up at the house, now empty. On the other side of the street, Madame Bax's window is lit.

"Hey! Aren't you waiting for me? Hey! Buddy!"

It is the drunk who is pursuing him.

"Hey! You there. Hey!"

Wallas walks faster.

"Wait a minute! Hey!"

The jubilant voice gradually fades.

"Hey there, don't be in such a hurry. . . . Hey! . . . Not so fast. . . . Hey! Hey! . . . Hey! . . ."

2

Eight short fat fingers pass delicately back and forth over each other, the back of the four right fingers against the inside of the four left fingers.

The left thumb caresses the right thumbnail, gently at first, then pressing harder and harder. The other fingers exchange positions, the back of the four left fingers vigorously rubbing the inside of the four right fingers. They interlace, lock, twist each other; the movement grows faster, more complicated, gradually loses its regularity, soon becomes so confused that nothing more can be distinguished in the swarm of joints and palms.

"Come in," Laurent says.

He rests his hands flat on the desk, fingers spread wide. It is an officer with a letter.

"Someone slipped this under the door of the concierge's lodge. It's marked 'Urgent' and 'Personal.' "

Laurent takes the yellow envelope the man hands him. The address, written in pencil, is scarcely legible: "Personal. Chief Commissioner. Urgent."

"The concierge didn't see who brought this letter?"

"He couldn't; he found it under his door. It may have already been there a quarter of a hour, or even more."

"All right. Thanks."

When the officer has left the room, Laurent feels the envelope. It seems to contain a rather stiff card. He holds it up to the electric light, but sees nothing abnormal about it. He decides to open it with his paper knife.

It is a picture post card showing a little house in a bad imitation Louis XIII style, at the corner of a long, gloomy suburban street and a wide avenue, probably at the edge of a canal. On the back is written, also in pencil, this one phrase: "Meeting tonight at seven-thirty." In a woman's handwriting. There is no signature.

The police receive messages like this every day—anonymous letters, insults, threats, denunciations—most often very involved, usually sent by illiterates or lunatics. The text of this post card is distinguished by its brevity and its precision. The meeting place is not indicated; it must be the street corner shown on the photograph—at least so one might suppose. If Laurent recognized the place, he might send one or two men there at the hour arranged; but it isn't worth the bother of doing a lot of research to end up—at best—laying hands on some fishing boat that is smuggling in five pounds of snuff.

It would be better to be sure that this minor infraction would be effectively punished by the inspector who discovered it. The chief commissioner knows that a good deal of minor smuggling occurs with the complicity of the police who merely take a modest share for themselves. It is only for serious misdemeanors that they are required to be completely uncompromising. At the other end of the scale of crimes, one wonders what their behavior might be . . . if, for instance, a political organization of the type described by Wallas were to appeal to their . . . Luckily, the question does not come up.

The commissioner picks up his phone and asks for the capital. He wants to have a clear conscience. Only the central services can inform him—if they have had time to perform the autopsy.

He gets his line soon enough, but he is transferred from office to office several times without managing to get in touch with the proper branch. The head of the department that signed the letter ordering the release of the body told him to speak to the medico-legal service; here, no one seems to know anything. Transferred from one to the other in succession, he finally reaches the prefect's office, where someone—he doesn't know precisely who—agrees to listen to his question: "From what distance was the bullet that killed Daniel Dupont fired?"

"Just one minute, please, hold on."

It is only after a rather long interval, interspersed with various noises, that the answer reaches him:

"A 7.65 bullet, fired from a distance of about four yards."

An answer which proves absolutely nothing, save that the lesson has been well learned.

Laurent then receives another visit from Wallas.

The special agent seems to have nothing to say to him. He has come back here as if he no longer knew where to go. He describes the escape of the businessman Marchat, the meeting with Juard, the visit to the former Madame Dupont. The commissioner, as on each occasion he himself has had dealings with the doctor, finds the latter's conduct rather suspect. As for the divorced wife, it was obvious to everyone that she knew nothing. Wallas describes the strange shopwindow the stationery saleswoman has made, and to Laurent's great surprise, takes out of his pocket the same post card the officer has just brought in.

The commissioner goes to his desk and picks up the card sent by the unknown woman. It is the same card. He reads Wallas the phrase written on the back.

3

The scene takes place in a Pompeian-style city—and, more particularly, in a rectangular forum one end of which is occupied by a temple (or a theater, or something of the same kind), the other sides by various smaller monuments divided by wide, paved roadways. Wallas has no idea where this image comes from. He is talking—sometimes in the middle of the square—sometimes on stairs, long flights of stairs—to people he cannot distinguish from one another but who were at the start clearly characterized and individual. He himself has a distinct role, probably a major one, perhaps official. The memory suddenly becomes quite piercing; for a fraction of a second, the entire scene assumes an extraordinary density. But what scene? He has just time to hear himself say:

"And did that happen a long time ago?"

Immediately everything has vanished, the people, the stairs, the temple, the rectangular forum and its monuments. He has never seen anything of the kind.

It is the agreeable face of a dark young woman which appears in its place—the stationery saleswoman from the Rue Victor-Hugo and the echo of her little throaty laugh. Yet her face is serious.

Wallas and his mother had finally reached the dead end of a canal; in the sunlight, the low houses reflected their old façades in the green water. It was not an aunt they were looking for: it was a male relative, someone he had never really known. He did not see him that day either. It was his father. How could he have forgotten it?

Wallas wanders through the city at random. The night is damp and cold. All day long, the sky has remained yellow, low, overcast—promising snow—but it has not snowed, and it is now the November mists that have gathered. Winter is coming early this year.

The lights at the street corners cast reddish circles just strong enough to keep the pedestrian from losing his way. It takes a good deal of care, crossing the street, not to stumble against the curbstones.

In the neighborhoods where the shops are more numerous, the stranger is surprised to find so few shopwindows lighted. Probably there is no need to attract customers in order to sell rice and brown soap. There are few notion stores in this province.

Wallas steps into a crowded, dusty shop that seems intended for the storage of merchandise rather than its retail sale. At the rear, a man in an apron is nailing shut a crate. He stops pounding to try to understand what kind of eraser Wallas wants. He nods several times during the course of the explanation as if he knew what Wallas meant. Then, without saying a word, he walks toward the other side of the shop; he is obliged to shift a large number of objects on his way in order to reach his goal. He opens and closes several drawers, one after the other, thinks for a minute, climbs up a ladder, begins searching again, without any more success.

He comes back toward his client: he no longer has the item. He still had some not long ago—a lot left over from before the war; they must have sold the last one—unless it's been put away somewhere else: "There are so many things here that you can never find anything."

Wallas dives back into the night.

Why not go back to the solitary house as well as anywhere else?

As the chief commissioner pointed out to him, Doctor Juard's behavior is not absolutely clear—though it is hard to see what his secret role could be. When he walked through the parlor-library, the little doctor glanced at Wallas out of the corner of his eye while pretending not to see him through his heavy glasses: yet he had walked through the room on purpose to have a look at him. And several times during their conversation half an hour later, Wallas was amazed at the strange way in which Juard expressed himself: he seemed to be thinking of something else and occasionally even to be talking about something else. "He has a bad conscience," Laurent delcares.

Perhaps, too, the businessman Marchat is not so crazy as he seems. After all, to go into hiding was the better part of valor. It is strange that the doctor's account does not make the least allusion to Marchat's presence in the Rue de Corinthe at the time of the wounded man's arrival; he has always claimed, on the contrary, that he did not need anyone's help; yet according to the commissioner, Marchat cannot have invented all the details he reports concerning the professor's demise. If Juard knew, one way or another, that Marchat was to be murdered tonight in his turn, it would certainly be to his advantage to conceal the businessman's presence in his clinic last evening He does not know that the latter has already mentioned it to the police.

Then the pneumatic message discovered at the *poste restante* window actually did concern this case—Wallas was convinced of it from the beginning. It is the summons sent to the murderer for the second crime—today's—which (according to this hypothesis) should take place in this same city. The conclusions of the inspector whose report Wallas read in Laurent's office could be correct about this: the existence of two accomplices in the murder of Daniel Dupont—the addressee (André WS) and the person designated by the letter G in the text of the letter. Tonight, the former would work alone. Lastly, Marchat was right to fear an attack long before the fatal hour—as confirmed by the words "all afternoon" also appearing in the pneumatic message.

There remains the post card mysteriously slipped under the concierge's door at the police station. It is extremely doubtful that the conspirators would have decided to inform the police of the time and place of their crime. It is part of their program to indicate the authorship of their crimes and to give them all the publicity possible (the Executive Services and the Ministry of the Interior have already received certain messages from the leaders of the organization), but the post card would constitute evidence capable of wrecking their plans—unless they henceforth felt so powerful that they had nothing further to fear from anyone. One would almost be led to suspect the commissioner himself of duplicity—which, from another point of view, is difficult to imagine.

It would be more reasonable to admit what Laurent, for his part, appears to be quite certain of: a reminder coming from

Marchat. The businessman, before leaving the city, would thus have made a final effort to convince the police to have the dead man's residence watched.

The suspicious behavior of the little doctor, the businessman's fears, various allusions contained in the pneumatic message . . . The deductions that can be made from such evidence furnish little opportunity for certainty. Wallas knows that. He realizes, in particular, the influence on him of the card left at the police station—though this card cannot logically constitute part of the structure. But after all, he has nothing better to do than show up at the rendezvous. Since at present there is no other lead, he will lose nothing in following this one. He has the key to the house in his pocket—the one to the little glass door—that Madame Smite gave him. Marchat has fled, leaving him a clear field: he himself will play the role of the businessman, to see if by some miracle someone will come to murder him. He congratulates himself on having brought his revolver along.

"It's true, you never know," Laurent has said ironically.

Wallas reaches the garden gate.

It is seven o'clock.

Everything around him is dark. The street is deserted. Wallas calmly opens the gate.

Once inside, he carefully pushes it shut, but not all the way, so as to leave some trace of his passage.

There is no use attracting the attention of anyone walking on the parkway at this hour by unnecessary noise. To avoid making the gravel crunch, Wallas walks on the lawn—easier than on the brick rim. He walks around the house on the right side. In the darkness, he can just make out the path, paler between the two flowerbeds and the neatly pruned top of the spindle trees.

A wooden shutter now protects the glass panes of the little
door. The key turns easily in the lock. Wallas surprises himself
in the attitudes of a burglar: instead of opening the door wide,
he has slipped in through a discreet gap. He takes out the key
and gently closes the door behind him.

The big house is silent.

To the right the kitchen, at the rear and to the left the
dining room. Wallas knows the way; he would not need any
light to guide him. He nevertheless turns on his pocket flashlight and moves forward, preceded by the thin pencil of light.
The tiling of the vestibule is black and white, laid in a pattern
of squares and lozenges. A strip of gray carpet with two garnet
stripes at the edges covers the stairs.

In the luminous circle of the electric light appears a tiny
dark painting that is obviously rather old. It is a nightmare
scene. At the foot of a ruined tower, illuminated by a flash of
sinister lightning, two men are lying. One is wearing royal
clothes, his gold crown gleams in the grass beside him; the
other is a simple peasant. The lightning has just dealt out the
same death to both of them.

On the point of turning the doorknob, Wallas stops: if the
murderer is actually lying in wait behind this door, it would
be stupid for a special agent to fall into such a trap; since he
has come to the rendezvous, he should play the game all the
way to the end. He slips his hand into his pocket to take out his
revolver, when he remembers the second one he has been carrying around since the morning—Daniel Dupont's revolver, which
is jammed and would be of no help to him if he had to protect
his life. He must be careful not to make any mistake about
which is which.

Actually, he runs no risk of doing so. Dupont's revolver is

in his left overcoat pocket: he had put it there first and then put it back in the same place when the revolver was returned from the laboratory. Since he has never handled both weapons at the same time, he cannot have confused them.

To be absolutely certain, he examines them on the spot by the light of his flashlight. He recognizes his own revolver indisputably. He even feels no apprehension about trying to fire the dead man's gun—it is, indeed, that one that is jammed. He starts to put it back in his pocket, but then decides it is no use encumbering himself with this heavy object any longer. He therefore goes into the bedroom and puts it back in the night table drawer from which he had seen the old housekeeper take it this morning.

In the study, Wallas presses the button of the light switch on the door jamb. One bulb in the ceiling fixture goes on. Before leaving the house, the old housekeeper has closed all the shutters; consequently no one will see the light from outside.

His loaded revolver in his right hand, Wallas inspects the little room. No one is hiding in it, obviously. Everything is in order. Madame Smite must have straightened the piles of books which the inspector had indicated as having been disordered. The white sheet on which the professor had as yet written only four words has disappeared, filed away in a folder or in some drawer. The cube of vitrified stone, with its sharp edges and deadly corners, is lying harmlessly between the inkwell and the memo-pad. Only the chair is at a slight angle, pulled out from the desk, as if someone were about to sit down.

Wallas stands behind the back of the chair and looks toward the door; this is a good place to wait for the arrival of the hypothetical murderer. It would be even better to turn out the light; the special agent would then have time to see the enemy before being discovered.

From his observation post, Wallas carefully notes the location of the various pieces of furniture. He goes back to the door, presses the light button, and in the dark returns to the same place. He checks his position by resting his free hand on the back of the chair in front of him.

4

If the murderer's trail has not been picked up, it is because Daniel Dupont has not been murdered; yet it is impossible to reconstruct his suicide in any coherent way. . . . Laurent rubs his hands together faster. . . . And what if Dupont weren't dead?

The chief commissioner suddenly understands the oddities of this "wound," the impossibility of letting the police see the "corpse," Doctor Juard's embarrassed looks. Dupont is not dead; it just took a little thought to realize that.

The motives of the entire story are not yet quite clear, but the point of departure is here: Daniel Dupont is not dead.

Laurent picks up his telephone and dials a number: 202-203.

"Hello, Café des Alliés?"

"Yes," a low, almost cavernous voice replies.

"I'd like to speak to Monsieur Wallas."

"Monsieur Wallas isn't here," the voice answers, disgustedly.

"You don't know where he is?"

"How should I know?" the voice says, "I'm not his nurse-maid."

"This is the police calling. You have a man staying there named Wallas, don't you?"

"Yes, I reported him this morning," the voice says.

"That's not what I'm asking. I'm asking if this man is in your establishment. Has he gone up to his room?"

"I'll find out," the voice answers reluctantly. A minute later it adds with a note of satisfaction: "No one's there!"

"All right. I'd like to speak to the manager."

"I'm the manager here," the voice says.

"You are. Then it was you who told an inspector that nonsense about some fictitious son of Professor Dupont?"

"I didn't say anything like that," the voice protests. "I said that sometimes young people came in here, they're all ages—some young enough to be Dupont's sons. . . ."

"Did you say he had a son?"

"I don't even know whether he had any! He never came in here, and even if he had I wouldn't have stopped him from getting into every whore in the neighborhood—excuse me, Monsieur." The voice suddenly grows gentler, making an attempt at correctness: "The inspector asked if any young people ever came in here; I said yes. Over sixteen is legal. Then he insinuated that maybe this Dupont had a son; I didn't want to say no, so I said it was perfectly possible he had come in here to drink one day or the other. . . ."

"All right. We'll send for you. But from now on watch out what you're saying; and try to be a little more polite. Monsieur Wallas didn't say what time he'd be back?"

A pause. The other man has hung up. A threatening smile is already spreading across the commissioner's face . . . when he finally hears the voice: "All he said was that he would sleep here tonight."

"Thanks. I'll call back."

Laurent hangs up. He rubs his hands. He would have liked to announce his discovery to the special agent right away. He enjoys in anticipation Wallas' incredulous astonishment when

238

he will hear at the end of the wire: "Dupont isn't dead. Dupont is in hiding at Doctor Juard's clinic."

5

"The car is here," Juard says.

Dupont stands up and starts for the door at once. He is dressed for the trip. He has been able to put only one arm through the sleeve of his heavy overcoat, which the doctor has buttoned as well as possible over the wounded arm, which is held in a canvas sling. He is wearing a wide-brimmed felt hat that entirely conceals his forehead. He has even accepted dark glasses so that no one will recognize him; the only pair to be found in the clinic was a pair of medical glasses, one of whose lenses is very dark and the other much lighter—which gives the professor the comical look of a villain in a melodrama.

Since at the last minute Marchat refuses to do him the favor he had promised, Dupont will have to go to the little house for the papers himself.

Juard has arranged matters so that the corridors of the clinic are empty when his friend passes through them. The latter has no difficulty getting to the big black ambulance waiting in front of the door. He sits down on the front seat beside the driver—it will be easier for getting in and out without wasting any time.

The driver has put on the black hospital uniform and the flat cap with the shiny visor. Actually this must be one of the "bodyguards" Roy-Dauzet uses, more or less officially. The man, moreover, has an impressive build, a sober manner, the hard, inscrutable face of a film killer. He hasn't opened his mouth once; he has handed the professor the letter from the minister proving that he is the man they have been expecting, and as soon as the doctor has slammed the door, he drives away.

"We have to stop at my house first," Dupont says. "I'll tell you where to go. Turn right. . . . Right again. . . . To the left. . . . Around that building. . . . Turn here. . . . The second on the right. . . . Now straight ahead. . . ."

In a few minutes they reach the Boulevard Circulaire. Dupont has the car stop at the corner of the Rue des Arpenteurs.

"Don't park here," he tells the driver. "I prefer not to have my visit noticed. Drive around, or park a few hundred yards away. And be back in exactly half an hour."

"Yes, Monsieur," the man says. "Do you want me to park the car and come with you?"

"There's no need for that, thank you."

Dupont gets out and walks quickly toward the gate. He hears the ambulance drive away. The man is not a "bodyguard": he would have insisted on following Dupont. His looks had fooled the professor, who now smiles at his own romanticism. The very existence of these famous guards is, moreover, quite uncertain.

The gate is not closed. The lock has been out of order for a long time, the key does not even turn in it, which does not prevent the latch from closing. Old Anna is growing quite careless—unless some child was playing here and opened the gate after he left—a child or a prowler. Dupont climbs the four steps up to the door, to make sure that the front door, in any case, is actually locked; he turns the heavy brass doorknob and pushes hard, adding the pressure of his shoulder, for he knows that the hinges are very stiff; since he wants to be sure of the result and mistrusts the unaccustomed movements imposed by his single good arm, he repeats the effort two or three times, yet without daring to make too much noise. But the big door is locked tight.

He has given Marchat the keys to this door, and the business-man has left without even bothering to return them. Dupont

has only the key to the little glass door left; he must therefore
walk around the house to the back. Under his feet, the gravel
crunches faintly in the silence of the night. It was a mistake to
count on that coward Marchat. He has wasted the whole afternoon waiting for him; finally he telephoned his house, but there
was no one there; at quarter to seven he finally received a
message that came from somewhere: Marchat was sorry, he
had had to leave town on urgent business. That was a lie, of
course. It was fear that had made him run away.

Mechanically, Dupont has turned the doorknob of the little
door. The latter opens without resistance. It was not locked.

The house is dark and silent.

The professor takes off his glasses, which are bothering him.
He has stopped in the vestibule and tries to figure out the situation. . . . Did Marchat come after all? No, since it was the front
door keys that had been given to him. And old Anna, if she
hadn't left, would be in the kitchen at this hour . . . that's not
certain . . . in any case, she would have left a light on in the
hall or on the stairs. . . .

Dupont opens the kitchen door. No one there. He presses the
light button. Everything is put away, as in a house where no
one lives any longer. And all the shutters are closed. Dupont
turns on the light in the hall. As he passes he opens the living
room and dining room doors. No one, of course. He starts up
the stairs. Perhaps Anna forgot to lock the little door when she
was leaving. She has been growing absent-minded the last few
months.

On the second floor, he goes to the housekeeper's room. It is
obvious that the room has been put in order for a long absence.

Having reached his study door, the professor holds his
breath. Last night, the murderer was waiting for him there.

Yes, but last night the little door was open: the man didn't need a key to get in; tonight he would have had to force the lock, and Dupont noticed nothing of the kind. And if the man found the door open this time too, it is because old Anna had not locked it, in any case. . . . It is impossible to reassure himself with arguments of this kind; with a bunch of skeleton keys, a specialist can easily open all ordinary locks. Someone has made his way into the house and is waiting, in the study, in the same place as yesterday, to finish the job.

Objectively, there is no reason to suppose this is not true. The professor is not easily frightened; nevertheless, at this moment he regrets that he was not sent a real bodyguard from the capital. However, there can be no question of leaving without taking with him the files he needs.

Marchat has told him on the telephone that the police commissioner did not think it had been a murder: he was convinced it was a suicide. Dupont turns around. He goes to get his revolver. Last night, when he departed for the clinic, he left it on the night table. . . . Just before he goes into the bedroom he stops again: it may be here that the trap has been set for him.

These successive, more or less chimerical fears annoy the professor. With an impatient gesture he turns the handle; all the same he takes the precaution of not opening the door at once; he quickly thrusts in his hand to turn on the light and glances slowly around the door, ready to draw back if he sees anything unusual. . . .

But the bedroom is empty: no thug is posted behind the bed, nor in the corner next to the chest. Dupont sees only his own face in the mirror, where the traces of an anxiety that now seems ludicrous to him still remain.

He walks straight over to the night table. The revolver is no longer on the marble top. He finds it in the drawer, in its usual place. He probably will not use it, any more than he had the night before, but you never know: if he had been armed last

night when he came upstairs from the dining room, he would
certainly have used it then.

The professor checks to see that the safety catch has not
been slipped back on and returns, walking steadily, his weapon
in his hand, to the study. He will have to use only one arm—
fortunately, his right. First put the revolver in his pocket, open
the door, turn on the ceiling light and, as fast as possible, grasp
the revolver while kicking open the door. This little farce—
useless as the one he has just executed—makes him smile in
anticipation.

Wallas listens to his heart pounding. Since he is quite close to
the window, he has heard the car stop, the garden gate open,
the heavy footsteps crunching across the gravel. The man has
tried to get in through the front door. He has shaken it a few
times, without success, then has walked around the house. Consequently Wallas could tell it wasn't Marchat who had changed
his mind and come for the dead man's papers; it was neither
Marchat nor someone sent by him—or by the old housekeeper.
It was someone who did not have the keys to the house.

The crunching footsteps have passed underneath the window.
The man went to the little door which the special agent has left
open for him on purpose. The hinges have creaked slightly
when he pushed the door open. To be sure his victim would not
escape, the man has looked in every room he passed on the
ground floor and then upstairs.

Now Wallas sees the slit of light widening along the jamb,
with unendurable slowness.

Wallas aims at the place where the murderer will appear, a
black figure outlined against the illuminated doorway. . . .

But the man obviously distrusts this room plunged in darkness. A hand moves forward, gropes for the switch . . .

Wallas, dazzled by the light, only distinguishes the quick

movement of an arm lowering toward him the muzzle of a heavy revolver, the movement of a man firing. . . . As he throws himself to the floor, Wallas pulls the trigger.

6

The man has fallen forward, his right arm outstretched, the left folded under him. His hand remains clenched on the butt of the revolver. He no longer moves.

Wallas stands up. Fearing a trick, he approaches cautiously, his gun still aimed, not knowing what he should do.

He walks around the body, keeping out of reach of a possible reaction. The man still does not move. His hat has remained pulled down over his forehead. The right eye is partly open, the other is turned down toward the ground; the nose is crushed against the carpet. What can be seen of the face looks quite gray. He is dead.

It is nervousness that makes Wallas lose the rest of his discretion. He leans down and touches the man's wrist, trying to find his pulse. The hand releases the heavy revolver and dangles limply in his grasp. The pulse has stopped. The man is certainly dead.

Wallas decides he must look through the corpse's pockets. (For what?) Only the right overcoat pocket is accessible. He thrusts in his hand and removes a pair of spectacles, one of whose lenses is very dark and the other much lighter.

"Can you say whether it was the right lens that was darker, or the left?"

The left lens . . . on the right side. . . . The right lens on the left side. . . .

It is the left lens that is darker. Wallas puts the glasses on the floor and straightens up. He does not want to continue the search. He feels instead like sitting down. He is very tired.

In self-defense. He *saw* the man aiming at him. He saw the finger squeezing the trigger. He perceived the considerable interval of time it took him to react and fire back. He was sure he didn't have very quick reflexes.

Yet he had to admit that he fired first. He didn't hear the other revolver fire before his own; and if the two explosions had occurred at exactly the same moment, there would be some trace of the stray bullet on the wall or in the backs of the books. Wallas raises the window curtain: the panes are also intact. His adversary did not have time to fire.

It is only the tension of his senses that gave him, at the time, that impression of slow motion.

Wallas presses his palm against the muzzle of his gun; it feels distinctly warm. He turns back toward the body and leans down to touch the abandoned revolver. It is quite cold. Taking a better look, Wallas realizes that the left sleeve of the overcoat is empty. He feels the shape of the arm under the material. Was his arm in a sling? "A flesh wound in the arm."

He must inform Laurent. From now on this is a matter for the police. The special agent cannot continue to handle the case alone, now that there is a corpse.

The commissioner will not be at his office this late. Wallas looks at his watch; it shows seven thirty-five. Then he remembers that it had stopped at seven-thirty. He raises it to his ear and hears the faint ticking. It must be the detonation that has started it going again—or else the shock, if he bumped it when he threw himself to the floor. He will call the commissioner at his office; if he is no longer there, someone can certainly tell Wallas where to find him. He has noticed a telephone in the bedroom.

The door is open. The light is on. The drawer of the night table is wide open. The revolver is no longer there.

Wallas picks up the receiver. Number 124-24. "It's a direct line." The ringing at the other end of the line is interrupted at once.

"Hello!" a distant voice says.

"Hello, this is Wallas, it's . . ."

"Oh good, I just tried to call you. This is Laurent speaking. I've made a discovery—you'll never guess! Daniel Dupont! He isn't dead at all! Do you hear me?" He repeats, separating each syllable: "Daniel Dupont is not dead!"

Then who said the telephone in the house wasn't working?

EPILOGUE

In the dimness of the café the manager is arranging the tables and chairs, the ashtrays, the siphons of soda water; it is six in the morning.

The manager is not altogether awake. He is in a bad mood; he has not had enough sleep. Last night he wanted to wait until his lodger returned before locking up; but it was no use keeping awake so late, for he finally closed up all the same and went to bed without ever having seen that damned Wallas come in. He has decided that his lodger was arrested, since the police were looking for him.

Wallas has come in only this morning—ten minutes ago— looking tired, his face drawn, hardly able to stand up. "The police called, they're looking for you," the manager has said as he opened the door for him. Wallas is not affected by the news; he has merely answered: "Yes, I know; thanks," and he has gone straight upstairs to his room. Too polite to be honest. It was a good thing he had waited until six to come in: if the manager had not been up, he certainly wouldn't have got out of bed to let him in. Besides, he's not going to take any more lodgers, it's too much trouble. It will be a piece of luck if this one doesn't make trouble with all his problems.

The manager has no sooner put on the light in the café than in comes a little man in shabby clothes, dirty hat and an overcoat too. . . . It's the same one who came yesterday morning at the same time. He asks the same question as the day before:

"Monsieur Wallas, please?"

The manager hesitates, not knowing whether his lodger will find it more disagreeable to be disturbed at this moment or to miss the man who has been looking for him the last twenty-four hours. From his face, the latter does not look as if he had very good news.

"He's upstairs, just go straight up. It's the room at the end of the hall on the second floor."

The little man with the woebegone face heads for the door indicated, at the rear of the café. The manager had not noticed yet how silent his footsteps were.

Garinati closes the door behind him. He is in a narrow hall illuminated by a vague light from the ground-glass pane above another door—opening onto the street. The staircase is opposite him. Instead of walking toward it, he follows the hallway to the door—which he opens noiselessly. He finds himself out on the sidewalk again. Wallas is upstairs, that's all he wanted to know.

Today he won't let him get away; he will be able to give Bona an account of his every movement. He has only too well deserved his chief's censure and contempt these last few days. As a consequence Bona had preferred not to mention to him the execution of Albert Dupont, the wood exporter that "Monsieur André" had performed last night. A good job, apparently.

But Garinati's own work has not been so bad as he had thought, after all. He has had to see his victim's body with his own eyes to be quite certain of his death. He had been getting ideas. The shot he fired at the professor was a deadly one all right.

Bona will be annoyed when he finds out (he always finds out, sooner or later) that Garinati, instead of following the special agent, has spent the night making dangerous expeditions through all the hospitals and clinics in town, looking for the corpse of Daniel Dupont.

He has seen the dead man with his own eyes. It is the last mistake he will have made. From now on he will not be so stupid about losing his confidence in Bona. He will obey his orders without hesitation. Today: follow Wallas like a shadow. It isn't very hard.

And it won't be very long: Wallas will leave the city by the first train. He is sitting on the edge of his bed, his elbows on his knees, his head between his hands. He has taken off his shoes, which were hurting him; his feet are swollen from so much walking.

This sleepless night has exhausted him. He has accompanied the chief commissioner everywhere, for Laurent had at once taken charge of the case again and resumed all his duties. Several times, during their nocturnal rides, Wallas fell asleep in the car. Now that he had recovered the missing corpse, Laurent was, on the contrary, quite at ease: he has displayed an energy which his one-day colleague scarcely expected from him—particularly after eight-thirty, when he learned of the murder of the millionaire exporter.

Wallas, on the other hand, has no longer concerned himself with anything. He has stayed on because no one had told him to leave.

When he telephoned the Bureau, Fabius himself answered. Wallas has reported on his case and asked if he could be transferred back to his old department. This was taking the initiative, for he certainly would not have been kept on at this delicate post after such an unfortunate incident. Since the court does not need him for the moment, he will return to the capital during the morning.

In his extreme exhaustion, snatches of his wasted day still come back to torment him: ". . . and if, at that moment, I had thought about . . . and if I had . . ." He chases away these obsessions with an impatient shake of his head. Now it is too late.

Forty-three multiplied by one hundred-fourteen. Four times three, twelve. Four times four, sixteen. Sixteen and one, seventeen. Forty-three. Forty-three. Two. Seven and three, ten. Four and three, seven. Seven and one, eight. Eight and one, nine. Four. Four thousand nine hundred two. There is no other possible solution. "Four thousand nine hundred two . . . that's not so good, my boy. Forty-nine square centimeters of surface: you need at least fifty, you know."

Only one centimeter—all he was missing was that ridiculous space.

He still has two tiny millimeters left over. Two last tiny millimeters. Two square millimeters of dream . . . It isn't much. The glaucous water of the canals rises and overflows, covers the granite quays, overflows the streets, spreads its monsters and its mud over the whole city. . . .

Wallas stands up: if he stays here without moving, he will really go to sleep. He tries to take his comb out of his inside jacket pocket, but his gestures are clumsy and in grasping the case he drops his wallet, out of which several papers fall. His *carte d'identité* shows him that face that once was his; he walks over to the dresser to see himself in the mirror and compares the image with the photograph: lack of sleep, aging his features, has re-established the resemblance. Besides, it would be no use changing this photograph, he need only let his mustache grow out again. He doesn't really have a narrow forehead, it's only that his hairline is low.

Putting the papers back in the wallet, Wallas cannot find the return train ticket. He looks to see if it is not still on the floor near the bed; he then searches through all his pockets; he looks through the wallet once again. He remembers having seen the ticket there during the day. He must have dropped it while taking out some money. It was also the only proof of the exact time of his arrival in the city.

On the telephone, Fabius did not have the dramatic reactions Wallas feared. He only half listened to his agent's account. The chief was on a new lead: now it was the next crime, tonight's, that was supposed to occur in the capital, according to him, at least.

Wallas begins to shave. He hears the throaty laugh of the stationery saleswoman—more annoying than provocative.

"I'm going to have to go. . . ."

"Sometimes you go through hell and high water to find a murderer, and the crime hasn't even been committed. You go through hell and high water to discover it. . . ." ". . . quite far from him, whereas one need only point toward one's own chest . . ." Where do these phrases come from?

It is not the stationery saleswoman's laugh; the noise is coming from downstairs—probably from the café.

Antoine is very pleased with his joke. He turns to the right and the left to see if his entire audience has had the benefit of it. The pharmacist, who is the only who has not laughed, merely says:

"That's ridiculous. I don't see why it wouldn't snow in October."

But Antoine has just noticed, in the newspaper one of the sailors is reading, a headline that makes him exclaim:

"There, what did I say!"

"What *did* you say?" the pharmacist asks.

"Hey, bartender, what did I say! Albert Dupont *is* dead. Look here, you can see for yourself that he's named Albert and that he's dead as a doornail!"

Antoine takes the newspaper away from the sailor and holds it over the bar. In silence the manager begins reading the article in question: "Walking home as he was accustomed to do every evening . . ."

253

"All right," Antoine says, "who was right?"

The manager does not answer; he calmly continues reading. The others have resumed their argument over the early winter. Antoine, growing impatient, repeats:

"Well?"

"Well," the manager says, "you'd be better off reading to the end before you start laughing. It'ş not the same story as yesterday. This was last night; and yesterday it was the day before yesterday. Besides, this one isn't a burglar that shot at him: it's a car that skidded and ran over him on the edge of the sidewalk. '. . . the driver of the truck, after pulling back onto the road, escaped toward the harbor . . .' Read first, instead of talking so much. If you can't tell the difference between yesterday and today there's no use talking."

He gives back the newspaper and picks up the empty glasses to rinse them.

"You're not trying to tell us," Antoine says, "that someone named Dupont gets killed every night."

"There's more than one donkey at the fair . . ." the drunk begins sententiously.

Wallas, after shaving, goes back downstairs to drink a cup of hot coffee. It must be ready by this time. The first person he sees when he comes into the café is the riddle-man whose question: "What animal in the morning . . ." he has been vainly trying to reconstruct all night . . .

"Good morning," the drunk says with his jubilant smile.

"Good morning," Wallas answers. "Will you give me a cup of black coffee, please?"

A little later, while he is drinking his coffee at a table, the drunk comes over and tries to start a conversation. Wallas finally asks him:

"How did that riddle of yours go yesterday? What animal . . ."

The drunk, delighted, sits down opposite him and searches his memory. What animal . . . Suddenly his face lights up; he winks and begins enunciating with an infinitely sly expression:

"What animal is black, has six legs, and flies?"

"No," Wallas says, "it was something else."

A wipe of the rag. The manager shrugs. Some people actually have time to waste.

But he mistrusts the friendly manners his lodger puts on so willingly. A man who dresses like that doesn't take a room and then spend the whole night out. And why did that man from the police station want to talk to him last night?

"I'm the manager."

"Oh, it was you! You're the one who told an inspector that nonsense about some fictitious son of Professor Dupont?"

"I didn't say anything like that. I said that sometimes young people came in here, they're all ages—some young enough to be Dupont's sons . . ."

"Did you say he had a son?"

"I don't even know whether he had any!"

"All right, let me speak to the manager."

"I'm the manager."

"Oh, it was you! You're the one who told that nonsense about the fictitious son of Professor Dupont?"

"I didn't say anything."

"Did you say he had a son?"

"I don't even know whether he had any. All I said was that young people of all ages came in here."

"You're the one who told that nonsense, or was it the manager?"

"I'm the manager."

"You're the one, young people nonsense, professor at the bar?"

"I'm the manager!"

"All right. Let me certainly have a son, a long time ago, fictitious young died so strangely. . . ."

"I'm the manager. I'm the manager. The manager. I'm the manager . . . the manager . . . the manager . . ."

In the troubled water of the aquarium, furtive shadows pass. The manager is motionless at his post. His massive body leans on his outspread arms; his hands grip the edge of the bar; his head hangs down, almost threatening, the mouth somewhat twisted, the gaze blank. Around him the familiar specters dance their waltz, like moths circling a lampshade and bumping into it, like dust in the sun, like little boats lost at sea, lulling to the sea's rhythm their delicate cargo, the old casks, the dead fish, the rigging and tackle, the buoys, the stale bread, the knives and the men.